# The Cottage

ALSO BY
JUDY PRESCOTT MARSHALL

BE STRONG ENOUGH
STILL CRAZY
THE INN IN RHODE ISLAND

# THE COTTAGE

Book Three
Be Strong Enough Series

**JUDY PRESCOTT MARSHALL**

THE COTTAGE. Copyright © 2023 By Judy Prescott Marshall. All rights reserved. Printed in the United States of America.

For information, please address
Writing Studio 12 May Knoll Dover Plains, NY 12522

ISBN 978-1-960278-00-5 (hardcover B&N exclusive)
ISBN 978-1-960278-01-2 (paperback B&N)
ISBN 978-1-960278-02-9 (paperback)
ISBN 978-1-960278-03-6 (e-book)
ISBN978-1-960278-04-3 (audiobook)
ISBN 978-1-960278-05-0 (mass market)
ISBN 978-1-960278-06-7 (boxset Amazon exclusive)

Audio read by Susan McGurl

For David
for loving me
and for never giving up on us.

# BE STRONG ENOUGH SERIES
## Book One – *STILL CRAZY*

A strong, loving and passionate wife discovers a handwritten note that has the power to either destroy her or make her stronger yet.

*Still Crazy* is the story of one woman's journey through pain, betrayal, and forgiveness as she learns to hold onto her faith and, for the first time in her life trust in herself. Julie Holliday has always had a dream – to be the perfect wife. After she gives her heart to the love of her life, all she wants is for Dan to adore her the way she adores him. With a high school equivalency in one hand and a fist full of ambition in the other, together they build a million-dollar empire. It seems Julie and Dan have a fairytale life – that is, until the day she discovers her love for him is not enough to stop him from having what she suspects is numerous affairs.

# Book Two – *THE INN IN RHODE ISLAND*

A powerful message about knowing, trusting, and believing in yourself.

At The Inn in Rhode Island, afternoons are reserved for soothing cups of tea while relaxing on one of the porch rockers. You're welcome to take an easy stroll among the many aesthetic gardens. If reading is your pleasure and the owner sure hopes it is, the library offers an array of books, a comfortable sofa and two wingback chairs on each side of the fireplace. From garden tours in the spring to author events in the fall, you'll be glad you stayed at the inn, especially for dinner. Chef Michael is passionate about food.

During the golden hour, Julie and Dan Holliday will renew their vows. The wedding will take place at The Inn in Rhode Island on what promises to be a magical evening surrounded by close friends, colleagues, gorgeous flowers, delicious food and a wedding cake baked by the bride's best friend.

A day guaranteed to be full of wonderful beginnings and everlasting memories to last Julie and Dan a lifetime.

Until best man Jesse shows up with an unexpected guest.

The twenty-three-year old and her son were found lying under a maple tree in their pajamas. Erin was weak, bruised and unable to carry her four-year-old son Kyle any further. How far would you run to find your safe harbor?

# Book Three ~ *THE COTTAGE*

D o you believe in second chances?

This small cottage once served as a safe harbor for Julie. It allowed her to find herself, restore her faith, believe in her dream and it is where Dan found her.

Soon the cottage will serve as the inn's bridal suite, a warm place for new beginnings and everlasting love.

Dan and Julie Holliday are looking forward to enjoying their retirement running The Inn in Rhode Island, a twenty-five room inn surrounded by tranquil gardens, a pond boasting serenity, peaceful hiking trails, and a brand new swimming pool. At the inn, weddings are special, author events are exciting and afternoon tea is a must. The staff at the inn are gearing up for their most profitable year to date. Best of all, Dan and Julie are building their dream home – a farmhouse in Julie's favorite harborside – Point Judith. First, the Hollidays are going on a long awaited vacation to Italy.

Just when life seems to be perfect, one of them is diagnosed with a life-threatening illness and everyone at the inn must come together to do whatever they can.

CAST of CHARACTERS
BE STRONG ENOUGH SERIES

Julie Holliday ~ Innkeeper
Dan Holliday ~ Contractor
Lady ~ Star of the series
Jesse ~ Arborist
Lynnae ~Baker
Sam ~ Lynnae's son
Max ~ Lynnae's son
Barry ~ Builder
Brooke ~ Cake Decorator
Stephanie ~ Artist
Aimee Jo ~ Babysitter
Barbara ~ Therapist New York
Book Two:
Kelly ~ Restaurateur
Geri ~ Real Estate Broker
Frank ~ General Contractor
Gina Marie ~ Budget Master
Jessica ~ Teacher
Sabrina ~ Architect
Teresa ~ Receptionist
Cathy ~ Spa Owner
Amanda ~ Daycare Owner
Kourtnee ~ Bookkeeper
Kevin ~ LandscaperMichael ~ Chef
Christine ~ Patissier
Mary ~ Bakery Owner

Christina Stellate ~ Model

Michelle Eggink ~ Nutritional Therapy Practitioner

Molly ~ Interior Designer

Tina ~ Writer

Debbie ~ Spiritual Shop Owner

Chad ~ Pilot

Erin ~ Survivor

Kyle ~ Erin's son

Rose ~ Therapist Rhode Island

Book Three:

Carmie ~ Librarian

Maryanne ~ Carmie's daughter

Francesco ~ Villa Manager

Nico ~ Francesco's Grandson

Aria ~ Francesco's Granddaughter

Dr. Eastwood ~ Dan's new therapist

When the fighter steps into the ring
she knows amongst her supporters
there are people who wish to see her fall.
Win or lose
The fighter always gets back up again.


~ Judy Prescott Marshall

# THE COTTAGE

# Chapter 1

"WATCH OUT. WATCH OUT. Dan!" I screamed as I braced myself. Traffic was coming toward us. The car in front of him had its blinker on to go to the left.

He gave me a pointed look.

"Stop!"

Dan slammed on the brakes. When he swerved to the right, he drove up onto the curb. We came within inches of hitting the vehicle, almost sending it into an oncoming pickup truck. I looked over at him. "What's wrong with you?" I shook my head. "You almost ran into her."

He glanced at me without saying a word.

I noticed he slowed down to a crawl the rest of the way home. When we arrived back at the cottage, he said, "I don't know what I was thinking."

We went inside. While I prepared dinner, Dan tossed a few logs in the fireplace and sat on the sofa staring at the flames. A half-hour later, I handed him his plate. "Do you feel better?"

"Yeah, I'm sorry about that. I don't know what happened to me."

My heart felt bad for him. We ate in silence. I didn't know what to say to him. It was not as if he was looking the other way. It appeared he was focused on everything in front of him. When we were done eating, I said, "Maybe you just need a good night's sleep. You've been working hard these past few weeks trying to get the pool ready."

"I'm looking forward to going away." He set his empty plate on the coffee table. "Three weeks in Italy will be good for both of us."

We took our plates to the kitchen. I was putting our ice cream in small bowls when Dan said he was going to the bathroom. He entered the bedroom but instead of continuing to the bathroom, he just stood there. I watched for several minutes, waiting for him to move. I opened the freezer, put the ice cream inside, and slammed the door shut, hoping to have startled him with the noise. Nothing. I set the bowls down in the living room, walked back to the kitchen, entered the bedroom, and asked him if he was okay. He looked at me as if he was lost. I told him to hurry up and go to the bathroom because his ice cream was on the table in front of the fireplace.

A few minutes later, he came back and sat down next to me. We were sitting on the sofa eating our dessert and watching a movie when his cell phone beeped. Jesse had texted him. I watched as he fumbled with his phone for a few seconds before setting it down. He never touched the icon to read his message, and I thought that was odd. I took our empty bowls to the kitchen, rinsed them, and set them in the dishwasher. When I went back to the living room, Dan had picked up his phone again, and I thought he was reading Jesse's message, but he was just looking at the home screen. The two men had been friends for more than thirty years, and they had never had an argument. They were so close, Jesse moved to Rhode Island to be near us. I had a lot of maybes going on— like did *they* have a fight? Could that be why Dan was acting so strange?

"How are you feeling?"

"I'm just tired. Why?"

"I was just wondering."

At nine-thirty, the movie ended, and I suggested we get some rest. As soon as Dan snuggled under the covers, he fell asleep. I tossed and turned for hours. Words like brain-fog, fatigue, stress, and dementia entered my mind. I prayed he was just excited and overwhelmed about moving to Rhode Island, retiring, and our new lifestyle. I had hoped in time he would fall into a routine and be happy about living in Point Judith. I made a mental note to ask Jesse if they had had words. I'll ask him to take Dan deep-sea fishing. Dan loved fishing, especially on the ocean. I'll remind him about going deer hunting next season. When we return from Italy, I'll show him my surprise, three new tree stands near the orchard, that will put a smile on his face.

I looked over at the clock, it was two in the morning. I could not get to sleep. I was awake the entire night, worried about Dan. I tried telling myself he was excited about going on vacation. We had never gone away for more than a long weekend. I told myself he had been working hard trying to get the new swimming pool finished before we left for Italy. Maybe, he had a lot on his mind. I wondered if he'd had a bad session with his therapist, Rose. Normally, he came home feeling good about his time with her. I could not figure it out.

I got up and motioned with my hand for Lady to follow me. I closed the pocket door between the bedroom and the kitchen. I made myself a single cup of Nespresso. I took my cup, and a throw blanket, outside. "Go to the bathroom," I told her and sat down on the front porch in one of the rockers. Lady came back onto the porch and laid down in the dog bed at my feet. As I sipped my coffee, I could hear an owl in the distance. The pond's reflection was bright enough for me to see a deer's silhouette. I thought about planting hosta for them to eat. The plant is literally candy to a buck and doe. I was sick to my stomach thinking about what could be wrong with Dan. Maybe, he was upset because he was not going turkey hunting. Perhaps we should have planned our trip at a later date. Dan lived for turkey hunting in the spring and for deer in the fall. Some men play golf, basketball, go to the gym; Dan enjoyed sitting in a tree stand. He loved being outdoors. I thought about canceling our trip. No, that could not be what was bothering him. Dan was the one who made our travel arrangements. Something was going on with him.

"Three weeks away could be the best medicine for him. Right, Lady?"

Our marriage needed the vacation I told myself. We

deserved the time alone. I tried to tell myself it was nothing, that he just had a lot on his mind, but then I thought about what he did, and it scared me.

The sun was starting to come up, and I heard the dawn's chorus getting louder. I could have sat there forever listening to the sound of those birds. I took my cup inside, checked in on Dan, snoring like a bear cub at four in the morning. I made myself a cup of tea, grabbed the first book I saw, and went back outside. Before I started reading, I said a prayer for Dan. I asked God to place his healing hands upon Dan's head, to ease his mind and relieve him of any doubts. I looked down at Lady and smiled; she snored like her father.

I was still sitting on the front porch reading the new novel when I heard, "Die a Happy Man" playing on the radio. I love when the singer tells a story. That song definitely had something to say. Thomas Rhett sang about a bottle of wine, Marvin Gaye, and the pouring rain. I stretched out my arms, knowing my husband was up.

# Chapter 2

THURSDAY MORNING, DAN LOOKED better, "Good morning, my love," I said as I set my book on the kitchen counter.

Dan kissed my temple, "You got up early," he said as he spread peanut butter on two slices of toast.

I snatched one of them and said, "I bought a new book, it was calling to me the entire night." Then I thought about how on Earth I was supposed to get through the day with no sleep. First, I had a breakfast meeting with my entire staff, then lunch with Frank, followed by a going away party in the large dining room. Then at nine-thirty, Jesse was taking us to the airport in Providence. Our plane would land in Italy sometime around ten Friday morning,

"Would you like another cup of coffee?" Dan asked, holding up an almost-full pot.

"No," I shook my head, "I'm so excited I don't need any more caffeine." I picked up my notepad and the list of things for Kevin to do while I was gone. I wanted him to wait for me to return, but he insisted he could plant the new garden on his own. I only agreed because of the warm weather approaching.

"I'm going in the shower and then we better get a move on," Dan said as he emptied the coffee pot into the kitchen sink. Maybe, he had just needed a good night's sleep.

"Okay, and then I'll take mine, but first I want to check my email to see if Erin replied."

While Dan showered, I read Erin's reply email. I took a deep breath, knowing she meant every word. She was thankful for Jesse, and she appreciated everything Dan and I had done for her and her son. I was happy for her. Glad she located her birth mother. Thrilled she had decided to stay in Ireland and make a new life for the two of them. I clicked on the photo of Kyle and his new puppy, a Bernese Mountain dog named Lady Madra. When I showed the picture to Lady, she wagged her tail. I set the tablet down remembering when Jesse found Erin and Kyle at the end of our driveway, beaten and distraught. I smiled knowing she was exactly where she belonged. Safe *and* far away from her ex-husband.

"Good morning," Jesse called out to me as he entered the cottage holding a case of Nitro cold-brew coffee from the RISE Brewing Company, his and Dan's new favorite morning beverage. "Good morning, little girl." Of course, Lady gave him more kisses than he deserved.

"Dan's in the shower. Take a seat. I have a few more things to do." When Jesse set the box on the coffee table, I asked him if he had words with Dan or if Dan had appeared upset yesterday, but he assured me they did not. "Oh, I didn't think so," I said and went back to the kitchen. "I think he's excited about going away."

"He told me he was glad the two of you are going."

Jesse sat on the sofa with his feet kicked up on the footstool, telling me about his dinner at Mulligan's Tap Room.

"Sherry loved it. She made me promise to take her there every Wednesday for happy hour. She devoured the boxty potato pancakes."

"Better than George's?" I protested.

"You're early," Dan said to Jesse as he tapped me on my derriere, adding, "You better get in that shower now or wait until after our meeting with Frank."

"I'm going," I replied and headed for the bathroom.

I took a quick shower, made the bed, dressed, and sat on the bed to tie my sneakers. I was near the bedroom door when I overheard Jesse telling Dan that Rose had sex appeal. "Not bad for—"

"Knock your shit off," Dan said. "Don't ever talk to me about another woman in that manner again. Rose is my therapist. And that is all she is. Got it?"

"I get it," Jesse said, adding, "I'm sorry. I didn't mean anything by it."

"What's wrong with you? You of all people know how hard it was for me when Julie left. Why would you even bring up another woman?"

"Dan," I hollered from the bedroom, "is my pocketbook out there?" I knew exactly where it was. Hanging on the back of the kitchen chair. When I entered the kitchen, both Dan and Jesse gave me a cold stare. "I found it," I said and grabbed it. "I'm ready if you are."

We were standing on the front porch when Jesse put

his hand on Dan's shoulder and said, "I'm sorry."

Dan closed the door and reached for my elbow. "Jesse and I have a few things to go over before the pool guys get here. I'll catch up with you after your meeting, and we'll go see Frank together."

I kissed him goodbye and told Jesse I would see him later, too. "Come on Lady, let's go see if the babies are in the daycare." Lady adored spending time with Delilah and Brin, but she loved the attention she got from Amanda even more.

I inhaled, taking in the scent of hyacinths and primroses planted in the garden bed along the path leading up to the inn. I knew Jesse felt bad for saying what he did about Rose. Truth be had, Rose was a sexy woman. Hopefully, a happily married woman. I dropped Lady off at daycare and told her to be good for Amanda. I saw she was on her cell phone, so I just waved and closed the door behind myself. I thought about Dan and hoped he worked everything out. It was obvious he was upset about something. I had never seen or heard him snap at Jesse like that. I took a deep breath and opened the door to the inn. "Good morning, Teresa."

"Morning, boss." She grabbed her tea and followed me to the kitchen.

My staff meeting went well. Everyone assured me they were in total control of the next three weeks.

"Oh, one more thing," I said before ending the meeting. "Erin and Kyle have decided to live in Ireland. She'll be going to college full time in the fall and helping her mother on the weekends in her dress shop, Erin's Threads."

"That's wonderful news," Kourtnee said. "She left her sweater in my office, I'll mail it to her with a card we can all sign."

"I have some beautiful stationery at the front desk we can use," Teresa said as she stood up.

"My goodness, Erin's mother named her business after her," Christine said, smiling. "I'll miss our little bake-offs."

I laughed, knowing Christine hated anyone baking in her kitchen.

Before I left, Michael reminded me, "Listen, I have plenty of help coming in to assist me in the kitchen for all of our events. I don't want you worrying about the inn. We have everything covered."

"Thank you, chef, that's very comforting." I handed my list of new plants to Kevin, and he laughed.

"I got this," he said and left the kitchen shaking his head.

At eleven-thirty, Dan and I went to Frank's for lunch. I was surprised when Dan didn't argue with me about my driving. Dan thought he was much thinner, but still happy-as-ever Frank. We ate our lunch, laughing about the time Dan hung up on Frank the first time he called him. I tapped Frank on the hand and said, "Thank God for caller ID." Then I told him, "I'm excited about going to Italy, but knowing you, Dan, and I will be working on a project together is better than ice cream on a hot day."

"My entire barn-raising team will be ready," Frank said to me and then shook Dan's hand. "Have the time of your life. You both deserve it."

On our way back to the inn, Dan told me what Jesse had said to him. "I shouldn't have yelled at him, but—"

"It's okay. Jesse knows you love him. I'm glad you put him in his place. Seriously, Rose is a happily married woman."

The entire day went by so fast, and before we knew it, we were celebrating and toasting to our long-awaited vacation. I noticed Jesse and Sherry sitting quietly at the corner table. I went over and asked them if they needed anything to eat or drink.

"You and Dan are a perfect couple," Sherry said to me as I sat down in the empty chair.

I moved the flower vase closer and sniffed the lilacs. "There's no such thing as perfect, but as long as you have love in your heart, faith in your home, and forgiveness in your soul, you have all you ever need in a relationship."

I felt Dan's hands on my shoulders. "Are you guys ready?"

"Yep," Jesse said, and they both stood up.

I hugged everyone else goodbye one more time. Kissed Lady on the head and told her to be a good dog for Jesse.

After Jesse and Sherry waved us off, we grabbed a few snacks and something to drink. I forgot about the no-water rule at the airport and had to toss two brand-new bottles in the garbage. As soon as we boarded, we both took a deep breath, put our heads back, and thanked God for traveling with us. Then I received a text from Barry. "Mother and daughter are doing fine. Dixie Lillith, six pounds, seven ounces, and twenty-one inches long. Big brothers Max and Sam are excited to bring their baby sister home." I showed Dan the photo. No tears. I was happy for her. Lynnae had found her prince and she had her little girl.

I looked over at Dan. He seemed fine. Quiet, but content in his seat.

About an hour into our flight, Dan started checking the news on his tablet when he read aloud, "Prominent Narragansett divorce lawyer Donato Russo was found dead in his car outside his law office earlier this evening. Russo leaves behind a wife and three children. Rose Russo had no comment."

# Chapter 3

I WAS STUNNED BY the news of Rose's husband. Why would a successful man, married to an equally successful woman, with three children all of a sudden turn up dead? Dan was motionless. "Dan?"

He set the tablet on his lap. Held his hands out, questioning me. "What do you think happened to him?"

I shook my head in the same bewilderment. "I don't know. Do you think he was sick?"

Dan let out a loud exhale. "Rose never said anything about him being sick or—"

"Oh, my." I closed my eyes and asked God to be with her and their children.

Dan reached over and held my hand in his. "I wonder if he had a heart attack?"

The flight attendant asked if either of us cared for a beverage or snack. We both refused, but then I changed my mind and asked for a diet Coke. Behind us, two women were speaking in Italian. They both ordered macchiatos. When he returned, Dan asked for a cold beer. Jackson the attendant told Dan his choice of beer. When Dan didn't respond, I nudged him. Dan snapped out of it and agreed to a Coors Light. Around three a.m., we both fell asleep.

I woke up at seven, logged onto Dan's tablet, and read the morning news. Nothing on Rose's husband or how he died. Dan tapped me on my leg. "Did you find out anything?"

I tut-tutted before asking, "Are you okay?"

"Do you think he was murdered?"

"I don't know. I read the *Narragansett Times,* the *South County Independent*, and the *Narragansett Patch,* nothing about Mr. Russo." I looked at Dan. "I'll Google his name when we get to the hotel."

Dan shook his head.

For the next few hours, we agreed to focus on our long-overdue vacation. It was hard to get excited knowing someone we knew had died. I know it's crazy and selfish, but I wondered how my heart was going to feel knowing Dan was spending an hour every week with a gorgeous single woman.

"Hey," Dan said as he tapped me on my leg. "Stop worrying about Rose, she'll be fine. What's the first thing you want to do when we get to the hotel?"

"Probably have breakfast and then go sightseeing," I replied.

"I need a couple hours of sleep and—"

"That's fine," I said, interrupting him and adding, "We'll grab a quick bite, take a nap, shower, and then tour the city."

"Sounds good. I'm so glad we're doing this." Dan took my hand and held it in his. "When you're working, I miss you and can't wait to see you again. My heart comes back to life every time you enter the cottage."

"I'm sorry about the time I was gone. I—"

"Julie, you don't owe me any explanations. You did what you had to do. I'm trying to tell you that I'm glad we have the next three weeks to be alone."

I thought about what Dan was saying, and I knew exactly how he felt. I too loved seeing him walk through my door. "During the day, when I'm busy with guests, I long for us to be curled up in front of the fireplace, talking about our day, planning for the future."

Dan cleared his throat. "I'm glad we're building a bigger house. Can you believe it, we're going to Italy?"

I leaned over and kissed him. "Finally!"

From behind, I overheard one of the women say, "Bellissimo," and I smiled at Dan.

The Leonardo da Vinci–Fiumicino Airport was just under a half-hour from our hotel. The concierge had arranged for a car to pick us up at the airport. We arrived at the Starhotels Michelangelo just in time to grab lunch. I ordered the fruit plate, scrambled eggs, and juice for both of us. The views from our room were so spectacular that we ate out on the balcony. We sat at the café table enjoying a breeze, watching what seemed to be a million Fiat Pandas go by. We had a deluxe room with a short walk to the Vatican. "You picked the perfect room," I said. "Lush, rich, velvety pumpkin fabrics, and we're only seven minutes from St. Peter's Square. I'm so excited to get outdoors, walk around, and see the sights."

Dan smiled. "I'll take a nap before dinner. Come on, we're in Italy. Let's go."

I jumped up, grabbed my purse, and followed him out the door. We walked by so many beautiful places, but seeing Vatican City was spectacular. I think Dan was feeling tired when he suggested we take the tram to the Trevi Fountain. The crowd was large, but every person was courteous and kind enough to let us get a closer look.

"The statues are even more realistic up close. You must see it at night," a man said to us in perfect English.

"Thank you," Dan replied. "We'll be sure to take a stroll one evening. Dan reached for my hand, and we moved close enough to smell the chlorine coming from the spray of recycled water.

When we arrived back at the hotel, I suggested we take a nap before dinner. Dan asked if I wanted to order room service, but I really wanted to go out for dinner. "I thought you made reservations at Acquolina at seven?" Actually, I was craving the pasta. Swirled high on the plate, surrounded by garden tomatoes, herbs, and fresh Parmigiano-Reggiano.

"Yeah, we better go. I had a hell of a time getting us a table."

I clapped my hands together several times as Dan sat on the edge of the bed. I looked at him, knowing he didn't get much sleep on the plane. "You know what? Why don't you lie down while I take a nice, hot bath?"

Dan was happy to oblige, and within minutes of lying down he was fast asleep. I sat at the desk and Googled

Donato Russo. My heart started beating in my chest when I read, "In an apparent suicide, a fifty-seven-year-old man shot himself once in the head." *Oh, no!*

I cleared all of the searches related to Mr. Russo, set the tablet on the dresser, tippy-toed past the bed, and went straight to the bathroom. I wanted to vomit. I was sick to my stomach. My heart ached for Rose and her children. *How? Why?* What would make a person take his or her own life when they had everything they could possibly desire in life? I turned the water on, added bath salts, oil, and a handful of rose petals. I didn't know Rose well by any means, yet I felt compelled to console her. I closed my eyes, said another prayer for her. I sank deep in the water, allowing my body to feel its warmth. I closed my eyes, trying to focus on where I was and who I was with. I remembered the evening I found out we were going to Italy. Together. I was elated hearing the news. When the water turned cold, I grabbed the robe hanging on the brass hook, went out to the bedroom area, and sat quietly in the corner chair looking out at the city.

Dan woke up an hour later. "How was your bath?"

I craned my neck to face him. "Wonderful, very relaxing." I smiled. "I was remembering when I opened your gift and the tickets fell in my lap."

"Did you sleep?" he asked and finally got up.

I shook my head. "Too excited."

"I'll get ready. We can have the driver take us to the restaurant early. I read about a little dress shop I think you might like. It's about ten to fifteen minutes from the restaurant." He looked at me intently. "What?"

"Nothing," I said, pleased to be alone with him.

# Chapter 4

WHILE DAN SHOWERED, I got dressed. I smiled when I looked at myself in the mirror. My dress matched the room's decor. A multi-tan, black-and-orange paisley, twist-front, boho maxi dress, knotted at the waist, with baggy sleeves creating an airy feel. The front slit definitely added extra interest. I paired it with a pair of high wedges. I set Dan's black pants, dinner jacket, and tan T-shirt on the edge of the bed. True to Dan, he'd only brought one pair of dress shoes, black.

"Sexy."

I turned around to see him standing in the doorway, hair still wet, wrapped only in a towel tied below the waist. I smiled. "I could always slip this off as quickly as I put it on."

Dan raised his eyebrows. "I'm going to make love to you every night for the next three weeks."

I chuckled softly. "Only at night?"

Dan dropped his towel, kissed me on my cheek, and patted my derriere. "Where's my underwear?"

I laughed. "I was only in charge of your wardrobe. You told me to make sure we didn't clash." Then I pointed to the dresser.

He smiled, moved closer to where I was standing,

rubbed his thumb across my lips, kissed me on the cheek, and said, "You look beautiful."

My heart melted. "Thank you."

Downstairs, Dan asked our concierge if he could call our driver to take us to the restaurant. In the car, I glanced over at Dan; he seemed happy, no longer upset or confused. I listened as he told our driver about the dress shop being a few blocks away from the restaurant. The man agreed, and Dan looked at me as if to say, "I know where I'm going." We got out of the car near a row of shops. The dress shop had an array of fabrics. I told Dan I would like to come back for a few items when we won the lottery.

We arrived at the restaurant early, so we sat in front of the fireplace enjoying classic Americanos. Served in a highball glass, the cocktail brings together Campari, sweet vermouth, and a dash of soda water. The spritzer was so good, we both ordered another before going to our table.

My pasta was an exotic excursion of flavors. Dan's veal piccata was so tender he could have eaten it with a feather. Dan ordered the tiramisu for dessert, and of course, I had to taste it. "Wow, I have to tell Christine about the chocolate-covered coffee beans. They not only look nice, they taste amazing."

Dan set his napkin on the table next to his empty plate. "I'm so full, I want to walk back to the hotel."

"Not on your life. Now I'm tired. You better hope I don't fall asleep in the car."

We sat in the backseat with the windows down. The cool night air felt wonderful. First Dan reached over and held my hand before kissing me on my lips. I felt a sudden surge of energy rush over me.

Right before our driver pulled up to our hotel, it started to rain. He said, "Tomorrow it will rain. You will want umbrellas."

When the hotel door attendant opened my car door, I stepped out and gratefully stood under his umbrella while waiting for Dan to pay our driver. Once in our room, we both fell backward onto the bed. I was the first one to move. I had to. My wedges needed to be untied. Dan kicked off his shoes and took off his pants, jacket, and shirt. I never saw him climb into a bed so fast. I followed his lead and joined him wearing only my panties. I don't think we cuddled for more than five seconds before we both fell asleep.

The next morning, I woke up to Dan wheeling a tray with coffee and something that smelled delicious. I sat up and stretched my arms over my head. "Good morning, do I smell coffee?"

He handed me a cup before telling me about breakfast Italy-style. "I thought we'd try a few new things. I ordered the ricotta pancakes, a frittata, and two crepes."

I inhaled. "I'm starving," I said before looking over at the clock. It was nearly noon, and the driver was correct, it was pouring outside. We were almost done with our breakfast when I heard a knock on our door. I shook my head wondering who it could be. Dan took a large brown box, then paid the concierge with a hundred-dollar bill. After he closed the door, I asked him, "Did you just tip him a hundred euros?"

Dan smiled, set the box down in the bathroom, and said, "How do you know what I handed him?"

I laughed out loud. "You took it from the stash side of your wallet. I swear you're the only person still using cash."

Dan approached the bathroom door. "Give me a minute."

I set the food tray to the side and hollered, "I have to pee."

He closed the door behind himself. I smiled when I heard water running.

A moment later, Dan opened the door wearing nothing, held his hand out, and said, "Care to join me?"

From the bed, I inhaled the scent of vanilla. Closed my eyes and smiled. "You're so romantic. Ahh, vanilla."

"Seriously? I'm standing here naked, and you only noticed the bath salts?"

I kissed him on the lips, ran my finger up from his belly button to his chin, and whispered in his ear, "Oh, I noticed."

The Greige bathtub, with its smooth round edges, was not only inviting, it was also a welcoming site. Surrounded by glowing candles, a bottle of Muscat on ice, two glasses, and chocolate-covered dried fruits. I stood in front of the tub, inhaling its aroma until I felt Dan's lips on my shoulder. A moment later, he pulled my panties down to the floor. One by one, we slowly entered the water. I sat in front of Dan, leaned back, and thanked him for making another rainy day romantic.

"I think the rain brings something out in both of us," he said. "I'll never forget that rainy day. Making love to you in the doorway." Then he handed me a glass of wine.

We joked about our neighbors walking by at any given moment. "We were young, wild, and in love. Now, we're older, wiser, and deeply in love," he said as he kissed the nape of my neck, sending a chill down my spine. "You have such beautiful breasts."

I turned around to face him, straddled my legs around his torso, leaned in, and returned the kiss. I licked his chin, telling him that I wanted to spend the rest of my life wrapped up in his arms. After we had made love, drunk the entire bottle of wine, and devoured the fruit, we promised each other to always take time for moments like this, to make every day special, meaningful, and passionate.

Dan inhaled deeply. "I miss bathing, showering, and being alone with you."

"Aw, I want that as well, and when we return, we are going to build the most spectacular farmhouse."

Dan gave me a wry grin. "You're just happy about working alongside Frank again."

"No, I'm glad we're at the age where we know exactly what we want." I tilted my head. "Double shower heads, a king-size bed, and a peek-a-boo fireplace, please."

"What?" he asked as he added more hot water.

"You can see the flames from the front and back. I was thinking it would look nice between the kitchen and the family room."

"Whatever makes you happy."

"Being with you makes me happy. Dan, you're going to love working alongside Frank and Gina Marie."

"They're good people," he replied. "You have surrounded yourself with Rhode Island's best."

Dan took my foot in his hands and began massaging it. I closed my eyes, remembering the first time we visited Rhode Island. "Do you remember what we did on our first trip to Point Judith?"

He grabbed my other foot and answered me. "We went deep sea fishing."

"That's right, and we stayed at the Lighthouse Inn where you taught me to shoot pool."

Dan dunked my feet in the warm bath; laughingly he added, "You kicked my ass that night."

"The next day, you settled your debt and took me out to dinner. You took me to George's of Galilee. It's still my favorite restaurant in the world. It's your fault I fell in love with—"

He kissed me tenderly on the lips, holding my face in his hands, gazing into my eyes. For a moment our eyes locked, and I thought he was going to kiss me again, but instead he said, "Let's go back to bed. We'll stay in bed all day, order room service, and talk about our new home and all the places we want to go and see."

I took a deep, shuddering breath before replying, "I

would love to spend this rainy day in your arms." My
heart was full.

# Chapter 5

THE NIGHT'S MOONLIGHT BLED into the distance as we fell asleep. We woke to sunlight streaming through our window. It was a quarter past seven, and we were both starving. I moved to the chair in front of the desk to look over our itinerary for the day. Dan made no sound walking from the bathroom as the Tuscan-style runner covered the hardwood floor beneath his feet. When he put his hand on my shoulder, I jumped.

"What are you reading?" He asked, adding, "Sorry."

"I didn't hear you come out of the bathroom. I'm checking our schedule." I set the paper down and moved to the bed to grab my robe. "Our first stop is Vatican City, then the Colosseum, and after lunch we're going to Villa Borghese Gallery and Gardens."

"You better get a move on if you want to eat before we—"

We heard a knock on the door. Our breakfast had arrived. "I ordered coffee and croissants. We'll save our calories for dinner." We had reservations at the Dome Restaurant at seven.

"Sounds good to me," Dan said as he opened the door for the woman to roll the cart in. He handed her ten euros and thanked her for also bringing him a map of Rome.

We took our breakfast out onto the balcony. The coffee was delicious. I laughed when I read the notecard, "Irving Farm, Millerton, New York."

"I assure you the croissants are freshly made in Italy." He reached for a second one. "Let's go. Seriously, we have to get a move on if we're going to see everything on our list today."

To my delight, Dan was able to get us reservations inside the Sistine Chapel. "Dan, I told you to surprise me. I should have said take my breath away, because this is amazing." I held my hands to my heart. "Standing here right now with you and seeing Michelangelo's masterpiece. I'm breathless."

He shook his head, gazing up, and replied, "I'm right there with you. I had no idea how magnificent it could be. I can't stop looking at all the details."

Three hours later, we were on our way. Lucky for us we passed the Mozart Café where we grabbed two tuna sandwiches, two cannoli, and a lemonade to share on our way to the Colosseum. From there we went to the Villa Borghese Gallery and Gardens. "Did you enjoy the gardens?" Dan asked as we made our way past a crowd of German-speaking women.

"I stole a few ideas," I said, smiling.

"I figured you did. It's about a twenty-minute ride back to the hotel. We have almost two hours before dinner, would you like to walk around Rome for a bit?"

"Somebody is well rested," I replied. "Umm, yes please."

Dan hailed a taxi, and we got out near St. Peter's Square.

"Ahh," I said holding my hands up in the air. "It is breathtaking today. Thank you, Lord."

"I could live with the low seventies all year round," Dan replied. Kissed me on my lips and added, "Rainy days aren't so bad either."

I returned his kiss and reached for his hand as we strolled past one magnificent piece of architecture after another. Dan wasn't the only person holding a map in his hand. People spoke Italian, French, German, Chinese, even Japanese. Oh, and English. "I can't believe we're here," I said.

Dan hugged me. "Wait until tomorrow. I promise you every day will be better than the one before."

We arrived back at the hotel by five-thirty. Plenty of time to change our clothes and get to the restaurant by seven. "Are you tired?" Dan asked as he took his shirt off. Standing before me wearing no shoes, only his jeans, taking my breath away one more time.

"No, but I'd love to take a shower with you if you don't mind."

He didn't have to say anything, I knew by his smile that he'd be joining me. Once inside, I turned every sprayer on. I chose rain for the overhead and for the sides a gentle mist. I took hold of the wall as if I were being interrogated. My stance was strong as he entered me from behind. When I felt his explosion inside of me, my head fell back with pleasure. Dan's groan left chills down my spine. I couldn't let go of the wall. My entire body was tingling. When Dan began to wash my hair, I allowed the suds to trickle. I turned around when he kissed my cheek.

With a devilish grin he said, "Remind me to tell Frank, we want multiple shower heads in our master bath."

I laughed. I kissed his lips and whispered in his ear, "In every bathroom."

For dinner, I chose a cocoa-brown V-neck wrap-dress with dolman sleeves and matching high heels. I put Dan's Tommy Bahama jeans, white T-shirt, and underwear on the bed next to his navy-blue dinner jacket.

When Dan picked up his T-shirt and commented on how soft it felt, I told him where I'd bought it.

"It's a knockoff," I said. Then laughed. "It still cost more than my dress. I ordered it from Amazon, it's supposed to be as soft as a Brunello Cucinelli. Umm, there was no way I was paying almost five hundred dollars for a T-shirt, but I'm glad you like it."

I curled the last strand, put lipstick on, and added a little mascara on my upper lashes before picking up the list of activities for the next day.

"Where are we headed?" he asked. "Julie?"

I closed my eyes, taking in the scent of his shave cream one more time before answering him. "Yes, my love. Umm, tomorrow we are going to see the Pantheon Monument, and we are going to visit the Santa Maria Maggiore church. And on Tuesday, we're going to Castel

Sant'Angelo by taxi. Your note says we have to get up early that day, you could only get reservations for nine a.m."

"Okay, and how about Wednesday?" he asked as he slipped his foot into his dress shoe.

I glanced down again and read, "Centro Storico and the Spanish Steps." I raised my eyebrows and added, "I can't wait to see all the gorgeous flowers."

"Do we still have Thursday and Friday open?" he asked.

"Yes, and I'm glad. I'd like to stroll around a bit. Be spontaneous for once in my life."

We arrived at the restaurant on time. I read the menu aloud: "We cook with love, we taste with passion, we always eat one hundred percent Italian. Eating is an emotional experience." Reading the menu and how they describe their pizza, I couldn't help myself. "I want the eggplant pizza. Fresh tomatoes, basil, and mozzarella, drizzled with olive oil."

Dan looked up from the menu practically drooling. "I want to order everything on here."

The waiter came over with a bottle of red wine and we accepted it with pleasure. Dan ordered the veal and a few appetizers for us to try. The wine was amazing, not too sweet and perfect in size. Dan also ordered a bottle of sparkling limoncello to go with our meal.

"Hey, I can't help thinking about Rose. Do you think—"

Dan reached for my hand, stopping me from asking

any further questions. "Julie, you are all I care about, want to think about. We're on vacation. Let's enjoy ourselves. This is our time."

# Chapter 6

DAN WAS RIGHT. IT was our time, and we were in Italy for heaven's sake.

The restaurant gave us a complimentary bottle of limoncello to take home along with a piece of ricotta pie and our many leftovers. We're both good tippers, and I suppose on nights like this it pays off handsomely. "Let's sleep in tomorrow, we'll eat breakfast out on the balcony and enjoy the sun's warmth on our faces before heading out for the day."

"You read my mind," he said as he opened the door to our room. Dan turned to face me, his eyes brimmed with compassion. His brow furrowed. "I don't want you to worry about Rose."

"I'm sure she has plenty of people who care about her. Right?"

"Yes," he said, pleasant and unflustered.

We set everything in the fridge and sat out on the balcony to watch the sunset. I was grateful for our unspoken words. We both knew each other too well to share empty conversations. And my worrying about his therapist had no place in our lives, or on our vacation. Directly out in front of us, the sky had shades of orange and red with a big round yellow burst in the middle high above the rooftops. My mind drifted again. We were living our dream, running an inn, and we were in Italy. I looked across the table, his eyes still vibrant blue. I prayed he was feeling better.

He looked back at me. "What?"

I smiled. "Nothing. Thank you for bringing me here, and for loving me."

He reached over, took my hand in his own, kissed my palm, and said, "I thank God every day for you. You're so beautiful." With a sultry grin he added, "Voluptuous, smart, and you're the love of my life."

"You, my love, are smarter than you know, you're still sexy as ever. You're kind and the most passionate person I ever met. You chose me. You made me your wife. You and I are together for a reason. I thank God every day for us." I exhaled slowly before leaning forward to kiss him.

A few minutes later, we went to bed. I fell asleep in the arms of the only man I had ever loved, and when I awoke, I was still wrapped up in his arms.

I kissed his cheek. "Good morning, handsome."

Dan stretched out his arms, then hugged me tight until I couldn't move or breathe. "Morning, beautiful," he said, and then let go of me. "How about I order scrambled eggs for breakfast with toast and coffee, then we'll go over the rest of our stay in Rome before we head up to Florence?"

"Sounds like a plan. I'm so excited to see the gardens."

Dan reached for the phone, ordered room service, and said, "I read that the Giardino Bardini Garden offers the most beautiful views of Florence. It's why I booked our vacation now."

"I love seeing all the tulips around town, in the restaurants, window boxes, and around the clock tower."

"Not to brag, but did you know Tulipark was Rome's first tulip farm?"

I gave him a smug look. "Okay, so you did your homework," I said laughingly.

First, we discovered the Pantheon Monument. We both found it to be magnificent, but then standing inside the Santa Maria Maggiore and seeing all the delicate artwork, splendor, and creativity left us both in awe.

"There isn't enough time in the day to take in all of this glory," I said, staring at the paintings on the walls and up on the ceiling.

"I'm mesmerized," Dan replied, adding, "How do you even describe this to someone? You can't."

"This trip gets better and better," I said.

When we stepped outside, we were met by a long line of people waiting to go inside. I wanted to tell them to enjoy every second because moments like this only happen once in a lifetime.

"We should have come here sooner," Dan said as we moved forward in line.

"I will treasure this vacation for the rest of my life." Dan's cell phone rang. "It's Jesse."

We moved out of the way for people to go by us. Dan

answered the call. "Hello! We're good. You have got to come with us next time."

I looked at Dan. Did he just say next time? I listened patiently as he spoke to Jesse. "Put him on speaker," I said.

Dan handed the phone to me. "Hey, is everything okay? How's Lady?"

Jesse said everything was great. He told me Kourtnee sent Rose a fruit basket from the Fruit Company and shared Rose's wishes for no public services, a memorial for the family only. "Thank Kourtnee for us please, and yes, I'll put Dan back on." I handed the phone back to Dan.

I heard him say, "Thanks, yes we are. Sorry, I forgot to let you know." Then he put his cell phone back in his pocket.

"Let him know what?" I asked.

"We were supposed to call and let them know we landed safely."

"Oh, my goodness. With Rose and all the excitement, I didn't think to call them. He's right, we should have called. Dan, I don't think my heart can take any more."

"I'm glad we came." He leaned over and kissed me on the cheek. "There's more to see. Are you hungry?" he asked as he waved a taxi driver down.

"Starving," I said, hoping to find an outdoor café.

We stopped at the Antico Caffè Grecco near the Spanish Steps. I ordered the espresso with cinnamon and an almond biscotti. Dan got a gelato that must have been good because he said "mmm" with every bite.

"We're coming back here tomorrow," he said as he licked his spoon for the last time.

I had to agree with him. "Everything looks delicious." Our stroll back to the hotel was delightful.

Forty minutes later. "I needed that walk, but now I'm tired," he said to me as we arrived back at the hotel.

After we kicked off our shoes, we both headed for the balcony. There was something special about the people in Italy. I watched a man stop and look in every window as he walked down the street. I wondered if he was lost or window-shopping. I thought about Dan being confused. The death of Rose's husband and immediately said a prayer for Dan.

"Julie. Sweetheart, are you okay?"

I glanced over to look at him, looked into the eyes of my husband, and answered him. "Yes, my love—"

"Where are you, because I've been talking to you for the past five minutes, but—"

"I'm right here with you. I'm sorry. What did you say?"

"It's not important," he said but then added, "What's your favorite part of being on vacation so far?"

"Everything," I replied.

"Are you sure? Because it feels like you're a million miles away."

I reached over the table and laced my fingers into his. "I haven't had one nightmare since we arrived."

Dan squeezed my hand. "That's great." Then he asked

me, "How often do you have nightmares?"

I thought about what Rose said to me the day I went to see her. *Dan can't help you if he doesn't know what's wrong.* "Several times a month," I said and took back my hand.

Dan tilted his head before resting it on his knuckles. "Is that why you wake up in the middle of the night and leave our bed?"

"Sometimes," I replied, hoping I didn't spoil the mood, but I could not help myself. My sense of being betrayed will haunt me till the day I die.

"What are they—"

"About?" I replied. "Every one of them is the same." I took a deep breath and found the courage to tell him. "I walk into a room and find you making love to another woman."

Dan's hand moved to his mouth. He went to reach for mine but stopped. "I'm sorry I did that to you. I promise, no more nightmares. Julie, we don't have to work. We're retired. We can travel, be together. We'll sell the inn. The hell with the farmhouse. We'll see the world."

I shook my head. "I can't sell the inn. Dan, the inn belongs to all of us. To Kevin, Kourtnee, Michael, Christine, Teresa, and Gina Marie. And what about Cathy and Amanda? They gave up their businesses to be with me. I would never sell the inn."

# Chapter 7

IT WAS RAINING OUTSIDE, so we picked up a pizza and had dinner in our room. I assured Dan I would have been lost if not for my employees. The Inn in Rhode Island was their home as much as it was ours.

"I'm so glad you had them to help you open the inn and to keep you company."

I looked over at him knowing he had our friends, Lynnae and Jesse, by his side. And he had our dog, Lady.

The next morning, our concierge handed Dan a roadmap with directions from Rome to Florence. He had even mapped out a few stops along the countryside for us to tour. "Your car will be here as well," he said.

"I'm so excited to tour Florence," I said.

"Me too," Dan replied and then added, "You're going to love my surprise."

It was so beautiful outside that we walked back to the café. Every table outside was taken, so we sat inside. I ordered another espresso and the tart with apricot jam, while Dan helped himself to an Irish coffee and the pistachio cake with ricotta.

"Not your everyday breakfast, but I'll take it," I said as I sat down, but then I turned around after hearing a woman crying. "Are you okay?" I asked, not knowing if she understood me.

She waved her hand at me. "I'm sorry," she said in perfect English. "I don't mean to cry, but I'm so lost right now."

"We'll help you," Dan said to her and stood up holding out the map.

She wiped her eyes and smiled. "I'm just being silly. I'm not lost, I'm confused as to why the hell I'm here in the first place."

I looked around. "Are you here alone?"

The woman shook her head and replied, "Only for the time being, my daughter is supposed to join me for the summer."

"Would you like to sit with us?" I asked. "I'm Julie Holliday and this is my husband, Dan. We're from Rhode Island."

"I shouldn't bother the two of you with my concerns. I'll figure it out."

"You're no trouble," I replied. "We'll just share a cup of coffee. I'm sure there's a solution to whatever it is that's bothering you."

"Can I get you something to eat?" Dan asked. "I'd be glad to buy you breakfast this morning."

"You're so kind. Both of you." She picked up her cup and said, "Carmela, but everyone calls me Carmie." Then she sat down at our table and asked us, "Are you on your honeymoon?"

I smiled. "No, but we're on a long-overdue vacation."

She looked at Dan and gave him a simpering smile. "You look like a hard-working man." Carmie sipped her coffee before adding, "My husband Eddie worked long hours. I'm from Troy, New York, by the way."

Dan and I both looked at each other. "We used to live in Dutchess County, about an hour south of Troy," I said. "We're here on vacation. Tomorrow, we're leaving for Florence."

"Umm, a three-week vacation," Dan said, smiling. "Does that make up for waiting so long?"

"No!" we both said in unison. And everyone laughed.

"Wait, did you say Florence?" she said, sounding bemused at the thought.

"Yes," Dan said to her as he put his fork down. "I'm supposed to leave for Umbria tomorrow."

Dan looked down at the map.

She was a tall, slender woman, and if I had to guess, in her late sixties. She had olive skin and dark brown eyes that appeared very nurturing to me. Much like my own mother's. "Is this your first time visiting Italy?"

"No, I traveled here with my sisters, Julia, Rose, and Josephine. We visited our grandparents in Calabria for an entire summer. I was only nine at the time. Now, I'm the only one still living. My two older brothers, my sisters, and most of my cousins have passed. I've always wanted to return, but not like this. My husband promised me we would travel, come to Italy together, visit my relatives, but when he suffered a heart attack..." I reached out and touched her hand. "I'm so sorry."

"I'm sorry for your loss," Dan said. "Carmie, I'm more than happy to drive you to Umbria. So you don't have to be alone." He held out the map. "Look it's on our way." Then he added, "Think about it." He smiled. Gave her that heart-piercing look of his.

She inhaled. "You know what I think? I will have some scrambled eggs," adding, "if you don't mind."

"You got it," Dan said as he got up from the table. "How about some juice? Julie, can I get you anything?"

"Orange juice, please."

"Three juices coming up."

"I'm glad we bumped into each other," I said and meant it. Then I noticed the map and saw where Dan had drawn a line to Florence along the Autostrada and our route passing through Umbria. "Oh, look, it's on our way."

Carmie looked at the map. "That's very generous of the two of you to offer, but I'm used to driving alone. I even have GPS on my cell phone. The man at the car rental facility said I can use my cell phone's GPS without using any data. I shouldn't have any problems." She looked over at Dan and then back at me. "Can I think about it?"

"Of course. So you mentioned you have a daughter. Just one?"

"Yes, but I have three granddaughters and five great-grandchildren." She reached down for her purse and pulled out a small photo album. "This is Maryanne with her grandson Hunter. He's so smart and such a good boy, especially with his little sister."

I looked at the picture she was holding. "I love his curls."

Carmie flipped to another picture. "This is Hunter reading to his cousins." She was beaming with pride when she added, "He does whatever he's told, he's handy around my house. Helps great-grandma all the time."

"He seems like an old soul."

"Yes, I think so too," she said as Dan set her plate in front of her. In addition to the juice, he had also grabbed three croissants.

"I ordered a latte, but they gave me a glass of milk."

Carmie laughed.

"Ooh, they're still warm," I said taking a bite of my croissant.

"Thank you, Dan." Her eyes were no longer red, and she appeared calmer, more relaxed. "My stomach was so upset before. I was telling your wife about my daughter and grandchildren. Do the two of you have children?" she asked and began to eat her breakfast.

"No," Dan said to her and then added, "but we are surrounded by a lot of good friends that we call family, and they have kids."

She smiled and helped herself to one of the croissants.

"Dan and I arrived in Rome a few days ago. Every stop along the way has been more magnificent than the one before. I'm so excited to go to Florence. We have reservations to see the Villa Borghese Gallery and Gardens. After that, we're hoping to just do some sightseeing along the countryside."

"And after the gardens, I have one more surprise for you to see," Dan said, smiling.

"It sounds wonderful," Carmie said. "Dan, I think I will take you up on your offer."

"Sounds good," he replied and then asked her, "Where are you staying in Rome? We're at the Michelangelo Hotel about fifteen minutes from here."

"I'm about ten minutes away, at the Royal Suite Trinità dei Monti."

"Here's our cell phone numbers." He handed her a napkin and told her to call if she had a change of heart or any concerns. "We can walk you back to your hotel, or you're welcome to join us for the day," he said.

"You don't mind?"

"Not at all," Dan told her.

"Carmie," I said as I stood up. "I believe we were put in each other's paths for a reason."

She squeezed my hand.

"We have tickets to see the Castel Sant'Angelo," Dan said. "Let me see if I can obtain one for you right now." Dan looked at his cell phone. "Quick and easy. We're all set."

"I don't know how to thank the two of you. I feel better already. I insist you let me buy lunch."

"Not a chance," Dan said.

We left the café and strolled together laughing and reminiscing about what we had seen so far on our trip. After Dan hailed us a taxi, we told Carmie about our plan to visit the Centro Storico and the Spanish Steps before leaving the next day. "You're welcome to come with us," Dan said. "I could have our taxi driver pick you up around eight-thirty."

"Are you sure?"

I looked at her. "Yes, we would love to have you join us."

She laughed out loud. "Do they serve wine?"

"Wine in a garden. I like that," I said.

# Chapter 8

As promised, Dan picked up our dinner tab that evening. Right before Carmie got out of the taxi at her hotel, she thanked us, and we assured her it was our pleasure.

"Bless your hearts," she said. "I'll see you both tomorrow morning."

"We're looking forward to it," I said. "Oh, we'll grab breakfast along the way."

When we arrived back at our hotel room, I told Dan there was something special about Carmie. "I can't put my finger on it, but I know in my heart we met her for a reason."

Dan sat on the edge of the bed and took off his shoes. "I'm glad you said something to her when you heard her crying. At least now she's not alone."

"She told me she believes there are still good people in this world, and we're some of them."

"Huh, did you tell her that you take everyone under your wing?" He got up, picked up his tablet, turned around, and asked, "Hey, is she going to visit family in Umbria?"

"I don't know." I slipped my nightgown and robe on and sat down on the bed to rub lotion on my hands. "I'll ask her tomorrow if she has family there."

It was nearly nine-thirty when Dan climbed into bed. He didn't say much, just that he was glad we were

going to see one more site before heading out. "I want to take our time tomorrow. I'm not in a hurry to get to Florence. We can stop along the way if the two of you see something."

I thought for a moment. "When is our reservation to see the Boboli Gardens?"

"Next Monday," he replied as he turned his lamp off. "Ahh, so we have a long weekend to visit the countryside." I kissed him on his cheek. "You did a great job planning this vacation."

When he didn't respond, I wondered if he was having second thoughts about Carmie tagging along.

As if he was reading my mind he rolled over, returned my kiss, and said, "No, I'm not upset Carmie is traveling with us. I wouldn't have asked her if I didn't want her to come." He kissed me again. This time on the lips. "She reminds me of my mother."

"Your mother? She's not old enough to be your mother."

"She's eighty-four," he said, and I think I choked on my own saliva.

"What?"

Dan laughed. "She said she drinks a glass of wine every night with dinner, and that's what keeps her skin looking so beautiful."

"From now on, I'm drinking wine with my dinner."

We spooned until we both fell asleep. When I woke

up, Dan was already out on the balcony, feet resting on the railing, hands clasped behind his head, leaning back as if he didn't have a care in the world. *Thank you, Lord, for bringing us here, he seems much better. I'm sorry about leaving him alone.* I never would have thought leaving Dan for those two years would have been so traumatic for him. Obviously, it still bothered him, and seeing Carmie alone was concerning.

I grabbed my robe and walked out to where he was. "Good morning, handsome," I said as I sat down next to him.

"Even the sunrise is more beautiful here."

"What time did you get up?"

"Around four-thirty."

I smiled knowing he was on his May schedule. My heart beamed about the surprise I was creating for him when we returned to the inn. "Ahh, you're on turkey time."

He reached over and held my hand in his. "You used to love sitting in the turkey blind, watching the deer come within inches of us, seeing the turkey's breeding rituals, strutting and gobbling."

I inhaled. "Yes, and watching the sunrise with you." I thought for a minute. "I still love being by your side." I remembered those mornings very well. "I loved listening to the early-morning birds as they woke the ground creatures. To see life unfold right in front of us." I smiled knowing that we would be doing it all again: turkey hunting, kayaking, fishing, hiking, and riding our motorcycle.

A half-hour later, the sun beamed on our faces. Dan stretched, got up, and headed inside.

I was still standing out on the balcony when I heard him say, "Great."

I turned around, stepped inside, and asked, "Who was that?"

He smirked. "Carmie. She's ready. Perfect timing, our car just arrived."

"What are you up to?" I asked knowing exactly what that look of his meant, but instead of pursuing, I got dressed.

"Carmie said she's not in a hurry to get to Umbria. She's agreed to see the countryside with us for a couple of days. Are you ready?"

"All set," I replied and grabbed my purse.

"You're both going to love my next surprise!"

We picked Carmie up at her hotel and headed straight for Centro Storico and the Spanish Steps.

"I have to say the Trevi Fountain was my favorite," Carmie said to us as she stood in front of a small gift shop gazing in the window.

Dan asked her if she wanted to go inside, but she declined. "I'd like to buy the two of you breakfast. How about over there?" She was pointing to La Buvette.

We crossed the street and sat at one of the outdoor tables. When Dan announced he was having two poached eggs over avocado and toast with the cheese sauce, Carmie and I both agreed to order the same. In addition to our breakfast, we ordered three cappuccinos.

Right before the waiter set our drinks down, I asked her, "Carmie, I've been meaning to ask you, do you have family in Umbria?"

"I used to. My godmother. Last November, I received a call telling me that I had inherited her home. Three days ago, I met with her attorney in Rome to sign the papers."

"I'm sorry about your godmother," I said, and Dan too echoed my sentiments.

"Thank you. I met her once when she came to America for my first holy communion. She never missed a birthday. Every year, I received a card telling me how much she loved me. I always called and thanked her. And on her birthday, I sent her her favorite flowers, lilies. She's the reason I became a librarian. Matilda told me that librarians are not considered professionals in Italy. She said librarianship suited her perfectly. We both love to read."

"She must have had some impact on you growing up," Dan said as he paid for our breakfast.

Carmie pointed her finger at him. "I was supposed to pay."

We ate our breakfast in time for us to get back to our hotels before check-out.

Dan waited for us in the car while I helped Carmie bring her suitcase downstairs and finalize her stay at her hotel. When we arrived at ours, I sat in the car with Carmie telling her about the inn and how blessed we were to have such great employees. "I met Teresa in a drugstore. She was singing like a songbird, and I knew she was perfect for the receptionist job."

"How many rooms do you have?" she asked.

"Twenty-five," I replied as I turned to face her. "When we return to Point Judith, Dan and I are building a farmhouse. I'll give you my email and our address, I would love for you and your daughter Maryanne to stay with us."

"We would love that," she said just as Dan set our bags in the trunk next to hers.

# Chapter 9

"ARE YOU LADIES READY?" Dan asked as he set his cell phone in the caddy and put the car in drive.

"Absolutely," Carmie responded.

Then Dan's cell phone announced, "Head north on Piazza della Repubblica toward Via Giuseppe Romita."

"It's pretty much a straight run," Dan said. "So feel free to talk, and let me know when you ladies want to stop for lunch, the restroom, or to take a break and stretch."

I looked back at Carmie and smiled. "I'm glad you decided to ride with us."

"I'll admit, I was a little nervous about driving more than two hours alone. When I called the car rental company to cancel, the woman said it was a good idea. What if I got into an accident? Or had a flat tire?"

I saw Dan look at her in the mirror. "You don't have to worry about that. I can set up an Uber driver to pick your daughter up at the airport in Perugia and bring her to Umbria."

"Julie, where on Earth did you find him?" she asked, and then promised Dan she would be fine driving to the airport. "It's only a half-hour from the villa. I'll be fine. Besides, Maryanne will want to go places."

"Okay, but if there's anything you need for either of us to do…"

"I'll be sure to let you know," she said and then tapped him on his arm. "I'd love to hear more about your new farmhouse."

I saw Dan smile. "We're both excited to start construction on the house. Did Julie tell you about her favorite builder?"

I grinned at Dan and then decided to move to the backseat. Like Gumby, I climbed over the armrest and sat next to Carmie. "Frank is the best contractor in the world. He's smart, diligent, and he knows how to build a house that makes all your dreams come true. His budget master is a pro with spending. Gina Marie knows exactly how to get the job done and stay within budget. Both Dan and I fell in love with Frank and Gina Marie. In fact, she bought a piece of property right next to our inn and built her retirement home on it."

"You'd like her if you met her," Dan said and then added, "She's the salt of the earth. She teaches at the inn. Every Saturday, she has classes down by the pond and shows our guests how to paint landscapes." Dan laughed. "And on Sundays, she makes Julie stop working so we can all go for a ride on our motorcycles."

"Your inn sounds wonderful."

"Thank you," I said. "It was a five-bedroom farmhouse when I bought it. Frank, Gina Marie, and their crew turned it into an inn in a little over a year. I love every aspect of running the inn. I have a chef, Michael, who knows how to run a kitchen and cook mouthwatering meals. His wife Christine makes all of our desserts. We also have a day spa. Cathy runs that, and Amanda operates a daycare on the property, too."

Dan looked back at us. "And she has a church on the property."

I smiled at the thought. "It's a small chapel. Frank and his barn-raising crew built it for me."

"I say my prayers at every meal and at night," Carmie replied. "Last night, I said a prayer for the two of you. The first day I met you, I asked God to allow me the time to get to know you more, and here we are."

I tapped her leg. "You are a blessing. Thank you for including us in your prayers." I winked at her. "I prayed for you, too. I asked God to watch over you during your new adventure."

"The lawyer's receptionist told me that Umbria is the most beautiful region in all of Italy. She said the views from the property are spectacular. The lawyer said the home was contractor-ready, whatever that means."

I Googled it and read aloud, "Builder's finish. Therefore the new owner can finish it as they wish."

"Oh," Carmie said. "I guess we'll see when we get there."

"Do you know how big the home is?" I asked, wondering if it was similar to my one-thousand-square-foot cottage.

Carmie looked over her shoulder. "I have a folder full of papers the attorney gave me, but it's in the trunk. I was so upset, I never opened it. At first, the idea of retiring to Italy and owning a small villa sounded like a dream, but then not knowing anyone scared me. I should have waited for my daughter to come with me."

"Carmie, you'll be fine," Dan said. "Julie was by herself when she moved to Rhode Island, and she did a wonderful job building a new life for herself."

I inhaled, wondering how I was supposed to explain to Carmie why I left the love of my life for an inn. I felt her hand tap my leg.

"You know, when my husband died, I told myself 'Get up, keep moving, you have a daughter, three granddaughters, and a life to live.' Now, I have my great-grandchildren to brighten my day. Women can be strong when they need to. They're stronger than men when it comes to their families."

I was grateful to have met her. "Sometimes, we just have to be strong enough," I replied.

For the next three or four miles we rode in silence, then Dan said, "Is anyone hungry?"

We heard the GPS announce, "Turn left onto Via Pastrengo then right onto Via Pinciana for nine kilometers."

Up ahead we saw a restaurant that looked nice. "Would you ladies like a glass of wine? We can stop at that restaurant. The Mezzo Ristorante," he said, sounding very Italian.

"Sounds good to me," she said and stretched out her legs, hitting the back of Dan's seat. "Dan, would you grab the manila folder out of my suitcase?"

It was three o'clock in the afternoon, and yet the parking lot was full of vehicles. It was a sea of Fiats. Dan parked next to the only Mercedes in the lot. The temperature outside was climbing. I looked at the temperature gauge and read aloud, "It's eighty-four degrees already. Summer is rolling in fast."

When we got out of the car, I asked Dan how far away we were.

"We're about a third of the way," he replied and then opened the trunk for Carmie to grab her folder.

I leaned in close to him and asked if he was okay to drive. "I can drive the rest of the way."

"I'm fine," he replied.

For lunch, both Carmie and I ordered the salad with fresh-grated parmesan cheese and a glass of red wine. Dan ordered eggplant on a baguette with fresh mozzarella and garden tomatoes. After we placed our order, Carmie opened the folder. "This is a copy of my dual citizenship." Then she handed me a stack of pictures.

I looked over at the first photo. "Oh, my word. Look at the views. They're spectacular. Are those olive trees?" Then I pointed to another photo. "How many trees do you think you have?"

Carmie didn't answer me right away, she just stared at the photo. "Where's the cottage? I don't see a home."

# Chapter 10

Aside from a few photos, the folder consisted of numerous legal documents. I too wondered how big the villa was, or if there was one at all. One picture showed several rooflines, but I wasn't sure if it was a shed, the villa, or a small barn. "Carmie, did your godmother ever talk to you about the property or the house?"

"No, mostly she wanted to know about me and how Maryanne was doing in school, or how things were going at the library."

I closed the folder and handed it back to her.

She set it in her bag and stared out the window for a second. "As soon as Maryanne was born, she would ask about her. Then life got in the way, and before I knew it, I had grandchildren of my own. Oh, wait. I called her when I won a trophy for ballroom dancing a few years back. I came in first place in all six dance categories. You know, the waltz, international tango, Viennese waltz, foxtrot, quickstep, and the American tango. That was another passion we both shared. She too loved to dance. I guess I inherited a lot from her."

"I did the cha-cha once," Dan said.

I rolled my eyes. "He dressed up in a costume and crashed my candle party."

"Hey, I wasn't alone," Dan said. "Our neighbor was right alongside me that day."

Carmie laughed. "I'd pay to see that photo." She turned to face me. "You got pictures, right?"

"Oh, yeah." I looked at Dan, he was beaming from ear to ear remembering how silly he was. Then I explained, "The party host not only sold candles, she also taught the cha-cha at her parties. When the music started, Dan and our neighbor came downstairs wearing hula costumes. We were in stitches watching them sway to the music."

Next, we heard the GPS announce, "Turn right onto SR147 for seven kilometers. Your destination will be on the right."

Dan glanced back at Carmie. "Are you getting excited? You're almost home."

When she looked out her window, I knew she was wondering what her future held. "It is beautiful here," she said.

Outside were rolling hills adorned by churches, massive homes, and vineyards. "Oh, my!" I said and pointed toward Carmie's window. "Look at that church. Have you ever seen a more gorgeous structure? The arches alone would make the devil enter." The beauty of the countryside amazed me, and we weren't even out of the car yet.

Up ahead, we saw two large stone pillars leading to a row of oak trees on our right and an entire town below on the left.

"It must be after this estate," Dan said to us but then

added, "No, it says we're here."

"You have reached your destination."

Dan picked up the GPS, held it in his hand for a moment and said, "Let me ask that gentleman." He pointed to an elderly man carrying a ladder.

"Let's get out," I said and motioned for Carmie to follow Dan.

Dan tried to ask the man where Matilda's home was when Carmie said, "Here let me try. Scusate, sto cercando la casa de Matilda Felitti?"

When Carmie said the name Felitti, she could have knocked me over. I had once baked a cake for a bride with the same last name.

"Ecco questa e la sua casa." He smiled at Carmie and nodded. "Sono il giardiniere." This time he grinned at Dan, "Francesco," and put his hand out.

Dan shook his hand as Carmie explained to us, "This is Francesco. He says he's the gardener."

"Scusami il mio inglese e cosi buono," he said to Carmie. "Miss Carmela."

She took his hand and said, "He said his English is not so good." Then she asked him, "You know my name?"

"Si." Then he pointed to a young man trimming a hedgerow. "Mi scusi."

Francesco came back to where we were and pointed to Carmie, "Carmela."

"Ah, it's nice to meet you. I'm Francesco's grandson, Nico. My sister Aria is here too. Grandpa doesn't speak very good English, and so we are here to welcome you and make you feel at home. Yes?"

Francesco nodded.

"Thank you," Carmie said. "Can you take us to my godmother's home?"

A broad smile appeared on Nico's face. "This is your home." Then he pointed to the end of the driveway. "I will show you."

We followed him up the slope and entered the property through a tall, stone archway. In front of us was a courtyard surrounded by several more archways. "This way, please." Nico walked through the center archway leading to a magnificent garden. "Grandpa wanted you to see how well he has been taking care of Matilda's olive trees. He said she loved them almost as much as you."

I looked back at Francesco and saw pride on his face. "Please tell your grandfather this is astonishing."

"Grazie," Francesco replied.

"Grandpa doesn't speak English, but he understands a lot more than he lets on. Come, I will show you your home and then the rest of the property."

"How did you learn to speak English so well?" Dan asked as we followed Nico through another archway.

"Matilda taught most of the children in the village to speak English." Nico pointed toward a small building made of stone and stucco. When he opened the door, we all followed him inside. On an entire wall and on every table, mantel, and bookshelf we saw photos of Carmie, Maryanne, her three granddaughters, and Carmie's great-grandchildren. Next to the Virgin Mary was a photo of Matilda standing behind Carmie in her communion dress. On the table next to it was Matilda's memorial card from the funeral home along with a letter. No envelope, just a piece of paper folded in thirds.

Carmie picked up the paper. When she opened it, the scent of gardenias filled the room. It was a watershed moment hearing Carmie read aloud the letter.

"Dear Carmie, if you are reading this letter then you know I can no longer be with you. My prayer is that you know how much I love you. You were my greatest gift in life. You brought joy to me every time I heard your voice. Listening to the stories about your beautiful daughter Maryanne, your three granddaughters, and your great-grandchildren warmed my heart. When you told me you wanted to follow in my footsteps and become a librarian, I was full of pride. This home is yours now. I hope you will visit often. Many years ago, my godparents gave it to me. Our family has gone through many wars and has fought hard to ensure the property remains in the Felitti family. I shall be watching over you from afar. May happiness surround you always. Love, Matilda."

"She loved you so much," Nico said before showing us the other rooms.

Matilda's bedroom was simple. A large bed with an enormous pillow top, one dresser, and in the corner, a small table and chair. "The lace is beautiful," I said.

The bedspread and pillows were adorned with hand-embroidered ivory lace.

Francesco opened two small doors exposing shelves hosting an array of lace products. From bed linens to tablecloths, and once again the scent of gardenias was prominent.

"Shall we take a walk?" Nico asked, holding his hand out.

Outside, the courtyard was circular, under each window rested a flower box filled with white cascading flowers. In front of us were ten archways. "Where do they lead to?" Carmie asked, pointing to the one on her right.

"That one leads to the main part of the castle," Nico replied.

"Castle?" Dan said with a look of shock on his face.

# Chapter 11

"CASTLE?" CARMIE SAID ALOUD. "Did you say—"

"Si," Francesco replied. "Castello."

An hour later, we completed our tour of Carmie's castle. The medieval construction consisted of three levels, and a basement full of bricks, wooden window frames, and over a dozen wheelbarrows. There were sixty rooms in total, all in disrepair. The first floor had several enormous rooms. We saw what could be a kitchen, but there were no appliances or dishes to eat from. But there was a beautiful stone fireplace in every room. On the second floor, we discovered thirty bedrooms and bathrooms. In one of the bedrooms sat a wheel barrel full of old bricks. "Do all homes in Italy require this many wheelbarrows?" I asked, rubbing my hand over the archway made of river pebbles.

"Julie, Dan, you have to see this," Carmie said to us, standing out on the balcony.

I caught my breath before it left my chest. "Oh, my."

"Wow," Dan said as he pointed toward a small tower. "The views are panoramic from here."

From where we were standing, we could see the olive grove, several courtyards, and rolling hills. "Where does that road lead?" Carmie asked.

"All around the castle," Nico replied.

"Carmie, did you know all of this was part of your inheritance?"

She looked at Dan as if to say no. "I read some of the paperwork. Not all of it. I thought it needed drapes, not—"

She began to cry.

I hugged her. "It will all work out. You have a beautiful residence."

"What am I supposed to do with all these rooms or the fact that I don't know the first thing about taking care of a damn castle?"

Francesco hung his head.

"Well, the views are spectacular," Dan said, trying to reassure her of its beauty.

I looked at her. "You can still enjoy the property with your daughter. I'm sure something good can come out of all this."

Francesco led the way to the courtyard where a beautiful young girl with long luscious curls and bigger-than-saucers eyes was serving coffee and biscotti.

Nico looked at Francesco before saying, "This is my sister Aria. Please sit and rest a moment, and I will get you one more thing Matilda left for you."

Aria was near sixteen or seventeen, and just like Nico she spoke perfect English. "I'm sorry about your loss," she said to Carmie. "Matilda was very special to all of us. I attended the Elizabeth English Academy and now I am going to an all-girls academy, thanks to her. I'm studying English and literature. Matilda said I should be a storyteller." She looked at Dan before asking, "Would you like some espresso?"

Dan inhaled. "Yes, please. Thank you."

As she poured his espresso, both Carmie and I held up our empty cups. A moment later, Francesco and Nico came back to the table, sat down, and opened a large, brown soft-leather attaché case. "These are the financials for the property. Matilda wanted you to get settled in and feel comfortable here. I wasn't supposed to give them to you until tomorrow, but Papa suspects that you are afraid. He wants you to stay."

"I'm a retired librarian, Nico. I thought I was going to spend my summer reading and touring Italy with my daughter, not playing caretaker to a castle."

"Excuse me for a minute." I stood up and moved toward the center archway. Before I took out my cell phone, I looked back at Dan. *It's perfect*, I thought. After I ended the call, I sat down listening to Nico explain to Carmie that she could take all the time in the world.

"Dan, may I see you for a minute?"

He stood up, walked over, and leaned up against the only tree in the garden. "How do you feel about Carmie coming with us to Florence?"

Dan smiled. "She would love it." Then he kissed me and said, "I know exactly what you're up to." Dan pulled his cell phone out of his pocket, dialed a number, and asked if it would be okay to add one more person to the tour.

We walked back over to where everyone was seated and sat down next to Carmie.

"Carmie, we would be honored if you came with us to Florence. I'd like to discuss a few things with you," I said to her.

Carmie was thrilled to tag along. "I'm so grateful to the two of you. I just don't know how I'm going to explain all of this to my daughter."

"You're going to love Florence," I said to her. On Monday, we're going to the Giardino Bardini Gardens.

"Yes," Dan said. "But first I am taking you ladies to the *Tenuta* Torciano Winery this weekend."

For the first time since we arrived in Umbria, Carmie smiled from ear to ear.

"Miss Carmie, would you like a glass of wine now?" Aria said with a smile.

"Please," she replied, and Aria motioned for Nico and her papa to follow.

I winked at Dan. "Carmie, don't give up on the property just yet. I may have a solution for you." Then I looked at Dan. "Gina Marie will be here next Wednesday."

Aria came back to the table rolling a two-tiered gold and glass teacart. After she opened the first bottle of wine, she set a charcuterie board down in the center of the table. "Please enjoy the rest of your afternoon. I have my studies, but Nico will be around if you need anything. First, I will prepare the guest room for the two of you in the villa."

"Thank you," I said.

"Yes, thank you," Dan echoed.

"Grazie," Carmie said, and we all laughed.

"Prego," Aria replied as she turned to leave.

After Dan, Carmie, and I drank two bottles of wine, laughed about her owning a castle, and finished the last of the prosciutto, we went back to our rooms to rest before dinner that evening.

Dinner was served outside. In the center of the olive garden, on a long table covered with lace and candles, we dined on homemade pasta, salad, warm bread, and marinated olives.

"I read most of the documents given to me by the attorney. I discovered a mafia war had been taking place between the *Intrieri* and the Bonanno families. They were fighting over who the olive oil company belonged to. As far as I can tell, the fight began in Cosenza, Italy. I didn't get to the part where it involved the Felitti family fortune yet, but I can tell you that according to the documents, the five families still exist in the mafia today along with their American allies."

"Wow, so how's your vacation going so far?" Dan asked.

Carmie replied laughingly, adding, "Oh, Maryanne, by the way, we have a castle to protect—"

I tapped her hand. "Relax, you're a long way from Cosenza." Then I told her about Gina Marie meeting us back at the castle. "Carmie, would you consider the idea of opening an inn at the castle?"

She immediately shook her head. "I could never. Not at my age."

# Chapter 12

THE NEXT MORNING, WE said goodbye to Francesco, Nico, and Aria. I reassured Francesco that we would be returning with Carmie before Wednesday. "I'll introduce you to Gina Marie when we return." I winked at him. "You'll love her, she's the mastermind behind all new construction projects."

We were in the car when Carmie announced she was expecting a shipment of boxes to be delivered. "There are some books I can't live without," she said to us.

"I'm sure Nico will put them away for you. We'll be back in time for you to open them and put them away before Maryanne arrives," Dan said.

Then we heard the GPS say, "Head northeast on Via Flaminia SR316 toward Via Carlo Maderno."

Ten minutes later, Dan pulled the car over and parked in front of the Falmina 38 café. "I'm going to grab a cup of coffee. Can I get you ladies anything?"

"I'll take a doppio cappuccino, please."

"Yes, I will too," Carmie said as Dan exited the car.

I glanced out my window noticing all of the buildings were made of stucco and bricks, and I thought, *A little color and decor makes for an ornate, gorgeously gilded, elegant design.* "I love Italy."

"I thought I'd be saying the same thing but—"

"No buts. Trust me, you're going to love being here even more when I share my ideas with you. Carmie, we're in this together, and for a good reason. Can I ask you what part of being a librarian you loved the most?"

"My authors," she said as Dan got back in the car.

He handed us both our cups and a small white bag. "I grabbed a few pastries for the ride," he said and put the car in drive.

We both set our drinks in the cup rest. I opened the bag and smelled cinnamon. Then I handed the bag to Carmie. "Something smells delicious."

She shook her head. "I'm good for now." Then she looked at me and added, "I've become pen pals with a few of the authors, and we have over two hundred members in our book club. Some of the women make me laugh with their stories. From memoirs to tales of fiction, they keep me turning the pages."

I saw Dan look at me through the rearview mirror. A cat-like smile came across his face. "Share your idea with her, I think she's going to like it."

"Idea? If you have a solution to this nightmare, please—"

"I wanted to wait for Gina Marie, but okay. Carmie, I was thinking the castle would make a great writer's retreat."

She never looked at me, but in a low tone she replied, "I'm listening."

"Last night, Dan and I toured the entire castle again,

and this time I took pictures and sent them to Gina Marie with my idea. She's excited and can't wait to talk to you about everything. Gina Marie agrees with me. Don't touch the walls or the floors. It's all part of the design. With very little money, you could turn the structure into a viable living space." I looked at her waiting for her to respond; when she didn't say anything I feared the worst. "Dan, go back," I shouted. "Turn the car around and park across the street, please. I'd like to go in a few of those antique shops."

Inside we saw bric-a-brac, miscellaneous items, and a few nice pieces of antiques selling for reasonable prices. I held up an iron rod and placed two matching pillows below it. "This could be a headboard." Then I pointed to a black-framed bed selling for less than one hundred euros. "You don't need much," I said adding a bed, nightstand, and a desk and chair. "All of the rooms have open shelves and a closet for clothes."

Carmie scratched her neck, looked at a few items next to her, curled her lip, and said, "Thirty. I'll need thirty bedroom sets, and how am I supposed to cook for all these people? The kitchen in the cottage is tiny. Certainly not big enough for me to serve... how many people?"

I picked up a tapestry. "This would be gorgeous hanging in the entryway."

Dan put his hands on my shoulders. "Let her think about it. Come on, we have a schedule to keep and wine to taste."

I felt defeated until Carmie walked up to a wooden

bed frame. "I'll bet Francesco could make these for a lot less, and with the right pillow top, you don't even need a box spring."

We stopped at three more antique shops along the way and a gift store for ideas. Carmie bought a small mirror framed in gold leaf to set on the end table in the living room next to Matilda's photo. "Every time I look in this mirror, I'm going to remind myself that I am a part of something wonderful. I'm going to make Matilda proud."

At three o'clock that afternoon, we checked into our hotel. Dan was able to get the room next to ours for Carmie. "I made dinner reservations for six o'clock, unless you're both hungry or tired."

"Sounds perfect," Carmie replied to Dan and then hugged me. "Thank you. I can't believe you're doing all this for me. You've done so much."

I smiled. "Maybe Matilda sent us both to that café in Rome for a reason."

While Dan lay on the bed resting, I searched for more ideas.

At a quarter to six, we knocked on Carmie's door. "Dinner time," Dan said as she opened her door wearing black trousers, a white blouse, and a satin scarf bursting with color.

"You look gorgeous," I told her.

"I feel invigorated," she replied and laced her arms through mine and Dan's.

After we sat down at our table, I noticed how simple

the decor was. Ivory walls, brick archways, and a single painting hanging on the wall. *Nice.*

For dinner, we chose the special paired with several choice wines.

The next morning, we met under a white tent in the middle of the vineyard. Brunch was served butler style. First, bread with olive oil, paired with a smooth white wine. "Fruity," Carmie said as she emptied her glass. "I like it, not too sweet."

Next a cheese board filled with grapes and more wine. We joined a private party for a walk through the San Gimignano countryside. When we got to the lobby at the hotel, a basket was waiting for us. Filled with three bottles of wine, bread, cheeses, and fresh fruit. "Grazie," Carmie said.

We spent the entire weekend touring wineries.

Monday morning, we left for Florence. "I'm so excited to see the Giardino Bardini Gardens," I said.

"Julie, tell Carmie about the gardens at the inn," Dan said as he drove onto the highway.

I gave Carmie a little of our backstory. Why I moved to Rhode Island, and how I built my inn one garden at a time. "Now, we host garden tours on our property every year."

"I'm glad Dan never stopped searching for you," she said. "You belong together."

I looked up at Dan. He was smiling back at me.

"I've been alone for a long time now. When you fall in love with the right person, no one else can or will ever take their place. I look forward to seeing my own husband again," she said nodding.

# Chapter 13

I THOUGHT ROME WAS the most spectacular place on Earth until we arrived in Florence. Mark Twain was correct. Florence was a "city of dreams." The views were mesmerizing and nothing short of spectacular.

"Oh, my," Carmie said as she got out of the car. "Florence holds the flame for sheer, unadulterated Italian beauty. Absolutely gorgeous."

"I agree," I said as I too looked all around. "I've never seen so much beauty in my life. Even the rolling hills are happy to be here."

Unlike our hotel in Tuscany, this one was lavish. "Dan, would you mind if I take a quick bath?"

From the other room, he said, "You have plenty of time."

As I sank deep into the clawfoot tub, I noticed there were no towel bars or shelves. Everything was placed in baskets: the soaps, washcloth, towels, even the toilet paper was resting in a basket. "Ahh, stucco. Hard to put a nail in it." There were so many ideas running around in my head.

Dan entered the room, knelt down next to the tub, and began washing my back. "What's hard to put down?"

I laughed. "They don't hang anything on the walls because of the plaster."

Dan stood up, got undressed, and joined me. After we made love, I asked Dan if we could stay in Umbria for the rest of our vacation. "Gina Marie is going to want us to be there."

"Only if you promise me you'll come back every year."

My heart was beaming, overflowing with happiness.

We met Carmie downstairs at the gift shop. She bought a box of notecards, a magazine, and a box set, *The Lighthouse Inn* series. She held up the book and said, "It's about a man who lives for the love of his life."

Dan, Carmie, and I spent the entire day at the Giardino Bardini Gardens. Four floors, two museums, and an art exhibition later, and we were all tired. We decided to rest our legs, sit in the Adirondack chairs, and watch the sunset together. "The wisteria was my favorite part of the walk," Carmie said.

"I loved seeing the statues in almost every garden," Dan said, and I had to agree.

"They set the tone for each flower bed. It's as if they were overlooking the plants."

"Tomorrow, we can make as many stops as you ladies would like," Dan announced as he stood and stretched his arms above his head. Dan handed me the keys and added, "It's your turn to drive."

I nodded without saying a word.

"I'd like to get back and hear more about your idea,"

Carmie said. "Perhaps I should see the entire property again along with the guest rooms."

I smiled warmly at her, and I too jumped to my feet. "I'm not a numbers person, but I have a lot of great ideas on how you can decorate for pennies and still have a classy retreat."

We didn't make any stops, in fact, I drove straight to Umbria. While Dan unloaded the car, Carmie and I went up to the bedrooms on the second floor in the castle. Except for all the bird poop, after a good sweeping in every room and a little help from my favorite interior designer, the place would look great.

"Julie," Carmie yelled from another room.

When I entered the room, she was standing in front of the window pointing with one finger, with her other hand on her hip. "Do you notice anything wrong with this window?"

I looked outside. "No."

She spun around. "There are no windows."

"Oh," I responded. "Yes, the window frames are all downstairs in the basement."

"Frames," she protested. There's no glass in them?"

I scrunched my nose, hoping to make light of it. "Glass is cheap," I said, hoping it was.

"I can install them," Nico said, standing behind us. "Actually, Papa and I can order the glass and put the windows in the bedrooms for you."

I looked back at Carmie and said, "I'll bet Francesco and Nico can do most of the work for you."

"Aria would be more than happy to help as well," he said and then shrugged.

On our way to the basement, Nico explained why they took all of the glass out. "Windows are primarily used as security. We enjoy the fresh air much better. You don't have to worry, Papa is a wonderful craftsman."

I began to tell Carmie about some of my ideas. "About a mile down the road, I noticed a woman selling baskets. At our hotel in Florence, they placed everything in baskets. All of your guest's supplies can be displayed in a basket. No shelving or expensive furniture. You could use the wood stored in the basement for tabletops." I turned to face Nico and asked, "Right?"

"Of course. The wood is from your olive trees. We cut down the trees when they no longer produce olives. Italian olive is very beautiful. Come, I will show you a piece Papa made with the wood he harvested a few years back."

We followed Nico downstairs to his grandfather's workshop. He didn't have to point it out, it was gorgeous. Nico picked up several small oval pieces of wood. "This is a biscuit." Then he rubbed his hand along the tall boards stacked up against the wall. "The biscuit holds the wood planks together. Papa makes a pocket hole in each piece of wood big enough for the wooden biscuit to go in and joins the two together, then he uses the vice to press and hold the adjoining boards."

"It is absolutely spectacular," Carmie said as she ran her hand over the table. "The knots, swirls, and colors are—"

"Si, spettacolare," Nico agreed.

When we left the building, we found Dan talking on his cell phone. "That was Gina Marie, she'll be here tomorrow. I'm picking her up at the airport at three."

"Wonderful," I said and placed my hand on Carmie's shoulder. "You're going to love her, if anyone can make this happen, it's Gina Marie."

That evening we ate dinner at a small restaurant that Carmie said she'd like to try. We invited Nico and Francesco to join us, but they declined. They said they both wanted to get ready for Gina Marie's arrival.

The food at Antica Trattoria San Lorenzo Simone Ciccotti was delicious. I ordered the puttanesca di baccala' e fiori di zucca.

"Julie, I noticed you order a lot of fish," Carmie said as she finished her decadent dessert.

"I love fish. If they don't have a good fish dish, I usually go with chicken."

"Oh, she'll eat beef if it's filet mignon or prime rib," Dan added as he asked for the check.

When the waiter came back to the table with our mints and receipt, Carmie said, "This one is on me. Thank you both for coming to my rescue."

I thought about Carmie's request to dine there. When she called to make the reservations, she must have given them her credit card information. I kissed her on the cheek. "Thank you. That was very lovely, but—"

"You're welcome." She smiled at Dan and winked. "Both of you."

When we arrived at the villa, Dan told Carmie and me that he would definitely come back every year and visit her. "I would love to see this place come to life. I can imagine how astonishing it must have been back in the day."

I thought about our inn and the joy it brought to me, especially now that Dan was living there.

# Chapter 14

OUR MORNING STARTED OFF with a loud bang. Dan and I both jumped out of bed and ran down the hall. Carmie was sprawled on the floor.

"Are you okay?" Dan said as he leaned down to help her up.

"The damn chair collapsed on me," she said. "I'm fine."

"You fell through the seat," I said and picked up the chair. Then I proceeded to gather the lace tablecloths she'd been putting down, adding, "They're all so beautiful." I set the pile on the end of her bed.

Carmie brushed herself off and said, "I thought maybe I could use them as bedspreads." She picked up one of her pillows, touching the end. "Most of them match."

I had to admit they were delicate, pretty, and perfect.

When Dan left that afternoon to pick up Gina Marie, Aria was gracious enough to set Carmie and me up on a Zoom meeting with my interior designer. We showed her the lace, a piece of wood, and one of the empty rooms on the second floor. "Do you think Carmie can get away with it?" I asked hoping she could until her finances picked up.

"Yes," Molly said. "I have a wholesale shop that sells duvet covers, inserts, pillow top mattresses, and the finest pillows. I also have a vendor that will drop ship to your door vintage-looking metal bed frames."

"I'm starting to get excited. Do you really think I can pull this off?"

"With Julie's help, I don't see why not," Molly said to her.

"Thank you, Molly. Thanks for taking time out of your busy schedule to lend us a hand." I waved goodbye.

"Bless your heart, sweetheart," Carmie said and blew her a kiss.

By the time Gina Marie arrived, Carmie was feeling good about hosting author events. She didn't waste any time showing Gina Marie her plans for the castle. It was an hour and a half later before I had a chance to say hello and give her a hug. "Thank you so much for coming," I said to her and then asked, "How is Frank?"

"He's good. He misses you. Actually, he's excited to get started on your farmhouse." Gina Marie chuckled, adding, "You better hope he doesn't start building before you get home."

We ate a late lunch in the olive grove, laughing as Carmie described in detail her vision for the grounds, the castle, and her future. "You don't have legs like this at my age from sitting on your ass and watching TV," she said, and then added, "The only time I sit down is to read a good book." Carmie shared with us her vision for one of the larger rooms in the main castle. "I could teach ballroom dancing."

Gina Marie smiled, and I knew she was up to something. "I'd like to see the rest of the castle. I have a few more ideas for you, and none of them will cost you a penny."

This time Carmie led the way. Dan and I were holding hands. From time to time, he would squeeze my hand listening to Gina Marie as she explained about keeping the castle's beauty and history intact.

Carmie stood in the middle of the room, raised her hands above her head, and said, "What do you think?" And then she began to dance. For several minutes, we watched as she waltzed around the entire room.

I nudged Dan to dance with her, but he said, "No. She dances beautifully all by herself."

Carmie was graceful to watch.

Gina Marie was giddy as she began to clap. "Bravo." Then I saw her look up and all around. "Maybe polish the floor that's it. Okay, what else?"

We followed Carmie to another large room. "In here I could host seminars and writing workshops. I was thinking I could teach a course on finding your sense of story and the passion to match." One by one, she looked at each of us.

I looked at Gina Marie. Once again, she appeared happy.

"Oh, and I could teach yoga every morning in the courtyard." Carmie smiled at Gina Marie. "I read Julie's website for the Inn in Rhode Island and about how other inns may have ocean views, but she has a library, front porch rockers, and gardens to explore."

Gina Marie touched her arm. "You have Italy. Imagine telling your guests they will be awakened by a gentle breeze that wafts through their window, enticing them to get up and write their next bestseller."

"Wow," I said.

"Wow is right," Carmie echoed. "What writer wouldn't want to stay here?"

"Okay, let me run the numbers and think about what exactly we need to do over the next three weeks." Gina Marie flashed Carmie a quick smile. "I wish I could stay longer, but I cannot."

I looked at her knowing Dan and I were leaving next week, starting our own project, and how much we needed Gina Marie. Then I noticed Carmie smiling and thought, *She needs her too.*

"You'll be fine," Gina Marie said to me as if she read my mind. "Everyone knows what to do. I'll be home in time for the first meeting."

"You'll stay with me to get everything up and running," Carmie said sounding more and more like she was onboard.

"Yes, for the next three weeks, I promise we will have all details worked out and finalized before I leave," Gina Marie replied and then asked me, "What did Molly say?"

"She gave us a few vendors to reach out to," I said.

"I can go online and get some prices if you'd like," Carmie said.

"No," Gina Marie said to her. "Let me go over the budget and I'll tell you what I think you should spend on each room. We'll start with the most important rooms first and go from there."

"Okay, will I see you for dinner?" Carmie asked before walking away.

Gina Marie raised both hands. "Hell, yeah."

That evening, while Gina Marie ran the numbers, Carmie ventured on her own through the entire castle.

Dan and I took a drive along the countryside. "Gina Marie told me Carmie should list the property as a rustic retreat," he said.

I looked at him. "Why, the rooms will have new—"

He snapped his neck looking at me. "And when they meander off down the hallways? Don't get me wrong, she can do it and everything she said sounds great, but she's not working with your budget or a well-maintained farmhouse."

I glanced out my window. "It's beautiful here. So relaxing. Did Carmie tell you how much money she has?"

Dan shook his head. "She said the castle comes with a trust fund, but she didn't think she could spend any of it on repairs. The money is reserved for taxes and upkeep only. I think Francesco is the only person on the payroll." He waved one hand my way. "You'll have to talk to her about it."

We drove by a flea market, and I saw a bunch of things Carmie could use to decorate with.

"Julie, can I just say being here with you and seeing you come to life creating all of this for Carmie makes me happy. I'm glad we bumped into her back in Rome."

"So you're not upset about being here?"

"No. Not at all. I'm having a great time. I told you, we'll come back. Besides, I promised Carmie." Then he pulled up to a shop, got out, and ordered us each a chocolate gelato.

"My favorite, thank you," I said and kissed him on the cheek before indulging in the creamy, gooey goodness.

When we arrived back at the castle, we saw Gina Marie sitting out in the grove with a glass of limoncello and a tray of biscotti. She waved to us. "I love this place. I especially love Nico and Aria. Look what she made for all of us." Gina Marie pointed to the tray. "She made a pistachio, a cranberry, and an almond. I'm going to get so fat. I ate all three of them."

I looked down at the assortment and noticed Aria had placed them on a silver tray lined with a lace doily. "The Doily Writer's Retreat in Umbria, Italy," Carmie said, standing behind us.

I looked up at her. "I love it."

Dan laughed. "You have enough of them. I like the name. It fits," he said and pulled out a chair for her to sit down.

First Gina Marie went over Carmie's budget of thirty thousand dollars, and then she explained to us how she thought Carmie should spend the money. "You have to stay within your budget."

"But, I have forty—" Carmie started to say.

"No." Gina Marie shook her head. "You need to set aside ten for advertising, marketing, and help the day your guests arrive."

Dan moved my hand from my mouth. "What are you thinking?"

"Gina Marie, what if I included Carmie's retreat in my advertising and marketing plan? I already have paid subscriptions for the year to *Propeller, Travel and Leisure, Coastal Living,* and *Condé Nast.*"

"Wow, that would help."

Dan touched the side of my face. "I knew you were thinking over there. She's always thinking of something when she breathes into the back of her hand."

Carmie jumped up and started clapping. "It's going to work. Dan, Julie, Gina Marie, you can all stay here for free," she said and then sat back down.

# Chapter 15

CARMIE WAS SO EXCITED she went back to her room to email her daughter. Dan said he was going to check on Nico to see if he had any dinner plans. "I'd like to take Nico, Aria, and Francesco out for dinner this evening."

"Sounds like a great idea," I said and moved over to the chair next to Gina Marie's. I wanted to get a closer look at her budget plans to see if any of my ideas fit. I glanced down, but she didn't have anything written on the paper. "Why the blank page?"

"She doesn't need a lot. She just needs to stay focused. Carmie has most of the materials right here at the castle. She can use the wood to create beautiful furniture, there's enough wood stored in the basement to build ten desks for every room, along with a large farm table for the kitchen." She closed the folder. "I'll write everything up later. I wish I could ship some of that wood home. I swear the fresh-cut pieces smell like olive branches."

"So, you think she should order the beds and—"

"Yeah." She looked over at me. "Did you see the way she danced in that room, all by herself? I remember seeing that same look on your face the day you introduced me to Dan. You can't put a budget on that. She needs this in her life."

I hugged her. "I agree with you. I told Carmie, God put her in our path for a reason."

Gina Marie laughed. "Path. I got a good path story for you. I almost ran someone over on my motorcycle last week. She was walking her damn pygmy goat in the middle of the road."

I couldn't help it. I had to laugh. "What?"

"Julie, she's beautiful, smart, sexy, and we enjoy a lot of the same things. She's perfect for me."

"Aww."

Gina Marie leaned back in her chair. "After she scared the crap out of me, I apologized for almost hitting her. She felt bad for wandering in the road, but her goat was trying to cross so he could eat something. Julie, it's the cutest thing I have ever seen. The goat wasn't even a foot tall. Tan with brown and black markings." She grinned from ear to ear. "Michelle knocked me off my feet—"

"You mean motorcycle," I said laughingly.

"Yeah, right. When I offered to make amends and take her out for a drink, she countered with buying me dinner for almost causing me to crash. The goat is her passion. Michelle wants a farm loaded with animals. From horses to chickens. I'll get used to the chickens. Apparently, her best friend has a house three doors down from mine. That's where she keeps her goat. That evening, she picked me up at my house, and I still can't stop thinking about her."

"I'm surprised you're willing to stay here for the next three weeks."

Gina Marie gave me a crimson smile. "She went back to work. She lives in New York City, but she wants to move. Wants a big house with enough rooms for her two sons, their wives, and her two granddaughters. I have to say, it wasn't easy saying goodbye to her."

"G—"

"I know. I have a big house. Plenty of bedrooms, and a backyard large enough to build a small barn."

"Umm, I could sell you more land—"

"Slow down. We'll see when she comes back in July. Apparently, she likes to play with fireworks. I'm going to her friend's house for a party on the fourth." She shook her head. "The first thing I thought about when I said I have to tell Julie about her was you're going to want us to get married at the inn."

"No, your backyard... hell yeah," I said. "Wait until I tell Dan and Jesse. Hey, does Michelle ride?"

"Ride? Huh! She owns a Harley Davidson, but she's never driven it. Said she likes riding on the back better."

"Me, too."

"Dan and Jesse are going to love her. I hope you like her."

"I'm sure I'm going to love her as much as you," I said and thought, *That's why she's not so concerned about every penny. She has something wonderful on her mind.*

We both turned around when we heard Carmie and Dan hollering for us. "Come here, I want to show you what we discovered," Dan said.

Gina Marie and I both stood up. She grabbed her

folder, and I took hold of our glasses and set them on the tray next to the remaining cookies. I set the tray down in the doorway before continuing to follow them through the main archway. The farther we walked, the darker it became. Dan opened a large door exposing an enormous number of chairs.

"Look," Carmie shouted. "Aren't they lovely?" She brushed her hand over one of them. "Francesco and Aria showed them to us earlier. Francesco said I could use them."

Dan pointed to the stack of gold Chiavari ballroom chairs. "I suggest we leave these for another day." The chairs had cane seats, much like the one Carmie fell through earlier that week. "Aria looked the chairs up online. If Francesco is correct, they date back several hundred years." Dan touched one of the chairs. "They are made from hand-carved wood. Francesco told Aria he believes it is walnut. Aria said the fabric is jacquard tapestry. There are twenty matching chairs with armrests in the back. Aria also said they could be worth a fortune."

"Like how much?" Gina Marie asked.

Carmie smiled. "To the tune of fourteen thousand."

"For all of them?" I asked.

"Each," Carmie replied. "Dan and I counted, I own three hundred, not counting the couple with broken legs. Oh, plus the twenty with arms." Carmie's eyes got big. "I could put in a new kitchen and hire a staff."

I turned to face Gina Marie and laughed. "Well?" I asked.

"I think you should hold on to them," Gina Marie said. "If you need to make money in the future, you could always sell a hundred or two. You should wait and see how the first year goes."

"Do you think I should use them? Francesco said I could. I mean they're mine. Right?"

In perfect unison, Dan, Gina Marie, and I said, "Yes."

That was it. She had enough money of her own to call the wholesaler and get her guest bedrooms set up. Francesco and Nico would build the tables, desks, and... I looked up. "What?" Everyone was looking at me. Carmie had tears in her eyes. I smiled. "It's as if the entire castle was waiting here just for you," I said and hugged her.

"Oh, the hidden treasures we shall find," Dan said leading the way back to the villa.

Dan said he was going to make dinner reservations and let Nico, Francesco, and Aria know what time and about Carmie's decision to use some of the chairs.

Gina Marie, Carmie, and I went to the villa for a cup of tea and to go over Carmie's game plan.

Gina Marie sat down first, but then she got up to grab a piece of paper and her laptop. I saw where she opened my previous email about Carmie opening a retreat for writers. She took a deep breath, smiled at Carmie, and started sketching something on the paper. "I like your idea of offering yoga classes, ballroom dancing, and maybe a day trip to a winery nearby." She paused, looking around the room. "I think you'll have enough to entice writers to stay here. For the first year, I want you to say the castle offers a full kitchen. Julie can advertise the castle as a thirty-day inspiring, creative, writing experience in beautiful Umbria, Italy. Carmie, I suggest you start with a thirty-day writer's retreat that includes their own private bedroom, complete with desk, chair, natural lighting, and an en suite bathroom. And a large classroom to partake in weekly group sessions."

"I could host a welcome party and serve some local wine along with cheese, grapes, and crackers. Oh, and an arrivederci party on their last day."

"How much?" I asked.

Gina Marie nodded. "I looked at a nearby inn. They offer breakfast and afternoon tea. They charge a hundred and ten a night. I think you should start somewhere in the neighborhood of twenty-four hundred dollars, per person for the thirty days. That's eighty-three dollars a day. Not bad for a night's stay in Italy."

"I could make breakfast," Carmie said, but then added, "Do you think I could get away with serving muffins?"

"Let's see how the first year goes. Perhaps next year you could offer more. How do you feel about hosting four events? One in the spring, two in the summer, and one more in the fall?"

"So I would have to be here for a hundred and twenty days, correct?" Carmie said.

"Yes," Gina Marie replied. "But remember, Aria will be here, and she's offered to assist you."

"How much?" I asked, knowing Gina Marie had all the numbers figured out.

"Huh, each season she'll make over seventy-two-thousand dollars. Carmie, if you book the castle all four seasons, you'll make almost three hundred thousand dollars." Gina Marie looked at me. "With Julie's help, I think you'll be just fine."

"A year?" she shouted, adding, "Do you really think people will want to come here just to write?"

"Yes," Both Gina Marie and I said in perfect unison.

"Wait." Gina Marie turned a page. "You have to use eight thousand for appliances, so no welcome party until you start making money."

# Chapter 16

FRIDAY NIGHT, DAN TOOK everyone to Umbria Restaurant where we sat at an outdoor table overlooking the village below. As soon as we sat down, our server delivered a large platter of fresh sliced tomatoes, mozzarella, and garden basil that smelled like heaven, all drizzled with olive oil and a pinch of sea salt.

When Carmie ordered the pasta e fagioli as her first course, we all asked for the same. Then we let Francesco order dinner for all of us. Aria smiled when he included her favorite, spaghetti alla carbonara.

First, Gina Marie spoke in English, then Aria or Nico would translate into Italian for Francesco. "The red clay floors and the wood ceilings are not to be touched." She held her hand out as if to say stop.

Without either of them translating, Francesco said, "Si!"

She smiled at him. "How soon can the two of you start building the desks and tabletops?"

Nico answered her, "Tomorrow."

"Si, domani," Francesco replied, adding, "Quanti?"

Even I knew what he was asking.

"Thirty," Aria said, followed by, "Trenta, Papa."

Francesco took a bite of his tomato and nodded. "Una settimana. Finito."

"Grazie," Carmie replied.

I looked at her, she was happy. In fact, there was something different about her. When we met her in Rome, she seemed weary, unsure of what lay ahead, now she had a new meaning and an adventure to look forward to. I felt good knowing Nico, Aria, and especially Francesco would all be at the castle with her. I wish I could have met her daughter, but I had an inn of my own to run, and I was building a new home for Dan and me to live in. As if he was reading my mind, he reached over and held my hand. I moved closer and rested my head on his shoulder. Gina Marie smiled at us.

During dinner, everyone laughed when Gina Marie told them about how she met Michelle and her miniature goat. For once, we were all too full to order dessert. We ended the evening with a stroll in the grove at the castle. Francesco told Gina Marie he hoped she would bring Michelle and return to the castle.

Aria explained to Gina Marie how Francesco said she reminded him of a woman he had met during the war. "He likes you," she said.

Gina Marie hugged Francesco and kissed him on his cheek. When he looked away, I thought he was going to blush, but instead he just said, "Buona notte," to her and walked away.

"I think you remind him of his first love," Nico said.

"Well, good night. I have tables and desks to make in the morning."

The next day, while Gina Marie and Carmie ordered the beds, linens, and toiletries for her guests, Dan and I took a drive to a little town called Spello, a beautiful village lined with bricks, red cascading flowers, and lush green plants dripping from window boxes. "I have to say every town is more beautiful than the last. I can feel the old-world charm seeping up from the narrow streets, shops, houses, and ornate buildings."

"I agree," Dan said before tugging on my hand to follow him inside. "Let's grab something for Gina Marie. I have an idea."

Inside, the scent of turpentine filled the room, along with used paintbrushes and oil-based paintings. On the walls, the most beautiful pictures were framed in dark wood.

"Benvenuti," someone said to us. When I turned around, I saw her standing behind a large canvas, holding a stack of pamphlets. "Posso aiutarla?"

Dan smiled at her and held up several smaller blank canvases and brushes and pointed toward the shelf displaying numerous tubes of paint. "One of each color," he said to her.

She smiled at me. "Do you paint?"

I returned her smile before replying, "No, but we know someone who loves to paint landscapes."

She looked pleased. "Ahh." Then she offered to take the canvases from Dan before putting one of each color in a large brown bag.

I couldn't take my eyes off her. She was gorgeous. Tall, long gray hair, deep blue eyes, and the most beautiful, flawless olive skin that I had ever seen. She didn't need to wear makeup, she was perfect.

"Thank you," she said to Dan as she handed him his bags.

"Grazie," he said in return. I was still looking at her when Dan turned to go out the door.

She gave me a cheerful, satisfied look before adding, "Arrivederci, bella."

When we got back in the car, I told Dan I wanted Carmie to have that look on her face the next time we saw her. "Did you see her? She was radiant."

"She should be. I just spent almost three hundred euros."

Dan asked if I was hungry, but all I could do was think about that woman. She reminded me of the innkeeper on Block Island. Ann had that same look in her eyes. "So?" he said. "What are you craving?"

"Let's eat with the others, I want to talk to Carmie when we get back."

Dan was stopped at the intersection. "I told Aria not to expect us for dinner," he said. "I thought we would spend the day together and go out for a nice dinner alone."

"Oh, okay. Sounds good. Whatever you want."

He put the car in motion. Looked over at me and said, "Are you sure?"

"Yes. I'm just thinking about Carmie and all the excitement coming her way." I looked out my window, wishing I felt it when I had started my inn, but instead I was missing Dan so much that I lost out. I glanced over at him. "You know what? I am getting hungry. How about we find a nice restaurant that offers outdoor dining? We can discuss our new home, swimming pool, and—" I stopped myself. I almost told him about my surprise.

"Right there," Dan said and turned the car around. He parked next to a Maserati, and I wished I could have just sat in the silver ride for one minute.

"I love the way they sound when they go by," I told him.

Dan opened the door, and I stepped inside. "Inside or out on the terrace?" the man said to us.

"Terrace," Dan replied. "Please."

We sat down, and I couldn't believe my eyes. The sun was beginning to set, and out in front of us was a lush green lawn leading the way to a few large farmhouses, an orange burst, and the most magnificent sky. When Dan handed me my menu, I read the name Ristorante Porta Venere and asked what he was hungry for. "What are you going to have?"

"Veal," he replied.

I read my menu and asked for a glass of Amarone. I looked over at Dan. "I'm going straight for the dessert." I knew when he said I could have whatever I wanted, he had no idea how sweet it was. "I'll have the cod with risotto, please."

After we ate, I swore I would take Italian cooking classes when we got home. "I have not had a bad meal yet. The portions are perfect, and every dish is cooked to perfection and oh, my word, so satisfying."

Dan gave me a sheepish look. "I think we should take the class together."

"Seriously?"

"Yes. Julie, we're retired. We can do whatever we want. Whenever we—"

I kissed him. "Ti amo."

# Chapter 17

DAN AND I SPENT the rest of our vacation at Carmie's. Before we left for Rhode Island, Gina Marie had painted eight landscapes, one of the exterior of the castle, and a gorgeous welcome sign bearing the name. They were all so beautiful. I wanted to take them back to my inn, but Carmie had already claimed them as hers. In fact, she hung them in her guest rooms. She used a fancy sword wall hanger pressed into the wood beam and a burgundy velvet ribbon attached to the back of each print. When Carmie was finished, she asked Dan to drive Gina Marie back to the paint shop for more supplies.

I finally got a chance to sit down with Carmie alone. We sat at the end of the driveway on the lawn, overlooking the hill town of Assisi.

"I could sit here for the rest of my life just staring at that beautiful white church," Carmie said as she poured our limoncello.

"Are you happy?" I asked as I accepted my glass filled with the delicious liqueur.

"For the first time since my husband..." she paused. "Yes, very much so. I feel like I have a purpose in my life." She lifted her glass. "Cheers." Took a sip and kissed my cheek. "Thank you." Then she moved a lemon cookie to the napkin resting on my lap. "I made these for you. I thought I would make them for my guests. Good Lord, don't tell Gina Marie. She's counting my every crumb."

I smiled from the inside out. She had yellow napkins, and a small tea plate that matched the bottle. In the center of the plate, a bottle with a cork stopper surrounded by lemons and olive branches. "It pleases me to know that you have a new-found happiness." I picked up my cookie and added, "Everything matches beautifully."

"I found them in the basement," she said and took a bite of her cookie. "Apparently, they were designed by a local artist. So many treasures to find. I plan on spending every day looking for my next vintage piece of history."

"Is there anything I can do for you before we leave tomorrow morning?"

She shook her head. "Don't worry about me. I'm going to be just fine. Wait, I want you to promise me that you and Dan will return someday. Watching the two of you was good for my soul. He loves you."

"And I love him," I replied.

"He's excited about the farmhouse. He told me about the first house the two of you built. He said he had so much fun driving around looking for antiques, appliances, and furniture. You're very lucky to have a husband who cares about his home." She sipped her limoncello, looked into the glass, and then proceeded to empty it. "I may have to trade my afternoon wine in for a glass of this sunshine more often." Then she poured herself a bit more.

"It's refreshing, that's for sure. Where did you buy it?"

"Buy it? I made it." She gave me an adorable smile. "Okay, Aria made it." She grinned my way and I smiled back, holding my glass up. As she poured me another drink, she gave me Aria's secret recipe. "She uses the peels of eight big organic lemons, soaks them in four cups of vodka for a month. Then she mixes three cups of sugar and four cups of water together to make the sweet syrup. When the vodka is ready, she strains the liquor into the syrup. Aria said you have to chill it in a frosted bottle for at least four weeks before serving."

"I like Aria, she's charismatic in an enchanting way."

Carmie laughed. "She's Italian, full of pizzazz and ideas." She played with the hem on her skirt for a moment before adding, "Gina Marie is a blessing. I had so much fun with her the other day." She laughed out loud. "You were right about one thing, she sure does know how to stay within budget. I wanted to order these beautiful, Mediterranean organic bath towels, and she canceled the order and made me get less expensive ones." Carmie smiled. "I actually like the ones she found better. They have a gorgeous edge in hand-knotted fringe at the bottom, perfect for hanging."

I too laughed. "How many did she allow you to order?"

Carmie shook her head. "Two bath, two hand, and four washcloths for each guest room. Do you think people will really come and stay with me?"

I gave her a wry grin before answering her. "I felt the same way. Believe it or not, they will come, and when they meet you, they'll be back every year. With every new novel, they will want to come and stay at your retreat." I tapped her on her leg. "I promise." Then I took out my cell phone and read a copy of the ad I sent to Kourtnee earlier in the week. "Inspiring, creative, writing retreat in an authentic castle in Umbria, Italy, introduces the writing experience of a lifetime. You'll begin your day in the courtyard for early morning stretches and yoga. Followed by a writing workshop on how to find your sense of story and the passion to match. Time to write your next bestseller, followed by afternoon tea in the grove, and then more writing. This thirty-day retreat includes your own private room with an en suite bathroom. The kitchen is open twenty-four hours a day to use at your leisure. Price does not include meals. Then I give them the price and link to your website."

Her eyes were on me. "You used my words perfectly. You remembered," she said.

"Of course I did."

"I better get to work. I need to start my daily planner. I have so many lessons to share. Do you think I need to order pamphlets?" She smiled and stood up before adding, "I'll write down everything I need and give the list to Gina Marie."

I handed her the plate, empty bottle, and stood up to follow her back to the villa. Once inside, she excused herself and went straight to her room to prepare for her students. I took the dish and bottle to the kitchen to clean. I was washing our coffee cups from earlier that morning when I saw Gina Marie and Aria getting up from the rockers in the backyard. Dan approached them holding several long pieces of wood. I tapped on the window to get their attention, but no one noticed or heard me. I wiped my hands dry and went outside. "Hey, what's everyone up to?"

Dan turned to face me. "These are the rods for the guest bedrooms. Nico is coming with the rest. I thought we could all hang them for Carmie." Then he asked Gina Marie if she had a chance to ask Aria about staying with Carmie until the fall. "I was thinking after Gina Marie leaves, Carmie will be alone."

I looked at Gina Marie and shook my head. "Her daughter Maryanne is coming for the summer, remember?"

Dan looked puzzled. "Maryanne. Yes, I forgot."

Gina Marie moved closer to him. "Carmie's daughter is coming four days after I leave. She'll be fine. We ordered everything for the retreat, I gave her a budget for toiletries and tea." She put her hand on the small of his back. "Hand me some of those. We'll help you hang them up."

Aria reached out and Dan handed her a few as well. "I'll be around all summer. I don't start classes until September, and even then, I only live ten minutes down the road. Besides, Nico will be here to help Francesco every day." Aria blushed before adding, "We get paid very well from the castle's funds. Papa is the best craftsman in Italy. That is why Matilda hired him."

After we hung the rods, Gina Marie pulled me to the side. "Hey, I wasn't going to mention this, but earlier when Dan and I got in the car to go shopping for more supplies, he asked me if I could drive. I asked him for the address, and he acted like he didn't remember." She shook her head and took a deep breath before adding, "When I asked him for his cell phone so I could check his travel history, he just looked at me. I tapped his pocket and told him I was sure the address was still in his phone."

"Did he give you his cell phone?"

"I felt bad and didn't want to ask him again, so I Googled the place on my own. Then I got out of the car and told him I would drive."

"This is disturbing to hear. I thought he was just exhausted." I reached out and touched her arm. "Before we left, he did a few things that made me wonder."

"Julie, where are you?" Carmie hollered.

Gina Marie and I looked at one another. I winked at her. "We'll talk later."

# Chapter 18

JUNE SIXTH, WE AWOKE to rain pouring down outside our window. I didn't want to leave. I wanted to stay in Italy. I wished I could be there when Carmie's first guest arrived. I wanted to be with her when she picked the olives. "Dan, are you awake?"

"Yeah, I'm just laying here listening to the rain. Hoping we don't have to fly during a thunderstorm."

I sat up, moved the covers back, and told him, "I want to come back at the end of October."

"For our anniversary?" he replied. "Why not?"

I smiled. "I was thinking about harvesting time."

"Oh," he said and got up. "Francesco said he didn't harvest until the end of November last year. It depends on the climate conditions. I'll ask Nico to keep me informed." Then he went into the bathroom.

I hollered slightly, "Can we stay for a month?"

Dan came back to the bedroom. "What about..." He sat down on the bed. "We can stay for as long as you'd like, but?"

"My inn?" I looked at him. "Will be just fine. I have the best staff in Rhode Island." Then I got dressed. I chose a wrap dress, low sandals, and my new sun hat in case the rain stopped. "Let's grab some coffee before we pack our overnight bags." Gina Marie had promised to ship our suitcases for us the next day. Our flight didn't leave until nine o'clock that evening. Jesse was picking us up in Providence around noon the next day. I sat down next to Dan. "I haven't slept this good in such a long time."

Dan slipped his foot into a new loafer. "You look beautiful." Then he asked me, "No nightmares?"

"No," I replied and kissed him on the lips. "Not one." I pointed to his feet. "Are they new?"

He winked. "Francesco gave them to me." Dan kissed me back. "I promise you only dreams from now on." He got up and looked out the window. I thought he was going to say something about the weather, but instead he asked if I wanted to climb back in bed for a quick one. I almost obliged until we heard Gina Marie walking down the hall singing, "Rain, rain, go away. Come again some other day."

"Hey, you two. Good morning," she said. "Coffee time." When Gina Marie says coffee time, what she's really saying is, *don't talk to me until I'm on my second cup.*

We followed her to the kitchen and watched her fill her cup and go straight out to the backyard. She sat down next to Carmie, who also doesn't like to talk until she's had a few cups. The women just nodded at each other. Aria came in holding a stack of folders. "Good morning, Dan and Julie." She set down what she was holding and explained to us, "Carmie completed the entire program.

I printed them out for her last night. I figured she should hand each student their own folder."

I hugged her. "Can I take you home with me?"

She gave me a little hip action. "Maybe." Then she poured herself a cup of espresso.

Dan sat quietly at the table nibbling on an Italian herb muffin. Carmie loved making them. She said they made the perfect savory treat any time of the day. "I could live on these things," he said as he grabbed a second one and spread it with fresh homemade strawberry preserves.

Aria sat down next to him. "I heat mine up. It makes the parmesan oozy."

I sipped my coffee watching Dan. He appeared to be fine, and I wondered if he truly had something on his mind that he wasn't telling me.

After I drank my coffee, I went outside to ask Carmie if she wanted to take a walk with me in the olive grove. I stood beside her. "Good morning, would you like to take a stroll with me?"

She held her cup up, emptied it entirely, stood, and told Gina Marie she would see her later to go over the budget one more time.

Gina Marie held up her cell phone and smiled. "I'll be ready." I could see she was FaceTiming with Michelle. I leaned in closer and whispered, "She's gorgeous."

Gina Marie beamed from ear to ear as she started talking again.

Carmie and I walked through the grove. "I told Dan I wanted to come back for the fall harvest."

She danced in front of me. When she held her hands high above her head and said, "Thank you." I smiled. "I hope I have a full house when you return," she added and swirled one more time.

Then I raised my hand and held it high in the air. "You can thank Him. You have fourteen reservations—"

I didn't get a chance to finish my sentence. She hugged me so tight. I think she was crying when she said, "Thank you so much." But then she pulled back. "Oh, my God. I'm so excited."

I put my hands on her shoulders. "I'm happy for you. It sounds like your retirement is going to be very busy, bright, and... " I looked around. "Beautiful."

By noon, Nico and Francesco had hung all of the rods, tapestries, and had put the first desk and chair in the first guest room. The bedroom sets were to be delivered by the end of June. Aria promised to be there to help Nico and Francesco set them all up. Then Carmie would be able to create her magic in every room. Aria also said she would take lots of photos for me to put in the advertisements. Her iPhone had three cameras all with built-in filters.

We sat down to eat around one that afternoon. Francesco had made his specialty—grilled fish and homemade spinach ravioli. He also made us his version of panna cotta. He explained that his mother only made desserts on Sundays, but he liked this so much he could eat it every day.

Aria smiled at him before she translated to us his love

for the rich, creamy, vanilla goodness.

Everyone got up and strolled through the castle, we went into every room. I imagined women writing their hearts out. Broadening their minds, following their dreams, their every desire. I hoped for them all to become bestsellers. To brag about their time spent at Carmie's writing retreat. To my surprise, Carmie had had Nico move one of the beds from the villa to one of the guest rooms. She had hand-sewn one of the lace doilies to the cover for the duvet, and to the end of each pillowcase. Aria had set the folder on the desk along with a handwritten welcome sign. In the bathroom sat a small basket full of toiletries. The scent of citrus blossoms filled the room. Carmie turned to face us. "The towels will be here tomorrow."

"When the beds arrive, I'll take this bed back to the villa," Nico said smiling. "For when you return in the fall."

I kissed his cheek. "I can't wait. How can I thank you? You, Aria, and Francesco have done so much to welcome us."

"Ci penso io, Carmie," Francesco said and bowed his head.

Carmie put her arm around him. "And I'll take good care of you."

While Gina Marie painted more landscapes, we spent the rest of the day helping Francesco and Nico move the remaining desks and chairs up to the guest rooms. I stopped in the hallway to thank Dan. First, I kissed him, and then I explained how much fun I'd had the past few days. "Thank you for changing our plans and staying at the villa."

"Villa?" he said laughingly. "It's a castle." Then he returned my kiss. "You're welcome. And just so you know, I had the best time here with you and everyone else. I'm glad we're coming back. I was going to suggest Alaska, but Italy works for me."

"Italy?" Gina Marie said holding up her best design ever. She had painted it during the golden hour.

Carmie immediately took it from her and showed everyone. "It's my church." She went to hug it, but Gina Marie stopped her.

"Hey, it might be a little wet for that." She took the painting from Carmie and said, "Julie told me how much you loved looking down at the church in Assisi."

"Gina Marie, you are remarkable. Julie, what am I going to do?"

I blew her a kiss.

# Chapter 19

THE EVENING GLOW WAS one to be bottled. I wanted to take it back with me. All of it, and all of them. I couldn't believe how sad I felt leaving. As we said our goodbyes to leave for the airport, both Nico and Aria had tears in their eyes. Francesco seemed to be comfortable in his space standing in the background. Carmie waved goodbye and said, "I will pray for you every night. You will be forever in my heart."

I stopped, turned around, and went back to hug her one more time. As we drove down the driveway, I saw Gina Marie hugging Carmie. I knew she would take care of her, make her feel better, and give her something to occupy her mind with until her daughter arrived.

Remembering my earlier conversation with Gina Marie, I decided to drive to the airport. "Now, I can say I drove a Fiat."

"I'm tired," he said and looked out his window. "I didn't sleep much last night. I stayed awake listening to the rain. I wish we didn't have to leave yet."

"I know what you're saying. Have you ever met someone you wanted to spend the rest of your days with? That's how I feel about Carmie, Francesco, Nico, and Aria."

An hour later, we boarded the plane. "I'm really going to miss Carmie," I said as I handed my bag to Dan.

"She's radiant for sure," Dan replied and took his seat. "I'm sure Francesco will take good care of her. He showed me his room at the castle. It's nice. An apartment, actually. He said sometimes Nico stays with him. Aria used to stay at the villa when no one was there."

"She should tell Carmie. I'm sure she would love the company." I immediately texted Gina Marie and told her to let Carmie know about Aria staying at the villa if she ever got lonely.

About twenty minutes later, we were up in the air. I turned to face Dan. "Back to reality."

He touched my leg. "I've asked Rose to recommend a new therapist for me. I told her I would feel better talking to a male."

"When did you talk to Rose?"

"I emailed her this afternoon. She hasn't replied yet."

"Why? I thought you liked her. You said you were comfortable—"

He kissed my temple. "I want you to be happy. I don't want you to have any more nightmares. I'm not changing my mind. It's done." He opened his tablet and turned to the news in Point Judith. We both gasped when we read about a developer tearing down the Lighthouse Inn of Galilee and turning the space into a parking lot. "No."

Dan closed his eyes, but I couldn't. I kept thinking about what he'd said. Wanting me to be happy. I looked over at him feeling grateful. I closed my eyes knowing the best years of our lives were ahead of us. I dreamt about us going to Bermuda in January for my birthday.

Dan and I were walking along the beaches every morning, dining out at night, and we were dancing under moonlit skies. When I opened my eyes, Dan was looking at me.

"You smiled several times. Were you dreaming about Italy?"

I inhaled. Leaned over and kissed his cheek. "I was dreaming about you."

He gave me a Cheshire grin. "Were we dancing? Because that's what we were doing in mine. We were at Carmie's, and she was teaching us ballroom dancing."

"I like that idea. When we go back, we'll have her teach us."

A moment later, the flight attendant came around with our breakfast. Potato wedges, scrambled eggs, burnt sausage, and bread that wasn't toasted long enough. I gave my starches to Dan and ate the eggs.

An hour later, we landed in Rhode Island, and forty minutes after that we were hugging Jesse and Frank.

"He wanted to surprise you," Jesse said.

I kissed both of the men and then put my arm around Frank. "I'm so glad you came. How have you been? I've missed you."

"I missed you too. And you," he said to Dan. He looked at me for a minute before telling me about his news. "Well, I've joined a book club."

"Book—"

"Yes, and I've met a nice woman who makes the best sweet potato pie and pan-fried chicken I've ever eaten."

"That's great," Dan said and then shook his hand.

"How long have you been going to the book club?" I asked.

"Three weeks," he replied. "We eat lunch, discuss the book of the week, and we all go home. You'll like Jan, she used to live in Connecticut when she was a literary agent. Right after she retired, she won the lottery and bought a house on the beach. No, I haven't seen it. One of the other ladies told me about it. But I did hear her say she might need a contractor to build her a new library."

"Oh, Frank. I'm happy for you. You need a little sweet potato in your life," I said, and both Dan and Jesse agreed.

"You better bring me some leftovers," Jesse told him.

"Make him go to the book club with you, Frank," Dan said and then put his hand on Frank's back. "I'm glad you have a new group of friends, but don't forget your promise to me."

"Promise?" I said.

"Sunday dinner at the farmhouse," Dan said as he approached Jesse's truck.

"Why didn't you drive my Explorer?" I asked.

"Hey, I was already on my way to get you when someone called and said he liked to go."

Dan and I climbed in the back so Frank could sit in the front.

"Oh, yeah, I forgot to tell you. I have a new puppy," Jesse said, glancing in the rearview mirror. "I named her Lucky."

"Now tell them what else," Frank said.

"Lady loves her. She may never want to go back to the cottage again. "

"How is my girl?" Dan asked.

"She's the best. Thanks to her, Lucky is already trained."

When we pulled up to the inn, the parking lot was full. Jesse offered to drop us off at the door, but we declined and walked from the employee parking lot. When we entered the lobby, no one was there. Frank said he could use a cup of tea.

"Come into the kitchen," I said. "I'll make us all one."

We were still in the hallway when I heard Teresa say, "Shush. They're coming."

"Surprise!" Everyone said as we entered the kitchen. Behind the counter were a welcome home banner, streamers, and an entire feast. Kourtnee was holding a tray of mimosas.

I gratefully accepted a glass and thanked her, as did Dan, Jesse, and Frank.

# Chapter 20

THE NEXT DAY, I must have slept in. I tossed the covers back and ran to the bathroom. Then I headed out to the kitchen hoping to find Dan, but he was gone. I found a note by the coffee pot. "Gone to meet Frank. I'll see you later, sleepyhead." I smiled, stretched, and poured myself a cup of coffee. I went outside to sit on the front porch. When I sat down, the rocker didn't move. Lady's toy was stuck under the rocker. I picked it up and wondered if I would ever get my dog back. After I drank my coffee, I headed down the new path for a jog.

I wasn't on the trail for five minutes when I saw them. A doe and two fawns. I loved summer for so many reasons. New blooms in my gardens, and seeing the deer old enough to follow their mammas. I waited until they were finished. I didn't mind they were eating the mountain laurel, alliums, and dicentra. When I got back to the cottage, I had hoped to run into Dan, but he wasn't back yet. I took a quick shower and headed up to the inn.

As soon as I entered the lobby, Teresa approached me with a magazine. "Recognize this person?" She handed it to me, and I couldn't believe my eyes. "Is that?"

"Christina Stellate. One of the models who stayed with us a few times," she said, and then proceeded to show me an article Kourtnee had given her a few days prior. "Michelle Eggink opened her own healing and meditation center."

Christina was on the cover of *Vogue*. "I remember the first day they came here."

Teresa shook her head. "So do I." Then she went back over to the reception desk. "Oh, I almost forgot to tell you. I was asked to sing at this weekend's wedding."

"Congratulations. What are you going to sing?" I asked, knowing she could bellow out anything her heart desired.

"I'm singing two. 'When God Made You' and 'I Choose You.'"

"You'll be great. I can't wait," I said and told her I was going into the kitchen for my list of herbs. Picking herbs was one of my favorite tasks. Actually, it was the only thing I was allowed to do. When I entered, I overheard Robert telling Christine that he had been homeless for a few months. She had tears in her eyes, listening to him share how hungry he was.

"I would go days without any food or water," he said.

Christine hugged him. "You'll never go without food again. I promise."

I cleared my throat. "Good morning, everyone."

Robert excused himself after saying, "Good morning."

"So, are you excited to be back?" Christine asked and handed me the list of herbs for the day.

I took the list from her and expressed my feelings. "I

overheard Robert telling you about being homeless. It's sad to think of the number of people who go hungry every day."

"It breaks my heart to think anyone has to go without food," she said and proceeded to turn the ovens on. "I hate poverty. I would give my last penny to feed someone."

"Me, too," I said and then asked if there was anything I could do.

"No, he's fine. Michael makes sure they both eat every day." She set a tray of biscuits in the oven. "I'll start sending them home with snacks."

"If you need me to up your budget."

She raised her hand. "I got this."

"Okay," I said and then asked where Michael was.

"He went into town again," she said, sounding flustered.

I went out to the herb garden and picked the herbs, then stopped by the daycare to see Delilah and Brin. I couldn't believe my eyes. They both grew an inch while I was gone. "Hi, how are my favorite munchkins in the world?" I said as they both ran to see me. I bent down and hugged them. Then I asked Amanda and Jessica if they had plans for the weekend.

Jessica smiled and pointed toward Amanda. "Actually, we're going to a party in Newport. A guy I met a few months ago invited me, and Jessica is going with me."

"Have fun. Hey, have you seen Lady today?"

"Jesse has her with him. Apparently, Lady is in love with his new puppy."

On my way back to the kitchen, I ran into Dan. "It's about time," I hollered.

"What are you doing right now?" he asked. "Let's go for a walk on the new path. I want to tell you about the plans for the farmhouse."

"Great. Let me bring this basket into the kitchen, and I'll meet you on the side porch in five minutes."

Dan and I hiked the entire path. Several times I had to wait for him. For a moment, I thought maybe it was because he was so excited about the new, bigger bathroom and the gun room he was finally getting, but actually, I think he was suffering from jetlag.

"Frank said we can start construction right after the pool party. Gina Marie told him to make sure his crew knew about the additional changes."

"What changes?" I asked.

"The new peekaboo fireplace, and the multiple shower heads in every bathroom."

"Ah, gotcha," I replied.

"So, I met with my new therapist this morning."

I stopped walking. "You did?"

"Yeah, before I met with Frank, I stopped by to introduce myself and schedule my first appointment. Let's go into town, I want to show you something."

Dan stopped again. This time he turned toward me and kissed me. "Thanks for doing this. It's good to be on the trail again with you."

"You're welcome. I love being with you, hiking, fishing, kayaking—"

"And hunting," he added. "Thank you for my new tree stands."

"You're welcome."

When we reached Dan's truck, I told him I would drive my Explorer. I got inside and waited for him for a minute. "Are you okay?"

"I'm just a little tired. After a good night's sleep, I'll be fine."

"Where to?" I asked.

I drove to the beach, parked in George's of Galilee's parking lot. Turned the engine off.

Dan got out and said, "Let's take a walk."

We held hands. Strolling down the beach until Dan stopped and said, "That's my therapist's house."

I looked up and saw a beautiful beach cottage with white trim and two Adirondack chairs on the back deck. "That's where he lives?"

Dan had a smirk on his face. "Yep. He's the coolest dude I've ever met. You're going to love him." Then Dan spun me around and started walking down the beach. "Let's get a bite to eat," he said, and I followed him inside.

We sat topside overlooking the crowd below and the ocean waves. "Is George's still your favorite?" he asked.

I didn't have to answer him, the smile on my face said it all. I did let him know how hungry I was. "I want one of everything, please." We started with a sampling of little neck clams and fried oysters. The honey chili aioli and side of cucumbers was delicious. Then I ordered the fish tacos. Dan said he couldn't resist the fish and chips with a side of coleslaw. "This was a nice surprise," I said, offering him the last oyster.

"Every day," he said. "I want to enjoy the rest of my life with you by my side. I never want to know a day without you—"

"And you won't," I said, reaching out to touch his hand.

When we arrived back at the inn, I saw Robert sitting on the front steps. I told Dan to give me a minute.

"I have to see Kourtnee about a few things, I'll walk down to the cottage," he said to me and got out.

I waved to Robert, went up, and sat down next to him. "How are you?"

He inhaled, nodded, and proceeded to tell me about what had happened while I was in Italy. "I was putting the mulch under the maple trees along the driveway when I saw this black Ford Expedition. The guy just pulled over to the side of the road, sat there, and watched me. After I did the last tree, he got out and asked me if Dan Holliday was around. I told him you were on vacation and wasn't sure when you would be back."

"That's odd, did he tell you his name?"

"No, but I told him mine when I reached out to shake his hand."

"It's okay. Can you remember what he looked like?"

"He had on a baseball cap and sunglasses with blue

mirrors. He was taller than me."

"It was probably one of Dan's customers. I'm sure he'll be back. Thanks for letting me know."

I went into the inn and told Teresa what Robert told me. "Who the hell would be looking for Dan in Rhode Island?"

"Do you think it was Chad?" she said as she stood up and came closer to where I was.

"I don't know. I hope not," I replied.

"I'll keep an eye out for him," Teresa said, and then the phone rang. "Damn phone."

I looked at the calendar and made a mental note of the date, June tenth. When I got down to the cottage, I called the Block Island Airport and asked if Chad Claremont had landed his plane there in the last month.

# Chapter 21

THE INN WAS BOOKED solid. We were hosting our biggest wedding to date. Guests started checking in on Thursday. You could feel the excitement buzzing everywhere. Until the bride showed up. She was the most demanding bride we had ever seen. She changed her room three times before she even got to the inn. Which was not a big deal, except one of her guests complained when Teresa told her the room's view had to be changed from the rose garden to the herb. Upon arrival, bridezilla instructed Teresa to make sure all the beds had fresh sheets each and every night. Friday, she screamed at Christine about the shade of blush roses for her cake, and she told Michael to piss off twice during the tasting.

"Julie," Michael said as I entered the kitchen. He moved in closer to me. "I'm done. That's it. She's a mad woman. I'm putting crazy glue in her douche. She's not allowed to give birth to another generation. "

I laughed. I probably should not have, but I couldn't help myself. "Stop," I replied.

"First, she fingered every hurricane globe under the tent, then she had Robert take down the lighting twice, only to put it all back up the way he had it the first time."

"I'll talk to her."

"You can't reason with her," he replied. "Don't waste your time on her. Warn the groom before it's too late." He shook his head and went into the food pantry.

"Hey, got a minute?" I heard Teresa say to me as she reached for a glass.

"Sure."

"Great, I'll grab some iced tea. We can sit under the shade tree behind the inn."

Teresa and I went out the back door, sat down, and sipped our drinks. "Ooh, I like this," I said.

She smiled. "It's part lemonade and part lemon tea. Don't worry about bridezilla, she'll be gone by Sunday. So are you and Dan settled in yet?"

"I am, but I'm worried about Dan. This morning we hiked around the property, and it felt like I was dragging him along. We've hiked before, and our usual time is forty-five minutes, this morning it took us an hour and a half."

"Maybe he should see a doctor," she said, and then took a sip of her tea. "Julie, this might not be the time to say this, but I saw Chad yesterday. I was in the drugstore, and I overheard him telling the cashier that he was flying in from Boston and needed to stock Dramamine in his airplane before he heads back."

"Did he say when he was leaving?"

"No. I thought you'd want to know in case he was here for the wedding." She looked at me and bit the inside of her lip before adding, "The groom's family is from Boston."

"Huh."

"You can stay at Sal's. We have a room available." She raised her eyebrows.

I thought about it for a minute. "We just got home. Dan would never agree. Besides, we're starting the cellar hole today. I'll stay down at the construction site with him. I want to keep an eye on him anyway." I tapped her on the leg. "Tell me about you. How are things with Sal?"

"He's great. We've learned to share our space and time together. He goes fishing after dinner while I sit in the lobby and read."

I noticed her expression had changed. "Why don't you go with him and read in the boat?"

"I enjoy my reading time." She twinkled from ear to ear. "I get to read my Bible, and he gets to fish." She moved the hair from my face and smiled. "I'm happy. I'm not alone at night anymore, Sal likes going to Walmart with me, and he enjoys eating pancakes at IHOP for dinner."

"What more could a woman ask for?" I said jokingly. "I'm so happy you and Sal met. Do you still go to church?"

"Every Saturday night," she said and stretched out her legs.

My cell phone rang. "It's Gina Marie." I set my glass down, and of course it fell over. "Hello." I listened to Gina Marie tell me about how excited she was to be returning to Rhode Island in a few days. "Okay, sounds good. Yes, I'll let him know. Miss you too. Give my love to Carmie, Francesco, Nico, and beautiful Aria. Addio."

The call ended.

"Who is Addio?" Teresa asked as she stood up.

I laughed. "It means bye in Italian." I too got up. "I need to ask Kourtnee to schedule a meeting as soon as Gina Marie returns."

Teresa held her hands out in front of her. "Hey, ask Kourtnee to check the guest list. Bridezilla gave a copy of the seating chart and place cards to Kourtnee in case her event coordinator messed up. Sorry I didn't think of this sooner. Geez, I'm getting old."

"Me, too," I replied. "I heard last week's wedding was the best ever. Michael said they invited you and Sal to attend after you sang."

She tilted her head. "Did he tell you what else happened to me?"

I shook my head. "Only that it was the most fun wedding."

We were walking back to the inn when Teresa explained, "I was on the dance floor. Waving my hands in the air, when I felt someone take hold of my hands and run their fingers down my arms. I naturally thought it was Sal, but when I turned around, it was a mature woman. She started dancing around me like she was performing some sort of ceremonial dance."

I didn't mean to laugh. "Oh, no."

"Yeah, well I got the hell off the dance floor quick."

"Thanks for the iced tea and for telling me about

Chad. I'll keep my eyes open for him." I hugged her. "I'm sure if he was attending the wedding Kourtnee would have let me know as soon as she read the place cards." I winked at her. "I'm not worried about Chad, but you better watch your back."

Teresa laughed aloud and looked at her Apple watch, which was reminding her of an appointment. "I'm meeting the group of ladies Kourtnee hired to change the bed linens this weekend. I have to run. See you later, Boss Lady."

She entered the inn. I was grateful. I knew right away when I saw her that I needed that beautiful friend in my life. From the first day I hired her, she had been sweet, intelligent, and a happy, humorous addition to the inn. Most importantly, I knew she had my back. I wondered if Robert saw Chad that day. Would he really come here, knowing Dan and I were together? And why would he ask for Dan and not me?

I didn't go inside, instead I went down to the construction site to check up on Dan. When I got there, he was standing next to the excavator talking to Jesse. I stopped and listened to them for a moment. Dan was telling Jesse about his new therapist. "He's really good. Picture Earl Stone from the movie *The Mule*. That's him. He's smart. I like him a lot."

I took out my cell phone and Googled Earl Stone. *Clint Eastwood?*

"Hey, moving along," I hollered. The cellar hole was complete. "That's a big hole," I said and moved closer to

Dan. I put my hand on his back. "How's it going?"

He kissed me. "You're looking at forty-two-hundred square feet."

"That's twice the size of my place," Jesse said.

"Stop complaining. You have plenty of room," Dan told him.

Jesse had enough room, even with all of Sherry's stuff. "You could build a room off the back of the house for her."

"I already discussed it with Sherry and Frank. Now to just come up with the money."

I felt Dan's eyes on me. I looked at Jesse. "I'll give you an advance. Pay you upfront. Right now. Just tell me how much," I said.

Jesse pulled out a check and handed it to me. It was a blank check signed by Frank.

Dan laughed. "How the hell did you go from I'll never settle down with one woman to needing a craft room?"

My heart smiled.

# Chapter 22

THREE WEEKS LATER, UNDER an early morning sky that appeared to have pink ribbons weaving in the clouds, Jesse started his addition. Sherry was happier than ever to be working alongside Kourtnee in the office. Michael had hired two servers for the dining rooms. He met them at one of our weddings and knew they would be a perfect fit. Kourtnee was delighted when she heard the women say being on call was their thing. It gave them time to enjoy riding waves. I was still spending my mornings hiking alongside Dan, picking herbs, and, on rare occasion, I would help serve lunch and dinner. I grabbed a second cup of coffee, took it out to the front porch, sat down with my book, and read three chapters while listening to the sound of birds and hammers in the distance. I went to get up but sat back down. I loved my cottage. It was my safe harbor. I knew it made sense to turn it into the bridal suite, but it broke my heart to think of others entering my space. I turned my thoughts to the farmhouse, knowing I would have more bookshelves, a bigger master bedroom for Dan and me, and a grand fireplace. I set the book down on the rocker and walked down to the construction site to check on the progress.

August first, Frank, Gina Marie, and Dan promised

me I would be hosting holiday dinners this year in my new home.

It didn't take the crew long to frame the entire house, build the porches, and put the metal roof on. When I approached the site and saw the new front door going in, I was elated. "This is incredible," I shouted. "I'm so happy we decided to wrap the porches all the way around."

Dan turned around, still holding one hand on the door jam. "We have a lot to do inside, but so far it's coming together as expected."

I entered the front room ahead of Dan. Once inside, I immediately saw my peekaboo fireplace. On one side was the family room and on the other the kitchen. The space was enormous. The open floor plan gave way to each adjoining room. Even though it only had plywood on the floors, it felt like a home. "This is wonderful," I said and brushed my hand along the stone.

"I knew you would walk right up to that fireplace," Dan said. "Come here, I want to show you something." I followed him to the back of the house, stood to his left as he pointed to the new swimming pool. "I cleared a few trees out so we could see the pool."

Seeing the pool and its gorgeous landscape out in the distance brought tears to my eyes. "It's everything I ever hoped for," I said.

I felt his hands as they crossed in front of me, hugging me. I leaned back against him. "I am so grateful."

He kissed the back of my head before telling me,

"Wait until it's done. You're going to love living here."

I turned to face him. "We're going to love living here.

"Oh, yeah," he replied.

Outside we heard the sound of trucks, men talking, and then the door opened. "Hey, where the hell is everyone?" It was Gina Marie followed by a dozen men and women all eager to get to work. "So, the cabinets will be here in an hour. I'm storing them in the basement for now. The tile crew is ready to get to work in the bathrooms, foyer, and in the kitchen."

"Great," Dan said and then asked, "When do they plan on putting the hardwood floors down?"

Gina Marie pointed toward the bedrooms. We followed her down the hallway. In the master bedroom, we saw a stack of hardwood. Gina Marie put her hand on Dan's back. "It was delivered last night. Come here." She walked down the other hallway toward the guest bedrooms and said, "Don't be alarmed, there's enough in here for all four bedrooms."

"Sounds good," Dan said.

"I forgot. Michelle is coming to the pool party on Labor Day."

I clapped my hands. "I'm excited to meet her."

Dan chuckled. "No goats in the pool."

Gina Marie tapped him on his shoulder. "If you held one in your arms, you'd allow it to sleep in your bed."

"Umm, no," I said and told her that I needed to ask her something. "How was Carmie when you left?"

"Nervous," she replied. "But she has enough rooms

booked that she can install a new dishwasher, so she's happy. I talked to her last night. Her daughter loves Italy. She might join Carmie for the holidays."

"Good, because Kourtnee wasn't happy I doubled my advertising budget for the year. I assured her I would see a return on it in good time. I'm glad her daughter is with her. Tell me about Michelle and your trip to Providence Town last week."

"She is amazing. She makes me happy. It's as if we have been together forever. We had a blast in P-Town. We met up with the owner at the restaurant. Ate dinner with her and her friends, toured the town at night, and sat on the beach every day. I told her to stop by the inn the next time she's in town."

"Thanks. What's the name of her restaurant? Maybe, we'll go there someday."

Gina Marie smiled at me. "You'd like her. She's a comedian and an actress, she owns The Club, it sits directly on the water. Gorgeous views, great food, and the best cocktails in the world."

"Gina Marie," Dan hollered from the front porch.

She put her hand on my back. "Hey, I haven't noticed anything lately, have you?"

I knew she was asking about Dan. "No, he seems fine," I replied.

We walked through the house and met him on the front lawn. Six trucks were sitting in front of the house. Dan pointed to the one with a photo of cabinetry on the side of it. "Do you want to do inventory, or do you want me to?"

"I got it," she said and told me she'd see me on Wednesday.

I waved goodbye to everyone and headed up to the inn. I smiled when I saw Teresa sitting on the front porch with a glass of lemonade. "May I join you?"

"Sure. Let me grab another glass." She got up and went inside. I was going to follow her in, but instead I sat down and picked up the book she was reading. "Huh, *the First Husband* by Laura Dave." When she returned, Kourtnee and Christine followed her outside. Christine had a tray of lemon pound cake slices in one hand and a glass of lemonade in the other.

Kourtnee sat down next to me, tapped me on the leg, and asked, "I'm not waiting for the meeting to hear about Italy. Spill."

I laughed. "There's nothing to spill. We had a great time. The food was delicious. The people are friendly, and Italy is gorgeous." I picked up a piece of cake and took a bite.

"And you met a business partner. How did that happen?" she asked.

"Carmie is just a woman Dan and I met in Rome one afternoon. She needed a little help. That's it. The poor woman thought she had inherited a villa when really, she was left an entire castle. I simply gave her the idea to turn it into a writer's retreat. What can I say?"

"Genius," Christine said, adding, "If that's not karma what is?"

"Sounds like a good idea to me," Teresa added. "Where would we be if Julie didn't turn this old farmhouse into an inn?"

I smiled. "A year from now, Carmie will be established, and, who knows, maybe her guests will want to stay with us someday."

# Chapter 23

LABOR DAY WEEKEND, DAN and I were hosting a private party. Michael had arranged for his crew from Friday night's wedding to stay an extra day and serve us. We were having a barbecue under the big tent for lunch, followed by dancing and dinner later that day. Nothing fancy, just a good old-fashioned get-together before we closed the pool.

"Good morning," Dan said as I rolled out of bed.

"Morning, my love." I leaned over and kissed his cheek. Grabbed my robe and told him breakfast was being served at ten in the large dining room.

"What's the attire for the day?"

I looked back at him. "Swimwear?" Then I laughed aloud. "You can wear whatever you're comfortable wearing. I'm wearing my bathing suit and this cover-up." I held up a white, cotton short-dress that was sheer at the top and bottom. Then I pointed to a pair of gold sandals and the large-brimmed hat Dan bought me in Italy. "I'm swimming in my new pool today," I declared and held up my new black two-piece. "I might change for dinner," I said smiling.

Dan grabbed his trunks. "I'll meet you up at the inn in an hour. I need to make a call first."

I looked at him wondering who he had to call.

He held his cell phone up. "Rose emailed me yesterday to see how I was doing and ask if I was satisfied with the new therapist."

I moved to the kitchen and sat down on one of the chairs. "How is she?"

"In her email, she said she was grateful for her children and her practice. She totally understood my reason for moving on. She said men are wired differently. Perhaps a man's point of view would be best."

"Please tell her I said hi and that I'm praying for her."

Dan nodded, poured himself a cup of coffee, and stared out the kitchen window before asking me if I wanted a cup.

I declined. "I'll grab a cup at the inn." I kissed him goodbye. "I love you." I turned back around and hugged him. "Thank you for finding a new therapist," I said, wondering, *Why on Earth does she have to know how he's doing? Couldn't she have called his new therapist? Is that why he's been acting strange these past few months? What the hell?* I wanted to scream, but instead, I stepped outside, feeling delighted with the day's forecast. Low eighties and no rain in sight. The flowerbeds were blooming, and the trees were doing their job. At least something was going right.

It was a quarter to nine, and people were checking in. First thing I noticed was Dan's old therapist from New York had arrived. Now her I liked. Barbara and her sister were staying with us in the Lighthouse Room. I didn't tell Dan her surprise. I promised her she could tell him about her decision to retire and move to Rhode Island herself.

When I stepped up onto the front porch, I heard Teresa singing, "Rolling in the Deep." I opened the front door, and we both heard laughter coming from the back of the house. Teresa and I both headed for the kitchen. Michael was hugging Amanda. Cathy was pouring champagne, and Christine was dropping a cherry in every glass. Cathy turned toward us. "I couldn't help it. I made her show them."

Amanda was beaming. When she held her hand out to me, tears formed in my eyes. "I'm so happy for you," I hugged her as did Teresa, Kourtnee, Kevin, and Jessica.

We each grabbed a glass and toasted to Amanda's engagement. When I sat down at the counter to grab a cup of coffee, Cathy sat down next to me. "I remember the day I met Steve," she said. "He played basketball at the college we were both attending. He was from Oregon." She blushed. "But when he chose me over his hometown, I knew I'd found the right man. When he makes love to me, it's the first time, every time."

I hugged her. "I'm so happy for you." Cathy is so loving and giving. Every person she comes in contact with is blessed for knowing her. She genuinely cares about people. When you step out of her salon, you are transformed. "I'm glad he moved here."

She leaned back. "Steve said a woman should be near

her family. The summer after we graduated, we got married. In my vows, I promised to always take him home for Christmas."

Dan reached in and took hold of my glass. "You started without me," he said jokingly. "Is anyone drinking coffee?"

"I'll take a cup," Jesse said as he and Sherry entered the kitchen.

"Everyone out," Michael yelled. "Breakfast is being served under the tent. Let's go." He used his hands to push us all out of the kitchen. "It's too nice outside to be in here."

Gina Marie, Michelle, Frank, Barbara, and her sister were already sitting at a table eating their breakfast. When I approached Gina Marie, Michelle stood up. I held my hand out to her. She gave me a hug and kissed my cheek. "Gina Marie has told me so much about the two of you. It's a pleasure to meet you."

Dan shook her hand. "It's nice meeting you," he said, and then excused himself to say hi to everyone else. Barbara introduced her sister to him. Frank nodded and continued to eat his breakfast.

"Enjoy your breakfast. I'll catch up with you all later," I told them. I kissed the back of Frank's head and said hello to Barbara and her sister. Then I joined Dan at the buffet table. I was glad to see everyone had dressed casually. I noticed Teresa, Kourtnee, and Christine had changed into their bathing suits.

"Did you see the rock on Amanda's finger?" Dan

asked me as he handed me a fork.

I glanced over at her. Her smile said it all. She had waited a lifetime to find true love. She deserved a fairy-tale wedding. "I did," I replied and inhaled, feeling happier than ever. I followed Dan to the table and sat down next to Jesse, Sherry, Kevin, Kourtnee, and Teresa.

Frank waved to Sabrina as she entered the tent. She was taller than most of the men, but that's not why they turned their heads; she's stunning, gracious, and captures your every attention. When he told me she was expanding, I wasn't surprised. She was the best architect on the east coast. Opening an office in Greenwich, Connecticut, and in Bronxville, New York, would put her on the map and expose her business to a much bigger, wealthier clientele.

The day was casual. It didn't require me getting up, greeting every person, or worrying about anyone, but when Geri entered the tent with her husband Rod, I stood up to say hello.

"Greetings," I said as I held my hand out to him. Rod was an attractive, retired executive. They were made for each other. "I heard you're pretty good on the dance floor."

"Oh, we'll see about that," he replied. "Thanks for the invitation. Geri adores you, by the way."

I smiled at her. "I love her more than she knows. Please help yourself and enjoy your day."

Later, when everyone gathered down at the pool, Geri

told me about her retiring to Maine. "Rod and I have decided to live full-time in Maine, he wants to write a book, and I've decided to spend my days reading on my tablet and discovering dabbling and diving ducks out on the lake."

"I'm going to miss you."

"I'm not giving up my beach house, I still have my annual birthday club that I host every year."

I looked at her.

She raised her eyebrows. "Every year in May, five of us gather to celebrate our birthdays together. We spend the entire weekend laughing, drinking, and playing cards. We cook together and have such a great time, I wouldn't give it up for all the money in the world," she said, and then followed Rod into the pool.

Before the inn, I didn't have a long list of female friends; I had Dan, and he was all the friends I needed. I looked over at him. His smile was still infectious. When he noticed me looking at him, he waved to me. I got up and approached him just in time to watch everyone jump into the pool together. Dan accompanied me to the lower end and we both walked in. The sun had warmed the water to perfection. I sat on the step and watched as Dan swam to the deep end. Gina Marie was swimming in my direction. When she sat next to me, I knew what she was going to say.

"Do you swim?"

I gave her a wry grin. "I can doggy paddle."

"Shut up. Who builds a pool and can't swim?"

"Shh, I'll splash around when everyone is out of the pool."

Jesse approached us, stood next to Gina Marie. "We're going to play volleyball, you in?"

"No, I'll stay here with Julie," she said.

"Stop, I can play from here," I replied and stood up.

"The salt water was a good idea," she said as she followed Jesse to the deep end.

# Chapter 24

WE WERE STILL LIVING in the cottage, and even though I was fine being there, I knew Dan couldn't wait to move into the farmhouse. The temperature was near eighty for the third day in a row. I had always loved Indian summers. Dan not so much. We were out on our hiking trail when I noticed his pace had slowed to a crawl. "Are you feeling okay?"

"The heat is kicking my ass," he replied.

When we got back to the cottage, I asked him again if he felt sick or tired. "How did you sleep last night?"

"I slept okay," he replied and went into the bathroom to take his shower.

I sat at the kitchen table wondering if I should take him to see a doctor. I made a mental note to ask Frank if he could recommend someone. We both needed to find new primary care physicians, perhaps now was the perfect time.

The farmhouse was near completion. The only thing left to do was install the kitchen cabinets. I looked around the cottage. "I'm going to miss my cottage."

"One week in the farmhouse, and you'll forget all about this little hut."

"Hey," I yelled at Dan before he bent to kiss me goodbye.

"I'm going to help the installers."

Before I went up to the inn, I ordered Brin's birthday present. Time was flying by me. I called Frank and asked him for the name of his primary care physician. "I can't believe we haven't gotten our yearly physicals this whole time."

"I just started seeing a new doc myself. Let me grab her card and call you back," he said.

"Sounds good. I'll see you at the birthday party, right?"

"I wouldn't miss it," he replied and then added, "I might bring a date."

"I'm excited to meet the lady who has been cooking for you," I said and hung up the phone. Before I could set my cell phone down, I received a text message from Molly. She wanted to let me know before the invitations went out in the mail that she was able to get the space for her new interior design studio. I texted her back. "I'm so proud of you."

I was almost up to the inn when Kevin approached me. "Morning. Do you have a minute?"

"For you? All day."

At first, he just stood there, but then he let it out. "Would you consider selling Kourtnee and me the thirty acres on the other side of our house?"

I looked at him. "Thirty?"

"Yeah, you left thirty acres between our houses and the road."

He was correct. I did leave a cushion. I purposely set the houses back from the road to keep people from entering the property. In fact, I left a little over thirteen-hundred feet of road frontage. "That's correct. I wanted to preserve the land as much as possible. It was important to me that people driving by not see houses."

"They won't," he said appearing nervous. "I want to buy it for Kourtnee. She's always had this idea to grow her own fruit, vegetables, and flowers."

I looked at him in awe, and of course, I remembered the previous owners and their farmer's market. "You have vision. I like your idea, but—"

"We'll both still work for the inn." He paused. "I already have two guys ready to run the equipment, and Kourtnee found a young girl to work the farm stand. What do you say?"

"So people will see farmland, crops, and—"

"Exactly. I'll have to build a small building to sell the products out of."

"Have you talked to Michael about this?"

"No, you're the first person I shared our idea with. Why?"

"I'm sure he'll want to buy all of our produce from you."

Kevin beamed. "Thanks. That will make Kourtnee happy."

"So what's the name of your farm stand?"

"She wants to call it the Barlow Farmer's Market in honor of her grandparents."

I smiled. "I love it. Tell my bookkeeper to make it happen."

Kevin hugged me, and I thought he was going to shed a few tears when he told me about the twins working for them. "They're only sixteen, but man, do they love farming."

When I returned to the cottage, I saw a note on the coffee table next to a vase filled with wildflowers. At first, I thought they were from Kourtnee and Kevin, but when I read the note, I smiled. "Date night with my wife." I took a long, hot bath, curled my hair, and put on a wrap dress. Sat down in front of the fireplace and waited for my man to walk through the door. Next to the flowers, I set up an ice bucket, two glasses, and a bottle of limoncello. At a quarter to five, Dan entered the cottage wearing a tight, baby blue T-shirt, blue jeans, and his Italian loafers.

"Are you ready?" he asked and extended his hand out to me.

"No drink? Not even one cocktail?" I asked.

He shook his head and waved me over to him. We got in his truck and drove to George's of Galilee.

"Topside or in the dining room?" the man asked us.

"Topside," Dan replied, and we followed him up the

stairs. We sat at a table along the rail, overlooking the ocean. Below, we could see the wild roses, people swimming and relaxing on their beach chairs.

We placed our order and our drinks at the same time. "I'll have a Corona with a pickle and a martini for my wife, please."

Our waiter pursed his lips. "You got it." When he came back to the table, both Dan and I were surprised to see the pickle in the beer. Usually Dan had to put it in himself.

A few seconds later, he returned with our clams.

"Cheers," Dan said as he held his bottle up.

"To us," I replied and tapped my glass to his beer. "How's the house coming along?"

"More and more every day. I promise we'll be cooking in that kitchen sooner than you can say—"

"Sous-chef," I replied and laughed out loud. I reached over and rubbed my hand on top of his. "How are you feeling these past few days?"

"I'm tired. It's hot outside. I never liked Indian summer. I told the painters to turn the air conditioner on today."

"I asked Frank if he knew a doctor we could both go see. We need our yearly checkups."

"Hey, I overheard one of the guys saying that Kelly bought the building next to her restaurant and is looking for someone to tear it down so she can have an outdoor dining room. I told Jesse to stop by and see if we can give her a hand with the project."

"Dan, you're avoiding me. I asked you how you felt. Hang on." I looked at my cell phone. I had a text from Kourtnee. I read it aloud, "No more Deborah Devine, love. She just eloped with one of our guests."

"Seriously?" Dan asked just as our food arrived.

I laughed. "I have no idea anymore." I looked down at my plate and forgot about the world. "This looks delicious." I'd ordered the Bourbon salmon, and Dan had ordered his usual little neck clams, lobster, scallops, and shrimp over linguine.

When Dan was done eating, he reached over and took my hand in his. "I love you so much. Every month, we're coming here no matter what. Tell me you're happy."

I looked into his eyes. "I have never been happier."

We paid for our meal, took a stroll down the beach before going home. As soon as we drove onto the property, Dan told me to close my eyes.

When he said, "Open them," I started to cry. The entire farmhouse was lit up. Dan got out of the truck, opened my door, extended his hand, and said, "I have something to show you."

I followed him inside. The fireplace was glowing. The kitchen cabinets were exactly as I'd imagined, and our king-size bed fit perfectly in our new bedroom.

# Chapter 25

WE SPENT OUR FIRST night in our new forever home. When I woke up, Dan was already in the kitchen with a fresh pot of coffee and breakfast. He smiled at me before setting our plates down on the table. "Good morning, beautiful. I can't tell you how happy I was spending the night here." He turned toward the stove. Raised his hands in the air. "I have room to move around." Held up the coffee pot before pouring me a cup. "I made you a new favorite—an omelet by Dan."

I kissed his lips before purring at my dish. "Looks delicious." I took my cup over to the counter and sat on the stool next to a fresh bouquet of lavender foxgloves. "The flowers are gorgeous." I took my first bite. "Mmm, this is tasty."

"You say that about everything," he said, and I laughed because I did. "Just so you know, I had to go all the way up to the August bed to pick you those flowers."

I tilted my head. "What is the August bed?"

Dan sat down to my right and explained. "Kevin marked the flower beds according to the month they bloom. It was Kourtnee's idea to stagger the plantings."

After breakfast, we hiked around the property and spoke about our plans to return to Italy in November.

"I'm excited to see everyone and to pick the olives. I want to see how they make the oil." Several times, I stopped and waited for Dan to catch up. "Hey, are you feeling okay?"

"I don't know. Last night, I felt warm. I got up around three, and I was soaking wet."

I felt his forehead. "You don't have a fever."

"Yeah, sometimes I just feel like I'm burning up on the inside."

"You need to see a doctor."

"I'll be fine. It's all part of getting old. As soon as cooler weather rolls in, I'll be back in the swing of things."

"Try to take it easy today. Maybe we can hang out by the pool this afternoon."

"I told Jesse I would help him put shelves up in Sherry's craft room, and I have to be back at the house for the furniture delivery."

"Okay, I'll go with you to Jesse's, and we'll come back to the house together."

"I'll take care of it. Besides, don't you have to meet Gina Marie to go over the budget for the year?"

I looked at him. "She never said anything to me."

He opened the door and said, "I forgot to tell you to call her."

I slipped my sneakers off and told him I would call her later. I was terrified. Not knowing what was going on with him. "I'll call her when I get up to the inn. Right now, I want to take your temperature." I went into the bathroom, grabbed the digital thermometer, and held it to his forehead. "Ninety-seven seven."

"See, I'm fine." Dan changed his clothes and told me he would meet me at the farmhouse around three if I wanted to help instruct the movers.

"Sounds good. Please be careful today, don't do anything too strenuous."

We rode in the UTV. I had him drop me off at the inn. "Morning sunshine," I said as I entered Kourtnee's office.

"Good morning, Boss Lady. Have a seat. I have something to tell you."

I sat down across from her, wishing I had grabbed a cup of coffee.

Kourtnee came around the desk and sat down next to me. "I got a call this morning from the COO of MetLife. They want to buy the inn."

I looked at her, not sure I heard her correctly. "Seriously?"

"Yeah. It's a good offer, but I told him I would have to talk to you and Dan before I could set up a meeting. Boss Lady, whatever you do, wherever you go, I'm going with you. I'm staying with you."

Her words brought tears to my eyes. Dan was correct. Last night was amazing. Our new farmhouse was perfect. Everything was falling into place for us. We were together, and we were living the American dream. Retired, enjoying life, and we were finally making time for vacations. "Tell him no. Thank him for his offer and tell him *our* inn is not for sale."

I glanced over at her, waiting for her response. When I saw her crying, I couldn't help myself. "This stays between me and you." I leaned over and squeezed her shoulders. "No one is breaking up our family."

Kourtnee handed me a tissue, and we both blew our noses. Laughingly, she said, "Good, because Kevin said you approved my new idea."

I smiled at her. "I love your plan for a garden along the road." I got up and reminded her to keep the ideas flowing.

She winked at me. "You mean growing."

When I went into the kitchen for my coffee, Michael showed me the dress he'd bought for Brin's birthday. "It's perfect," I said as I poured my coffee. "She's going to love it." Then I picked up my list of herbs to pick for the day.

Michael laughed, "Christine said Brin's never going to take it off. She's obsessed with unicorns."

The dress was colorful. Rainbow tulle, satin bodice with a big, bright unicorn in the center, and a unicorn headband to match.

I met Dan at the house and gave him a hand instructing the movers. Unlike the inn, our home was easy. The living room, family room, and dining room went off without a hitch. We'd decided not to put a media room in the house because of the one up at the inn. Never mind, Gina Marie had said there was no room in the budget for extras. Considering I got my swimming pool, I was more than happy to walk up to the inn for movie night. That left the guest bedrooms. Dan and I still had to go shopping for the furniture. I told him we could put it off until after the holidays.

Dan collapsed into a chair in the family room. "I never realized we had thirty-seven Hayden Lambson prints?"

I handed him a bowl of chili. "Yes." I smiled and sat down next to him. "And for Christmas this year, you're getting me two more." I raised my eyebrows and took a bite of my cornbread.

Dan shook his head and his finger at me. "Tomorrow, we'll pack up the cottage."

I picked up my spoon. "I'll do it. Seriously, I can gather our belongings myself. I'll use the Polaris Ranger."

"Okay, let me know if you need a hand. I'm tired. What do you say we get some shut-eye soon?"

A few days later, I passed Kourtnee in the lobby with a teenager. The girl was telling her that she'd brought her working papers with her along with a permission slip from her parents. She stopped in front of her office door and introduced me to her new helper.

I held my hand out to her. "It's nice to meet you. You're welcome to eat breakfast and lunch in our kitchen anytime you're hungry. Oh, and you're going to love working with Kevin too." She blushed. "Okay, I'll let the two of you talk." As I walked away, I heard her tell Kourtnee that she turned fourteen last month, but not to worry because she also had her special limited permit to work signed by her school. She was sweet. Reminded me of a younger Kourtnee. Slender, blonde, and full of energy.

Later that day, Kourtnee told me her helper was a farm girl just like her. "Her grandfather taught her how to take care of the farm animals and how to milk the cows by the time she was seven. As soon as she told me she was a member of the 4-H Club, I knew she was perfect for the job and that she had good work values."

"You're really doing this. Aren't you?"

She nodded. "I have always wanted to run my own farm. Being able to feed people fresh produce every day will be—"

"A blessing for our community. I'm so proud of you. Let me know how I can help," I told her and then headed down to the farmhouse.

# Chapter 26

SEPTEMBER TWENTY-FIRST WAS HOTTER than the middle of July. Everyone wanted to stay indoors and turn their air conditioners up. The ornamental grasses didn't seem to mind the heat. They were loving the humidity. I especially liked the white, feathery blooms surrounding the north side of the pool. I was sitting in a lounge chair when my cell phone rang. "Hello. Hey, no, everyone is in the pool. How is everyone?" I listened to Lynnae tell me about the baby, Sam tutoring other kids online, and about Max almost meeting his real father at a baseball game. "Did he see you?"

"No, I saw him leaving with his family. Barry and I decided to wait a few more years. Max has been doing so well in school, and he's amazing with his little sister. Julie, I have something to tell you, and it can't wait."

I sat up in my chair. Hung my feet over the side and waved back to Dan. He was lying on one float, and Jesse was on another. Sherry was sitting on the side of the pool, dangling her feet in the water, while reading a book on her tablet. "I'm listening," I told her.

"Barry took a new job. It's a lot of money."

"That's great!" I was excited for them. "I'm so proud of all of you. Gosh, Lynnae, I'm happy for you—"

"Julie." She paused for a second. "We're moving to Montana."

"Montana?" I said loud enough for everyone to turn their heads toward me. I waved them off and stood up. "For how long?"

"At least five years," she replied, and my heart sank.

"I still haven't met the baby yet. I—"

"Julie, you can visit us any time you want. The house is beautiful. It sits on the side of a mountain overlooking a lake. The boys are excited about moving. They can ride the horses, swim in the pool, and go out on their quads on trails that roam for miles."

Silence. I knew Barry would take care of them. I also knew he was a hard worker, but what I didn't realize was that he was in such high demand.

"Are you okay?" she asked and then added, "I'm excited about staying home and taking care of my family—"

"I'm happy for you. Dan and I will come to see you when you get settled in. I'll bring the baby's gift and the boys' presents when we come."

"You're going to love the new house. It's a huge ranch, three stories with wrap-around porches. We leave next week. Barry is flying out tomorrow to meet the developers and then coming home to get us. We're all driving out there together. He rented a motor coach for us to drive in. The boys have their maps pinned to a corkboard so they can mark every state as we travel through them."

As she spoke about her new venture, memories of her flashed before me. Asking her to work at the bakery, being pregnant with both of her boys, tossing my offer to buy the business on the floor before finally saying yes, blushing the first time Barry came into the bakery, and I remembered the day she told me she was in trouble for letting him play with the boys. I was so grateful that day. Lynnae had found true love. "Love is taking you on a journey. I'm happy for you. Call me when you reach Montana."

"I will. I love you. Please tell Dan I love him, and I will see him soon." She hung up the phone.

I sat back down, but I got up again and went into the pool house. I put the lid down, sat on the toilet seat, and cried. When I heard Dan call my name, I went back outside. He was pale. I asked him if he ate lunch yet. When he said no, I suggested we fire up the grill. "I'm going to make some burgers and hot dogs," I said to everyone.

"There's potato salad in the fridge," Sherry said. "I'll help." She got out of the pool and dried off.

Jesse stayed in the pool until Sherry sent him to their house for watermelon, buns, and rolls.

"Sit down, I'll make you a hamburger," I told Dan and turned the grill on.

When Jesse came back, I pointed over at Dan. He sat down next to him and asked him if he was okay. "How are you feeling old man?"

"I have a headache," Dan replied, and I thought,

*That's a first.* I went into the pool house and got two Tylenol for him.

By the time everything was nearly ready, Gina Marie and Michelle had joined us. I told them to help themselves and handed Dan his plate and the pills. "Lynnae called me. They're moving to Montana for a couple of years."

Dan touched my arm.

Jesse snapped his neck back before asking why. "What the hell is in Montana?"

"Barry got a big job," I said.

"Huh," Dan replied as he reached for his glass of iced tea.

Michelle said, "Montana can be beautiful in the summer, but extremely cold in the winter. Don't get me wrong, it can be just as nice if you're into winter sports."

"If we move, we're heading south," Gina Marie said laughingly. Then she went over to the porch and turned the music up. Luke Bryan was singing, "Country Girl Shake It for Me" on the radio. Sherry and Michelle both stood up and started dancing alongside Gina Marie.

I stayed in my seat next to Dan and Jesse. A moment later, Kevin, Kourtnee, Michael, and Christine joined in on the dancing.

The next day, Dan went to help Jesse move a few boxes into Sherry's craft room. When he came back to the house, he told me he had to sit down for a minute. "By the time I carried the last box, I was exhausted."

"Get in the shower. I'm taking you to the emergency room."

When Dan didn't argue with me, I knew something was wrong. We got in the car and drove to the hospital without telling a soul. I was so glad I signed up for the portal program. I was able to see every test and the results as they came in. After they hooked up the oxygen line, they ran an IV. When they took him down the hall for an MRI and a CAT scan, panic set in. I paced the hall. I was too nervous to call anyone out of fear they would ask me if he was going to be okay. I found the strength to pray. I had to stop myself from imagining a terrible outcome. I went back into his room and waited. As I watched the clock go from one hour to two, I begged the nurses to tell me what was happening. They kept telling me the doctor would be right in. I started to cry again, but then I stopped when I heard Dan's voice. He was asking the nurse for some water. I wiped my face and smiled as they rolled him in.

Five hours later, I looked at Dan and said, "It's not your heart or your lungs. Dan, I think it's your liver."

The attending physician came in, handed me a bunch of papers, and explained she would release Dan on one condition. "You have to promise me you will go directly to your primary care doctor after leaving here."

Dan looked at me before answering her. "We just moved here, but I give you my word I will see one as soon as I can."

She tapped his hand. "Your primary care doctor should be able to recommend a gastroenterologist." She looked back at me. "This needs to be taken care of."

"Thank you, I'll make an appointment as soon as we get home," I told her.

# Chapter 27

WE LEFT THE HOSPITAL shocked. Dan was diagnosed with cirrhosis of the liver. As a result, his spleen was enlarged, and fluids were building up fast. I looked down at his discharge papers, wondering how, why, and what this meant for his future. Dan opened my door, and I got in. I sat in the driver's seat numb. I glanced down at the papers again. When Dan sat down and closed his door, I put the vehicle in drive and drove straight to the farmhouse. We both sat in the family room. When darkness fell around us, I stood and turned on a few table lamps. Dan offered to cook dinner. I looked at the clock. It was almost seven.

"I'll cook, you rest," I said, but he wasn't having any part of it.

He went into the kitchen and made his delicious beef tenderloins with fresh mushrooms, Vidalia onions, and peppers on a club roll. We ate in the family room in front of the fireplace. I poured us each a glass of his signature iced tea. Afterward, Dan wanted to go for a walk around the property. I suggested we sit out back in the porch rockers, but Dan wanted to walk. We set our dishes, glasses, and pan in the dishwasher and put on our hiking shoes. Neither one of us said too much. We held hands and allowed the moon to rise above our heads. That night, Dan went to bed first. I sat in the corner chair and read his discharge papers again.

Cirrhosis of the liver—scarring over time, causing the liver to stop functioning properly. I had to look up splenomegaly, which meant enlarged spleen. I remembered the doctor saying Dan's ascites was fluid building up in his abdomen. Then I read the word thrombocytopenia, and again I picked up my cell phone to find the answer. Low platelets. My heart came to an abrupt stop. I glanced over at Dan. I knew he was still awake, just lying there thinking about his prognosis. I emailed my entire staff including Gina Marie and Frank. I told them about our trip to the emergency room and that I was not strong enough to talk to anyone, to please give us the weekend to gather our thoughts. I also texted my friend from Long Island the same message adding, "Rita, I am distraught texting this message to you. What am I to do?" Rita was the best registered nurse we knew.

She immediately texted me back. "I'm praying for both of you. Let me check with Margaret."

Margaret was her daughter-in-law. An anesthesiologist at New York-Presbyterian Hospital in New York City. I set my phone down on my lap and grabbed a tissue, but before I could blow my nose, Rita texted me back. "Margaret said to call Dr. Lorna Dove, she's the best and she's the head of gastroenterology."

I texted her back. "Thank you so much."

As soon as I got in bed, Dan held me tight. I

whispered in his ear. "You're going to be just fine. We got this."

He reached over and squeezed my hand. "I'm glad we were able to go to Italy. I'm sorry we didn't take a lot of vacations." He brought our hands to his lips, kissed my thumb, and said, "I'm sorry I ever cheated on you."

My heart was heavy. "I'm taking you to see a top specialist. It's my job to do whatever it takes. Your job is to get better."

The next morning, I was up by six, took my shower, and got on the phone and scheduled an appointment in New York to see Dr. Dove. I also found a doctor in town accepting new patients.

I didn't hear Dan come into the room. When he put his arms around me, I leaned back for a kiss. "Monday afternoon, we're going to see Dr. Jee, and on September twenty-third, we're going to the city to see Dr. Dove at New York-Presbyterian Hospital."

"Have you been up all night?" he asked as he turned the coffee on.

"No, I took my shower, called the doctor's office, and just came out here to make you breakfast."

Dan gave me a wry grin.

"Okay, you can make breakfast," I said smiling. "Dan, I looked her up, she's highly qualified, and she's the head of gastroenterology."

He took hold of the frying pan, eggs, mushrooms, peppers, and onions and asked me to pour him a cup of coffee.

I poured our coffee and put two Thomas' *English Muffins* in the toaster. "I thought we could take a drive today. I want to take my truck so I can get some pumpkins, gourds, and corn stalks for the inn."

"Only if I can drive?" he said, and I laughed.

Truth was, I wanted to be alone with Dan. I needed time to think. His appointment was more than two weeks away. I needed to make a game plan. I had to do my research. I wanted to be as informed as I could before our meeting with Dr. Dove.

I ate my breakfast while listening to Dan tell me about being diagnosed with hepatitis back in 1970. "Back then, they only tested for hepatitis A and B," he said. Dan took his last bite before adding, "I pray it's not contagious."

I set my fork down. "I'm fine. Stop. Don't think like that. I'm as healthy as an ox."

For a moment, he was lost in thought, then he said, "I remember being one of three guys. We all worked in the hospital for the state. We were put out on worker's comp. I went to old Doc Halsburger in Millbrook. I think he gave me an antibiotic and sent me back to work after a couple of weeks. He said there was nothing they could do for it."

Dan got up from the table, put his dish in the sink, and said he was going to take a shower before we headed out. I washed the dishes and logged onto the portal. I was in shock. Dan's symptoms were all from a tick bite. He tested positive for all three Lyme diseases. "That tick saved his life."

While Dan took his shower, I looked up hepatitis C. He was correct, they didn't even test for it until 1991. I closed my laptop. I was glad Dan agreed to go for a drive. I could care less if we bought one gourd. I just needed to be alone with him. Dan came out of the bedroom wearing blue jeans, a tan Carhartt shirt, and his work boots. "I'm ready if you are," he said looking better.

Dan drove the Ford truck out of the garage and headed out on the main road. "Take the highway heading toward South Kingstown," I said. Dan drove about thirty-five miles an hour, and that was just fine with me. When I asked him to stop at Carpenter's Farm Stand, Dan smiled at me.

"You're not buying, you're spying on Kevin and Kourtnee's competition."

"Get out," I replied and closed my door. The only thing we bought was a bushel of apples. "I'll make an apple pie today if you promise me that you will take it easy until we meet with Dr. Dove."

He smiled from ear to ear.

Sunday morning, we were in the kitchen eating lunch when we heard a knock on the front door. Through the glass, we could see Gina Marie and Michelle standing on the porch holding bags, boxes, and an armload of groceries. Dan opened the door.

"I know you said to give you some time, but I couldn't wait any longer," Gina Marie said as she walked right past us. "From now on, you're eating organic."

I gave Michelle a kiss on her cheek and said, "Thank

you for doing this."

"Oh, she's not done," Michelle said, before telling Dan he was going to be okay. Michelle pointed back to her truck. "There's more."

Dan was still holding the door open when he offered to help. "Here, let me give you a hand."

"Oh, hell no!" Gina Marie shouted at him from the kitchen and then went outside. When she reentered the foyer holding a stalk of Brussels sprouts, Dan became emotional. I took the vegetables from Gina Marie as she hugged him, telling him she loved him and that she was not leaving his side. "I'll do whatever I have to."

Michelle went back to the truck and came in with fresh-baked pies, muffins, and scones. "No preservatives," she announced.

Together, we unpacked the bags and boxes. There were frozen organic meats, poultry, seafood, fruit, vegetables, and fresh berries. Everything was handpicked with love in their hearts and intended for Dan's road to recovery.

"This is incredible," I said at least ten times as I put each item away.

# Chapter 28

MONDAY MORNING, WE TOOK an easy stroll around the pond before going up to the inn. Jesse was standing on the front porch. When I saw his tears fall, I turned to Dan. "He needs you. Jesse needs to hear from you that you're going to be okay."

I saw as Dan took a deep breath, hugged Jesse, and slapped him on the shoulder before saying, "I got this."

Jesse stood there looking at him. I motioned for them to come inside. Teresa stood up as soon as she saw us. She too walked past me and hugged Dan.

"You're going to be okay. You have all of us to lean on," she said.

Dan patted her on the head. Sherry came in and asked if anyone else needed a cup of coffee. We gathered in the kitchen. Gina Marie, Frank, and my entire staff gathered around the counter watching Christine as she put fresh-baked pastries on a tray. Michael served coffee and tea to anyone who held up a cup. On the table sat carafes of orange and grapefruit juice.

I grabbed a cup of coffee and sat down at the table between Kevin and Dan.

Kourtnee sat next to Kevin and immediately started the meeting. "Okay, from now on we all have to stay on point. Dan, you're to do nothing until the doctor says so. Got it?" She looked at him until he agreed.

"Good, in the meantime, Kevin is going to send Robert down to the farmhouse to give you a hand with anything that needs to be done. I don't even want you mowing the lawn."

When Dan turned from her and looked at me, I thought he was going to give her a hard time, but he simply thanked her. "Thank you. Seriously, you've all been great. Take care of Julie, and I will be—"

They stopped him cold. "You," they all said in perfect unison.

"You are our priority right now. Lord knows Julie can take care of herself," Kourtnee said, and Gina Marie agreed with her.

Gina Marie took a sip of her coffee before saying, "Dan, Kourtnee is right. We're family. Julie made sure we all knew that when she opened the inn. You're just as important to us as she is. We can and will take care of you."

I swallowed the lump forming in my throat, seeing and hearing the love they had for him. As we ate our breakfast, Gina Marie assured us that even after installing the new swimming pool and building the farmhouse, we had enough money to start another project. "Oh, I saw Deborah. She's coming back. She said her husband is building her a new house along the ocean, but she still wants to run her shop if that's okay."

Frank looked at me. "What did I miss now?"

I laughed as I explained that Deborah closed her shop so she could elope with a rich man. "She met him at one of our weddings," I added.

Christine handed Frank another slice of carrot cake and told him, "They've been dating for six months. The guy is crazy for her. Sends her flowers every day, buys her jewelry, and now he's building her a dream home. Do you blame her?"

Frank laughed. Replied, "I better step up my game," then took a bite of his muffin.

Dan tapped on the table. "Is that it?"

"No," Michael said. "One more thing, at the end of October we have our biggest wedding to date, almost four hundred people." He was looking at me when he said, "I'm telling you this now, because I don't want you to worry about one detail. I have my own staff. You don't need to do anything. I just wanted you to know in case you get any ideas."

Both Cathy and Amanda agreed with Michael. "We got this," Cathy said.

"Yes, take care of Dan," Amanda said.

I rubbed my hand on Dan's leg. "I told you we have the best of Rhode Island all around us."

"Oh, and don't forget you're all invited to Brin's birthday party on Sunday," Christine said, adding, "Two o'clock in the large dining room."

Frank smiled. "I bought my present the day I received my invitation."

"Me too," Gina Marie said.

"Okay, I have a few more announcements to make before we all get back to work." I told everyone about Kourtnee's idea to start a farm stand.

"Don't worry," Kevin said. "We hired a couple of guys to tend to the crops and a young lady to open and close the stand every day."

"That's right, we'll still be here doing our usual jobs," Kourtnee added.

"One more thing," I said. "Lynnae and Barry have decided to move to Montana for a few years so they won't be joining us for the holidays."

"It's temporary," Dan added. "Lynnae deserves a little family time."

"What about her bakery?" asked Teresa.

"Stephanie and Brook will continue to run the bakery." I thought about what Dan said. He was right. She deserved some time to herself. "She's leaving the bakery in capable hands."

Everyone agreed. I turned to Teresa and asked if she was singing at this weekend's wedding.

"No, thank God." She got up and poured hot water into her teacup. "Last weekend was a nightmare. I sang the whole song before I realized my mic wasn't on."

"Wait," Michael said. "If the inn has the money for a new project, I'd like to build an outdoor kitchen down at the pool." When he looked at me, I pointed to Gina Marie and Kourtnee.

They looked at each other. Kourtnee announced she had plenty of funds available.

Gina Marie said, "Write up a proposal, and I'll get to work on ordering the material."

Frank stood up and announced, "I might be retired, but Gina Marie is on my account and gets to use my discount at the lumber yard, and if you need any stonework done, be sure to call Stone Resource, Sam's a personal friend of mine."

"I still have a couple thousand dollars left over for plantings," Kevin added to the conversation.

"Anyone else?" I said as I went to get up.

"I'm good," Teresa said, standing on the other side of the kitchen, and everyone laughed.

"By the way, I'm taking Dan to see a new doctor this afternoon. I'll let you all know what he says when we get back. I also made an appointment with a specialist."

"Dan, you're in good hands," Michael told him. "Julie will make sure you're taken care of."

Dan inhaled, stood up, and thanked everyone.

At one p.m., we entered Dr. Jee's office. I handed Dan's previous discharge papers to the nurse and asked her to make a copy so I could keep the original. After they weighed him, checked his vitals and temperature, we were told the doctor would be right in. Fifteen minutes later, a small, broad man wearing a white coat came in, sat down, and opened his computer. I looked at Dan wondering if he was thinking the same thing. *Is he the doctor?*

He slid his stool closer to Dan and offered a fist-bump. Then he moved back over to his computer.

I couldn't wait any longer, I had to know. "Are you Dr. Jee?"

He closed his computer, stood up, and approached Dan. "Let me listen to your heart."

Dan read the nametag on his coat and waggled his eyebrows at me.

He looked in Dan's eyes, ears, and throat before saying, "There's nothing I can do for you." Then he sat back down.

I looked at Dan. He was pale. I was pissed.

"Do you have any children?" he asked.

"No," Dan replied.

Then he looked at me and said, "You'll need to get your affairs in order. This man is sick. His liver doesn't have long."

I swallowed the very large lump in my throat and said, "You're supposed to recommend a gastroenterologist." When he left the room, I told Dan to get up. "Let's go. Now," I said.

As soon as we got back in the car, I told Dan, "That man had no right saying any of that to you."

Saturday's wedding went off without a hitch. Everyone was happy. The bride's father paid for the entire event, and when the wedding was over, he handed envelopes to everyone on the wait staff. I will say one thing about that weekend. The music was louder than normal. The flowers were over the top. The archway was at least three feet wide, covered with expensive white flowers. The head table was adorned by a blanket of hanging Dendrobium white orchids that gave the appearance of a waterfall.

On the twenty-third of September, Dan and I went to see Dr. Dove. When she came out to the reception room and called his name, I felt honored. I knew it was her by her picture on the Internet. We sat in the chairs next to the examination table. While a nurse took his vitals, I explained to Dr. Dove about what had happened in the past few weeks and why we chose her to be his liver specialist. "I took him to see a new primary care doctor, but I wasn't happy when he told Dan there was nothing he could do for him and that I needed to get our affairs in order."

Dr. Dove snapped her neck and replied, "You're never going back to him." She looked at Dan.

"Got it," Dan replied. "Not ever."

Then I looked at her and said, "You are an answered prayer."

"Me?"

"Yes, I prayed for a miracle and for thirty more years with my husband, and God gave me you."

She laughed, looked at Dan, and said, "No pressure on us." She sat down and told Dan to sit closer to her. She pulled the paper out on the examination table and drew a picture of his internal organs. She explained everything to him in plain English. She wanted to relieve his mind of any worry, to make him understand how the liver worked, why he had fluid building up, and she told him not to stress about his enlarged spleen. Dr. Dove went on to say, "Based on your previous visit to the emergency room, I'm going to schedule a series of tests. In the meantime, I want you to rest, and I will see you in one month." Then she handed me a printout of the tests to be performed at New York-Presbyterian Hospital and a list of classes we could sign up for to better educate ourselves on liver disease. "It pleases me when my patients have a good caregiver."

After Dan thanked Dr. Dove, I told her, "His job is to get better, mine is to do everything and anything to make sure that happens."

# Chapter 29

IT WAS ALMOST NOON when we left the doctor's office. "Are you hungry?" I asked before we got to the parking garage. We walked one block up from Fort Washington Avenue to Broadway. We had several options to choose from. Not wanting fast or fried food, I pointed to a restaurant.

"Let's grab a slice of pizza," he said.

We went into Broadway Pizza, placed our order, and sat outside. I took one bite and my eyes lit up. "Oh, my goodness." The pizza was so good I ate the entire piece. "This is the best pizza, I have ever eaten."

Dan agreed with me. "I can't believe you ate that whole thing. It was the size of your plate."

"I know," I replied wishing I could take home a dozen more. I drove back to the inn. Considering I'm a country girl at heart, I navigated the streets of New York City very well.

"I love Dr. Dove. When she told you to sit closer, I was amazed at her bedside manner."

"I can't believe she allowed you to take her picture," he said. "I like her too. I'm glad she's my doctor. I trust her. I feel better already."

I glanced over at him. He was looking out the

window, and I wondered if he truly was feeling good about everything.

We stopped in Connecticut to go to the bathroom. "Would you like to go inside?" He asked and pointed to an antique shop.

"Sure," I said, turning toward the row of shops.

We both stood under an enormous, round vintage clock that read Holliday in the center. Dan reached up and read the price tag. "Four hundred and fifty dollars?"

I smiled like a child seeing her first baby doll. Dan asked the woman to take it down for us.

"I love the roman numerals," I said and clapped my hands.

"You like it because it says Holliday," he jokingly replied and then kissed me. "It's going to look great in the family room."

I hadn't thought about that, I was thinking of hanging it in the kitchen, but the family room worked for me too. I knew what Dan was doing. Every time something upsetting happened, he would discover ways to make me feel better.

"Do you want to look around?" he asked as he sat down on a wide armchair. I thought the chair would look great in one of our guest bedrooms.

I shook my head. I didn't want to say how much I liked the chair out of fear he would offer to pick it up. "Let's go home. We have plenty of antique shops in Point Judith. I want you to get some rest." What I didn't say was, I need a moment.

The man carried the clock out to our SUV, set it in the back, and thanked us for our purchase. When Dan offered to give him a tip, he declined and told Dan he was the owner. Then he handed Dan his business card and said, "We have a catalog on our website, I can ship anything under two hundred pounds within the United States."

Dan looked at the card. "Thank you. This will make her happy."

"Thank you," I shouted over the top of the vehicle.

I was still driving in Connecticut when Dan fell asleep. I turned the radio down to a whisper and drove all the way to Narragansett Pier before Dan woke up. He stretched out his arms and said, "I didn't sleep much last night." He turned toward me and added, "Thanks."

I touched the side of his face. "For?"

When he didn't reply, I said, "I love you with all my heart. God has plans for us." Then I thought about Carmie, and my heart sank because I knew going back to Italy was off the table.

"Have you heard from Lynnae?" he asked. "Did you tell her?"

"She's holding you in her prayers. She said to tell you that she loves you and if you need anything to let her know."

He nodded and closed his eyes for a second before telling me, "Sherry told me Jesse cried after he read your text message."

"Jesse loves you. You're his best friend. Everyone

says the same thing about the two of you, you're closer than most brothers. Maybe you should go see him when we get back and let him know how pleased we both are with Dr. Dove. It will ease his mind. He's probably more scared than you are, the big lug."

"He is a big baby. I remember when he got your note. He came to the house in tears. Demanded we go looking for you."

I reached over and took his hand in mine. "When you're family, it's hard to think of someone you love being sick, but you're going to be better before they can say, 'Where's Dan?'"

When we got to the farmhouse, we saw an enormous fruit basket on the porch. I picked it up and handed the card to Dan. Then I opened the front door. I set the basket down on the coffee table and went back out to get the clock. I set the clock down in the doorway. Dan was sitting on the couch. He handed the card to me. "That's so sweet," I said.

Dan had tears in his eyes. "They're all special to me, but Frank and I will always have a special bond." Dan took his cell phone out of his pocket. "I want to call and thank him."

I gave him a crimson smile. "Okay, I'm going to run up to the cottage. I want to make sure it's ready for the bride and groom this weekend."

"Sounds good," he replied, adding, "After I talk to Frank, I'm going to lie down for a while." He dialed his cell phone, and I went outside.

I walked to the cottage knowing I was having a meltdown. So much was happening. I wanted to feel happy for Sabrina, who was expanding her architectural business. Molly for opening a new interior design studio. Amanda for getting engaged, Geri for retiring to Maine, and Barbara for retiring to Rhode Island, but my heart was heavy. On the porch sat a new loveseat that matched the two rockers. I opened the door and almost fell over the boxes stacked between the doorway and the coffee table. I looked down and read the bride's name, wondering what could be inside. In the kitchen sat even more boxes. I looked in the open one and saw ivory pillar candles. "That's a lot of candles."

I went into the bedroom, sat on the edge of the bed, and cried. I couldn't lose him. Not then or ever. "Lord, please. Place your healing hands upon him." I took hold of several tissues before sliding myself to the floor. "Dear God, we have been through so much. You showed him where to find me. Please don't take him from me." I sat there for nearly an hour, crying, praying, before I realized Dan was up at the farmhouse by himself. I didn't want him to be alone, to be afraid, I wanted him to know that I was by his side, and that together we were going to get through this.

# Chapter 30

I WAS MORE THAN grateful for my staff. They always knew when to take the reins. The next day, Dan, Lady, and I skipped our morning hike and went to the beach to be alone. We sat on our blanket and watched the sunrise. In the distance, we saw shades of aquamarine, the color you might imagine a painter writing about when she's trying to describe her water scene. The ocean at Narragansett Beach is that color right before the sun bursts from orange to yellow.

"If you don't mind, I think I'm going to pass on helping with the new outdoor kitchen," he said, and I thought, *Please send me a living donor.* "I told Jesse and Kevin they could use whatever equipment they needed."

He was deflated. I remembered feeling the exact same way when I arrived in Rhode Island without him. For me, I always needed a new project, something to look forward to. I looked over at him. "I was thinking about building a new pole barn next year for all of your tools and smaller pieces of equipment."

He gave me a wry grin. "Let's see what happens."

"You need to start designing it," I replied and rested my head on his lap. "It would mean the world to Frank if you ask him to help you." I waited for him to say something, but he just stared out at the waves. "I could sit here with you for the rest of my life." He didn't say anything, and that was okay too because I was just as scared.

Dan and I stayed at the beach until nine-thirty. When we got back to the farmhouse, Gina Marie was there waiting for us on the front porch. She waved her hand as we got out of the SUV. "Good morning," she said and stood up.

"Morning," we replied as Lady ran to greet her.

I opened the front door, listening to her tell Dan about the new outdoor kitchen. "It's going to be insane. We're putting a big flat-screen TV over the fireplace in the gazebo and a ceiling fan so you can sit comfortably day or night. Kourtnee got a fantastic deal on patio furniture."

Dan sat down on the sofa. "Sounds nice. Who designed it?"

"Michael," she replied. "He did a damn good job too. It has a pizza oven, grill, warming drawers, and an eight-burner stove."

"What?" I shouted from the kitchen.

I saw Gina Marie turn to face me. "He's so damn meticulous. This thing has two refrigerators, a wine rack, an icemaker, and two sinks. You're never going to see him in the kitchen again."

I handed her a glass of lemonade. "I can't wait to see it." I sat down next to Dan and handed him a glass. I saw Gina Marie look at me. Dan wasn't saying too much.

"Dan, tell Gina Marie about your new tree stands."

He hitched his chin my way. "When we were in Italy, Julie had Jesse, Kevin, and Robert put up a few tree stands for me."

"I'll go deer hunting with you," she said. "Seriously, I know how to be quiet in the woods."

I felt his eyes on me. "I think it's a great idea."

I waited for Dan to tell her no, but instead he told her she could sit in the ground blind. "I'll take you on the last day, we'll sit in the new Educator, it's made for more than one person. You can't talk out loud, and you have to sit still," he told her.

"I'll be fine," she replied. "I'm so excited. I've always wanted to go."

Dan laughed aloud for the first time in weeks. "I'll meet you on the porch at three-thirty."

"In the afternoon?" she replied.

"Ha ha, in the morning," he said, adding, "and don't be late. We have to be in the blind before the sun comes up."

"Oh, crap." Gina Marie stood up. "Seriously?" She laughed. "I'm kidding. I'll be ready and waiting for you."

Dan laughed again. "We'll see." He looked at me. "I'm going to go for a swim before Kevin closes the pool. Come on, Lady."

"The salt water is good for you. Maybe we'll join you." I looked up at Gina Marie.

"I'm game. Let me grab my suit, and I'll meet you all down at the pool in a half hour."

When we got there, Kevin, Kourtnee, Michael, Christine, Teresa, Cathy, and Amanda were all swimming, laughing, and playing a game of volleyball. "Hey," Kourtnee shouted to us. "The water is magnificent."

"Is anyone up at the inn?" I asked.

"Sherry and Jesse," Michael replied. "Sherry is covering the phones, and Jesse is making pancakes for Brin and Delilah."

Christine waggled her eyebrows as she hit the ball, sending it to the other end of the pool.

I saw Gina Marie stop in front of the pool house and turn the music up a little louder. Travis Tritt's, "It's A Great Day to Be Alive" was playing on the radio. She jumped in the deep end, causing a splash.

A minute later, Kourtnee got out of the pool and said, "I want to show you my drawing." She dried herself off and went inside. When she returned, she handed me a composition notebook. She had the entire garden laid out. On the first page was her budget. Next, was a photo of the farm stand. She pointed to the picture and explained how the two flaps opened up, creating shade for the customers to stand under. "At night, we can close it up and lock it down."

I turned the page to look at her design. "This is amazing. You didn't miss a thing."

She pulled a piece of paper from the back of the book, showing me an example of what it will look like. "We wanted to protect the view from the road. The pear trees won't be ready for four to five years, but they'll be beautiful to look at as people pass by."

"I love the white blossoms behind the white split-rail fence. Gorgeous." I turned to another page and saw a different white post. "What are these for?"

"For the berries. That's a vineyard trellis. Turn the page, I want to show you my chicken coop design."

"Chicken?"

She laughed. "Yes, chickens. We need them for bug control. We're getting a dozen of each: Hamburgs, Leghorns, and Dominiques. They love Japanese beetles, squash bugs, and a whole slew of other invertebrates. That's where chickens get their protein from. It will probably take us four years before we can officially open. Kevin still has to meet with Frank and the Board of Health about the irrigation and sprayers. He said the water source needs to be tested before we do anything. I applied for our organic certification from MOSA. I already started my seedlings. I'm planting seven different types of apple trees, three types of pear, and one of each: plum, peach, nectarine, fig, and cherry." She took a deep breath. "A total of six hundred fruit trees."

"Did you say fig? They're my favorite. What type of apple trees are you planting?" Hoping for McIntosh and Granny Smith so I could buy them and bake Dan's favorite pie.

Kourtnee turned to a different page and showed me, I was pleased with her entire list. "Umm, what does MOSA stand for?" I laughed, thinking I should know, but I didn't.

Kourtnee smiled. "Midwest Organic Services Association. They're great. They've been helping me fill out all the paperwork and addressing all my concerns."

"It sounds as if you have everything under control."

"Huh, tell that to Kevin, because he's driving me crazy. He wanted to plant the apple trees in seven long rows. I told him no way. Two rows of each. Can you imagine the confusion come picking time? One-hundred and twenty-six feet is long enough for any picker." She tapped me on my leg. "Hey, how's Dan been feeling? Is there anything Kevin and I can do for him?"

I glanced up and saw him talking to Michael and Christine. "He's great. If he hadn't been bitten by that tick, we would never have known he was sick." I thought about the online classes Dr. Dove told us about. "I have to get back to the farmhouse and take care of a few things. I love your design and idea. I'm rooting for you." I got up to leave, but I turned around when I heard Dan call out my name.

I went over to where he was. "What's up?"

"Are you coming in or chilling out?"

"I have to go back to the farmhouse for something." He shrugged and leaned back, allowing the jets to massage his lower back. Gina Marie gave a thumbs up, and I knew she would keep an eye on him.

# Chapter 31

I WENT BACK TO the farmhouse and read the documents Dr. Dove had given me, and then I logged onto the hospital's website. I read everything they had on liver disease. I wasn't about to sit still and wait. I blogged about Dan needing a living liver donor. I started the post by writing: My husband's life is in danger. Please help. I went into details about Dan being bitten by a tick that brought him to the emergency room, and from there we found out he had liver disease. If he wasn't sick from that tick bite, we never would have known he had a liver problem. Liver disease is a silent killer. A living liver donor is most desirable because it provides immediate organ availability to those awaiting transplants. Thus patients can avoid long wait times, avoiding complications. A donor can be between the ages of eighteen and fifty-nine. Living donors can expect to be hospitalized for about five to ten days. The liver portion of both the donor and recipient will grow to nearly full size in twelve weeks. Liver donors are able to donate their right or left lobes. Common complaints are fatigue and incision pain. I made sure to include the hospital's website, a clickable link, and the phone number to call. I also put my cell phone, email, and mailing address at the bottom. I used every hashtag I could think of that would draw attention to the article. Within five minutes, I had seven women send me an email. I answered each of them as best I could, thanking them. At first, I thought it was strange they were all women, but then I realized—women are used to giving life. I answered one woman's concerns about how long she might be out of work. According to New York-Presbyterian Hospital, the donor could be out of work for up to three months depending on their job. My heart exploded at another woman's message. "I just completed the online questionnaire, and I made my appointment at Quest lab. I too am A-Positive."

I sat at the counter and cried until I heard Lady barking. I closed the laptop and opened the refrigerator to grab a glass of limoncello. Dan came in and said he was taking a nap before dinner. I told him I was going to sit on the porch and drink my beverage. As soon as I sat down, my cell phone alerted me to another email. I replied to her by thanking her for trying. I told her God would bless her for stepping up. She was not a good match because she had a blood disorder. I glanced at my calendar and saw we had a Zoom class coming up. The topic was pre-transplant preparation.

During dinner, I told Dan to make sure he was home at four so he could attend the class with me.

On Thursday afternoon, the bride and groom checked into the bridal suite so they could set everything up for the rehearsal dinner. Friday morning, the inn was buzzing with guests. Jesse had taken Dan to see the finalization of the new outdoor kitchen, and they were having breakfast with Frank and Gina Marie at Meldgie's Diner. I had just picked the herbs for the day when I saw Michael, Kourtnee, and the couple who were about to get married standing on the front porch talking about the swimming pool. By accident, they stumbled onto the pool and asked Michael if they could host their Sunday brunch poolside. Michael and Kourtnee both explained that we were not insured for guests using the pool yet. "Let me look into it and get back to you," Kourtnee told them. The bride clapped her hands. "Thank you so much. I promise no more than twenty."

"I'll do my best," Kourtnee said and then added, "I'll call the insurance company now and get back to you by this afternoon."

When the couple went into the inn, I picked up the basket of herbs and waved to Michael and Kourtnee. "She's such a lovely person," I said. "I remember when she came in for her tasting and her meeting with the florist, she was so appreciative about everything. I don't have a problem with them using the pool area."

Michael looked at Kourtnee. "I have to go into town. Good luck with everything."

"I'll let you know how I make out when you get back," she said.

Then she took me by the arm. "He's not happy today. I think he's pissed they'll use his new grill or something." She shook her head. "I have to meet with Sherry, and then I'll call the insurance company and tell them to add one more thing to the policy."

Kourtnee went to her office, and I continued toward the kitchen to set the herbs in the vegetable sink. I didn't see Christine, but I did meet one of Michael's sous chefs. "Hi, I'm Julie," I said and extended my hand out to her.

She shook my hand and told me her name. Then she offered to wash the herbs as soon as she completed preparing the marinade for the barbecue chicken.

"Thank you." I hung the basket up in the pantry and noticed Christine's apron. "Is Christine around?"

"She went to the daycare for a moment."

I didn't see Dan until two that afternoon. He looked good, happy in fact. "Hey, there's my sunshine," he said as I stepped up onto the front porch.

I sat down next to him. "How was your breakfast?"

"Good. I told Frank you have a big wedding this weekend and that you owe him a dinner."

I went to say what a great idea, but instead asked, "Is that our new furniture?" A delivery truck was rolling down the driveway.

"Yeah, I forgot to tell you. The final delivery is coming today."

Dan and I both stood in time to see Kevin, Robert, and Jesse. Jesse got out of his truck while Kevin and Robert climbed out of the Polaris Ranger. Dan yelled to them, "I told you the delivery guys were going to set everything up."

Jesse snapped his neck. "Yeah, and I told you not to lift a finger. Now sit your ass down."

I laughed. Dan signed for the furniture, and he was right—the men from Cardi's carried everything in and set the beds up. I didn't have to tell them one thing. And Dan didn't have to do anything either. As the furniture truck was backing out of the driveway, a FedEx truck was pulling in. Dan nodded to the man and pointed to Jesse. "You can get that one, if it makes you happy."

Jesse and Kevin grabbed the chair wrapped in plastic.

My heart smiled when Dan kissed me on the cheek. "I knew you liked it," he said.

It was the chair from the antique store. "Well, you did look comfortable sitting there that day. Thank you. I love it. In the first guest room on the right," I told Jesse and Kevin. Robert held the door open for them, and the three men unwrapped it.

When Jesse sat down, Dan told him to get up. "That's for guests."

"No one is coming to visit you, old man." Jesse stood up and said, "It's comfortable. Why didn't you order me one?"

"Next time," Dan replied.

"Anything else?" Kevin asked before leaving with Robert.

"Thanks," Dan told them both.

I asked Jesse if he wanted something to drink, but he declined and said he had to help Sherry with something.

"Do you have to go back to work?" Dan asked me.

"No, everything is under control. Tonight's rehearsal dinner is small. Michael and his staff are all set for tomorrow's wedding. Would you like to do something special?"

"I thought maybe we would stay home and watch a new series on Netflix this weekend."

We started watching *Ink Master*. Saturday morning, Dan made breakfast, and we ate in the family room in front of the TV. In fact, we ate our lunch doing the exact same thing. "I hate it when they allow someone to bully another artist. They should kick him off," I said.

Dan set his plate down on the coffee table. "Why, it's good for the ratings. People love drama."

I shook my head. "Drama isn't about knocking someone else's work down to the ground."

"It would be nice if they lifted each other up and were supportive of one another, but that's not life."

"Well, they'd never work for me," I replied and took our dishes to the kitchen. I washed the dishes and put the dry rub on the pork roast. I put it back in the refrigerator. Before I realized he was sound asleep, I said, "The roast is resting—" I turned the TV volume down a little and continued to watch the series. At three o'clock, Dan woke up and asked who won.

"No one yet," I replied. "But the mean one is in the top three."

Dan got up and went to the bathroom. When he came back with two glasses of lemonade, I smiled. "I was just about to get up and grab a glass," I said and took mine from him. "Thanks."

Dan yawned before saying, "Tomorrow's episode has three female contestants. I vote Malarkey is the winner."

He turned the TV off.

I pulled the bedspread down to the bottom of the bed. "I actually enjoy watching the show. Some of them are so talented."

"I agree, but some of them should have waited a few more years before entering a contest like this with so many heavy hitters."

Dan kissed me goodnight.

"Goodnight, my love," I replied and closed my eyes feeling happier than I'd felt in days.

A few minutes later, Dan was sound asleep. I didn't want to move out of fear I would wake him. I was thinking about the women who were quick to answer my cry for help. I could hear the sound of music in the distance. I must have drifted off to sleep because I woke to the sound of sirens. I glanced over at the clock and saw that it was midnight. The sirens were getting closer. We both sat up.

"Is that?"

"Yes," I declared.

I jumped up and grabbed my robe. Dan put his pants on, and we both headed for his truck. Dan was driving toward the inn when black smoke began filling the air all around us. I'm not sure why he stayed to the left of the pond, but he did.

"I hope the electrician didn't wire the new pool house wrong," Dan said and began driving faster.

I almost hit my head on the windshield when he slammed on the brakes. "No," he shouted and pointed across the pond.

# Chapter 32

WE WERE THE FIRST to arrive. The flames were ferocious, savagely violent. Orange, red, and yellow hotness shot up from the ground. We could hear the fire trucks in the distance. Someone with a handheld scanner must have been close to us because I heard him say, the cottage at the inn. The man kept repeating himself. For the first time in my life, I wished I had named the driveway leading to the cottage.

Dan tried to pull me away, but I refused to budge. I stood there watching, listening to the crackle of flames as windows popped, walls collapsed, and my floors groaned. When the roof caved in, my heart fluttered.

The firefighter kept telling the other men to follow the driveway north of the inn to the end, to stay to the left of the pond, but it was too late. My safe harbor was gone.

Five minutes later, several fire trucks, EMT vans, and two police vehicles pulled up to the pile of residue. Within minutes, they had put enough water on the burning embers to make it go from flickering flames to gray smoke everywhere. The young man with the handheld device tried to put a blanket around Dan and me. We assured him we were okay.

"Were you in there when it caught on fire?" he asked.

"No," Dan replied. "My wife owns the inn. That was her cottage."

Then I felt someone's hands on my shoulders. I turned around and saw Gina Marie. A moment later, Jesse and Sherry jumped out of his truck. Michael and Christine both ran up to us. "Oh, no," she shouted.

Kevin jumped off the Polaris and told Christine she should go back up to the inn with Kourtnee and the babies. "Tell Kourtnee everyone is fine."

When he said that, my heart stopped. "The bride and groom, where are they?" I shouted.

Michael approached me and said, "I just left them. They're dancing. Everyone is under the tent."

I collapsed to the ground. When I opened my eyes, I was in the back of an ambulance. I sat up and told the two men I was fine and wanted to go home. I could hear Dan and Jesse talking to Gina Marie outside. "I'm okay," I said and stepped out.

I stood next to the young man and extended my hand to him, but he hugged me instead. "I'm glad you're okay. I saw the flames from the main road. I wish I got here sooner."

"Thank you for everything," I said and took hold of Dan's hand. When I turned back my heart sank. The bride and groom were talking to Michael. "Excuse me, I need to take care of something." I approached the couple, and Michael pointed toward me.

The bride was in tears. I reached out to her. "I'm so sorry," she said.

I looked at her. "It's okay, it's not your fault. I'm sorry you lost whatever you had inside. I'll pay for everything." Then I looked at her. She was young, innocent, and so beautiful.

"I'm sorry I ruined your wedding night. You can stay at the farmhouse with Dan and me. You'll have your own private quarters."

The groom reached out his hand and thanked me. "My parents have a summer house in Point Judith. We can go there." Then he glanced back at the cottage. "I'm sorry you lost your cottage."

I put my hand on his shoulder. "It's just a building. I am so grateful that no one got hurt."

Michael offered to give them a ride back up to the inn in the Polaris Ranger, and they accepted. The fire marshal handed me his card and told me he would be back in the morning to assess the situation. I thanked him. When he turned to leave, he shook his head as if he already knew the cause.

I stood there watching the fire trucks leave, the police cars, and finally the EMT van. Dan motioned to me to follow him, Gina Marie, Jesse, and Sherry back to the farmhouse. Then I recognized the young firefighter. "You were here before," I said to him.

"Yes, ma'am. I was one of the volunteers who built that cottage."

Tears filled my eyes.

He nodded and walked away. I believe he felt as bad as I did about seeing that beautiful cottage burn to the ground.

When we stepped inside the farmhouse, Dan asked if anyone wanted a glass of water.

Gina Marie raised her hand. "Not like any of us are going to sleep tonight. I'll make a pot of coffee."

I followed her into the kitchen and took out a loaf of zucchini bread, sliced it, warmed it in the microwave for a few seconds, and then set a dish of whipped butter on the tray next to it. "I'll call Frank in the morning," I said to her, but then we both looked up as we heard his voice coming from the family room.

Gina Marie carried the tray of drinks, and I followed behind with mine. As soon as I set the tray down, Frank told me he was building me a new cottage. "Closer to the inn," he said.

"I'm okay," I tried to say.

"Dan and I already decided," he replied and accepted a cup of coffee from Gina Marie.

"How did you hear about it?" she asked him.

"A co-worker called me and offered to help out again. Your cottage was his first barn raising. He said he was here before anyone else arrived."

I set the tray down and kissed the top of his head. Which always smelled like coconut. "What am I going to do with you?"

"The bridal cottage is on all of your advertisements, you can build it close to the chapel," Dan said, and Gina Marie agreed with him.

Jesse took a slice of zucchini bread. "I'll bring the bulldozer down and clean everything up tomorrow."

"I'll order a dumpster," Dan said.

"Sounds good," Frank said then pointed his finger at Dan. "I don't want you to worry about one thing. My team will assist Jesse with whatever he needs."

Dan pursed his lips. "Normally, I'd be upset if someone told me not to be concerned." He put his hand on Frank's shoulder. "Thank you."

We spoke about the design, and everyone agreed it no longer needed built-in storage compartments or window seats. "A simple four-room cottage, maybe a few Murphy beds would be nice," Gina Marie said.

"I liked the idea of Murphy beds," I said. "The bride, maid of honor, and bridesmaids will love it."

About fifteen minutes later, Gina Marie suggested everyone go home and try to get some sleep. "We have a busy day ahead of us."

The next morning, I received a phone call from Italy. "Dan, hurry. It's Carmie." I cried so hard, I handed the phone to Dan.

"Thank you. I don't know what to say. Yes, of course," he said and handed the phone back to me.

"I love you too," I said and hung the phone up. "I can't believe it?" Dan said. "I have to call Jesse."

"Dan, wait." I thought about the other women who had volunteered and were turned away. "Let's see if Maryanne is truly a match."

"But Carmie said she's type A like me." He was smiling, and I couldn't take that away from him.

"You're absolutely right. Call him and then let Gina

Marie know too."

I listened to Dan tell first Jesse then Gina Marie. "Hey, Carmie flew her daughter to New York after they found out she was the same blood type as me. Yeah, Maryanne is in the city right now being tested. She still has to have an MRI and some other tests," he said. He smiled at me. "I will. Me too." He set his phone down. "They're both excited."

"So am I," I replied.

"You said we met them for a reason. Remember?"

I smiled back at him. "Yes, I'm happy for you. Hey, we have hope."

# Chapter 33

Sunday morning, I met with the bride, groom, and her father up at the inn. Michael had called me and said they needed to talk to me. I opened the front door, and Michael pointed toward the library. I rolled the cart inside. "Would anyone care for some coffee and a Danish?"

The father of the bride motioned to me, and I poured him a cup of coffee. "Good morning, everyone," I said and sat down in my favorite wingback chair.

"Mrs. Holliday, I want to say how sorry I am for burning down your cottage," she said.

I shook my head.

She raised her hand as if to say stop. "Please, give me a moment to explain. Our wedding night was very special to both of us." She blushed. "I wanted the night to be special. One that neither of us would forget. I lit all the candles and left them to burn, unattended. I shouldn't have. I'm sorry. I didn't think. I thought it would be romantic."

"I'll pay for the entire—" her father started to say, but I stopped him.

I got up and reached out to his daughter. When she stood up, I took her hands in my own. "You listen to me.

Last night was an accident. I can replace the cottage. I am so grateful that the two of you were not asleep when it happened." I wiped away a tear on her cheek. "Promise me the two of you will come back next year for your first anniversary." I glanced past her and nodded toward the groom. "You can stay in the new bridal suite for the entire weekend. It will be my treat." I turned toward her father when I said, "Life is more precious than brick and mortar any day." Then I reminded them. "Besides, I have a wonderful insurance agent."

Out in the lobby, Teresa was talking to the fire marshal. "If you'll excuse me, I have someone I need to see. And I believe you have a pool party to attend."

"Thank you, Mrs. Holliday," they both said.

"Julie, please call me Julie." Then I winked at her father. "It was a pleasure to meet you."

"Pleasure was all mine," he replied.

I took the fire marshal by the arm and led him to the kitchen. There he explained the cause of last night's fire. "A candle on the nightstand in the bedroom."

"Thank you for your quick response. You can go now. I'll take care of it from here." I showed him the back door.

When I turned around, Michael asked me if I was okay. "You realize you just kicked that man out?"

"Do you have my list for the day?" I winked at him. "Yes, I did." I took the list of herbs from his hand, and I too left the kitchen through the back door. My guests will always come first. I didn't care about his report. Candles burn, fires happen. I stopped on the back terrace, gazed at every flower, vegetable, and herb planted in my gardens, and when I saw the guest parking lot full of cars, I thanked God for blessing me with another day. "Lord, please." I stopped. "Thank you," I said instead. I knew in my heart that God would make sure Dan received a perfect liver.

After I picked the herbs, I went straight back to the farmhouse to find Dan. He was sitting on the front porch. "Is everyone okay?" he asked.

"I think so." I sat down next to him. "The fire marshal stopped by. He said a candle in the bedroom started the fire." I turned to face him. "No more candles. I'll fill the bridal suite with flameless candles."

"Yeah, and post a note by the door."

When he said that, my heart stopped. I started to cry. My safe harbor was gone, and so was my gift from Frank.

"Are you okay? What's the matter?"

"The sign Frank bought me. It was hanging by the door in the cottage."

Dan sat up. "The one that says, 'To forgive is the highest, most beautiful form of love. In return, you will receive untold peace and happiness?'"

I wiped my eyes. "Yes."

Then he took me by the hand and led me to the master bedroom. "Sit down." He went into his closet. When he came back out, he handed me a large brown package. "Open it. I was planning on giving it to you for

Christmas, but I think you might need it now."

I ripped it open. It was Robert Muller's quote on a pale blue canvas with a silver anchor lying in the sand.

Dan sat down next to me. "I like it too. By the way, Frank gave me one to carry in my wallet. When he gave it to me, he told me to forgive myself for what I had done, and to never look back."

I was surprised when he opened his wallet and showed it to me. Then he sniffed my hair, and I laughed. "Did you just smell me?"

"You need a nice, hot bath. You smell like smoke," he said and got up.

I gave him a crimson smile and replied, "I think we need to test the new hot tub out together."

I placed our towels on the teak accent table, added vanilla bath salts to the water, and took a deep breath, watching as my gorgeous husband stepped in. I sat in front of him, leaned back, and inhaled the scent of smoke rising from our bodies. My insides surged when Dan began washing my hair. After his hands moved from my neck to my back and arms, I turned to face him. I took the other warm washcloth and washed his face before straddling him. Dan closed his eyes, rested his arms on the side of the tub, and when he leaned back, I felt his erection. Dan spun me around, spread my legs open, and entered me. My head fell back. I closed my eyes and allowed myself to reach a beautiful climax.

# Chapter 34

WE ALMOST FORGOT ABOUT Brin's birthday party. I was standing in the kitchen listening to Patsy Cline sing, "Just A Closer Walk With Thee" when I shouted, "We need to be up at the inn in an hour."

I put my new, blue-paisley dress on and asked Dan if I should wear my white slip-on Keds or the brown boots. "Which ones go better with my dress?"

He laughed. "I say leave one of each on. The white sneaker," he said, and I agreed.

I saw myself in the mirror and asked, "Do you think this dress is too short for a one-year-old's birthday party?"

Dan smiled. "It's perfect. Right, Lady?"

On our way up to the inn, we heard laughter coming from the pool area. I was thankful for the wind blowing in the opposite direction, away from the burnt rubble. Dan was still holding my hand when I felt a tug. "I'll have Jesse order the dumpster tomorrow for the debris. Kevin can run the excavator while Robert runs the bulldozer. They'll be fine with Jesse's supervision."

"Sounds good." I knew it bothered him not being able to do anything. I thought about his next doctor's appointment. "Remember, we have a Zoom meeting with the nurse practitioner a week from tomorrow. If you have any questions for her, let me know and I'll write them down so we don't forget to ask her."

"October fifteenth, right?"

"Yes," I replied and waved to several women touring the Japanese garden. "I promise we won't stay long. If you don't feel good, let me know."

"I'll be fine," he said as he opened the front door, but then he asked, "How many kids are coming?"

"I have no idea," I replied.

Dan chuckled when we entered the dining room. It was decorated in rainbow colors. Unicorns were everywhere. The only other child at the party was Delilah. Brin was sitting in her high chair wearing the new dress Michael had bought for her. I was surprised she kept the headband on. I gave her a kiss on the cheek and we both told her happy birthday.

Dan sat down next to Frank who was already drinking a glass of fruit punch. "I added a little ginger ale to it. Too sweet for me," he said and motioned for me to grab the bottle of soda.

I set two glasses down in front of Dan and myself, and I added a splash of soda and a few ice cubes. The entire menu was kid-friendly. We ate lunch, enjoyed a slice of—you guessed it—rainbow cake, and watched Christine and Michael hand out goody bags.

"Thank you," Frank said and then opened his. Inside everyone's bag was a box of four mini pies. "Is that?"

Christine winked at him. "Sweet potato pie."

She thanked Dan for coming. "I know you don't feel very well, but it means the world to us that you're here."

"Yes," Michael said. Then they moved closer to Kevin, Kourtnee, Jesse, and Sherry's table and handed each of them a bag. "Thank you for coming," he added.

After the party, Frank, Dan, and I went outside and sat at a table on the terrace with glasses of iced tea. Frank told us about the day he saw Michael in Newport. "I saw the lad sitting alone outside Belle's Café. He asked me to join him. We had a nice lunch. I tried to give him the best advice I could," he said and sipped his beverage.

Dan's eyes opened wide. "He'll figure it out."

"Or, she'll swat him in the head with a rolling pin," I added.

A moment later, Jesse, Sherry, Teresa, and Sal came outside and sat down at our table. Before anyone could say a word, Gina Marie and Michelle stepped onto the terrace. Gina Marie pointed her finger at us. "I've been looking all over for you."

I pointed to my chest. "Me?"

"No, not you. Dan," she said, and they sat down in the empty chairs. "I thought we could go fishing tomorrow."

Jesse started to say I want to go, but instead he told Dan, "I'll go next time." Then he got up, went back inside, and returned with eight slices of cake and a pitcher of fruit punch. "What?" He set the tray down and took a slice for himself.

Sherry laughed as he ate it. "He bakes every night. Last night he made peanut butter and chocolate chip cookies." Then she touched Dan on his arm. "How are you holding up these days?"

"I feel fine. If I didn't get bitten by that tick, I never would have known I was sick. I thought it was my age, the heat, and being overweight that was kicking my ass." Then he brushed his hand on the back of my head. "I can't tell you how thankful I am to Julie for taking me to the emergency room that day."

Gina Marie reached over and tapped his hand. "That's scary. How many other people are walking around with cirrhosis of the liver?"

"And they don't even know it," I said.

"Hey, let's hope Maryanne is the one."

Monday morning, we received a call from Maryanne. She had bad news. She wasn't a good match. "The doctor said Dan was in better health than me. I'm sorry my diverticulitis and its damn inflammation and infection are not suitable for liver donation."

"You tried," Dan told her. "Thank you for stepping up."

"My mother is going to be heartbroken." Maryanne started to cry. "She tried to donate hers, but they told her she was too old."

Dan's eyes filled up fast. "We love your mother. I'm sorry we won't be able to go back for a while. But I promise we will."

I took the phone from him. "Maryanne, thank you so much."

She ended the call sobbing.

I immediately sent Jesse and Gina Marie a text message letting them know. Then I called up to the inn and spoke to Kourtnee. "Please let the others know. Kourtnee, tell them I will find a suitable donor."

Dan was sitting on the back porch. I asked him if he wanted something to eat or drink.

He laughed. "You always try to feed me when I'm upset."

"Well, they don't call it comfort food for nothing."

He stood up. "Let's make cheeseburgers."

I turned the radio on, and when we heard, "Let's Get It On" playing, Dan held out his hand. I still want to make love to him every time he holds me in his arms, dips me low, and rocks my hips. And when he whispers in my ear... time stops. All sadness goes away.

# Chapter 35

OCTOBER FIFTEENTH, AT PRECISELY noon, we sat in the kitchen in front of the laptop listening to Dan's nurse practitioner, Lauren. She was also his go-to person for all of our concerns. She started the meeting off by asking Dan, "How are you feeling?"

"I feel good," Dan replied. "If you didn't tell me about my liver disease, I never would have known."

"I'm glad you're not in any pain or discomfort. Okay, we're going to start you on a new medication to see if we can lower your hepatitis score. I'll send you a copy of the schedule with your transplant evaluation team. In the meantime, I have you on the calendar for November fifteenth at NY-P for an echocardiogram, a bilateral carotid artery ultrasound, and a stress test."

"Will we have to stay overnight?" I asked.

"No, just be here by eight. You should complete everything by three or four in the afternoon."

"Sounds good," Dan said. "Julie's been printing everything out for me to read. Anything else we need to do, please let us know."

"We've been taking the classes every week," I added. "They're informative and very educational. Aimee is very knowledgeable about before and after liver transplants."

"The classes are not mandatory, but the more you can learn the better," she said, and we both agreed.

"Anything we can learn about pre-op and post-op is definitely a plus." I turned toward Dan. "Right?"

He nodded. "Yes."

We both thanked her. When the meeting was over, I closed the laptop and told Dan that I liked Lauren. "I do too," he said and turned around.

"Hey, what's going on in here?" Jesse yelled. "I brought someone to see the two of you. Delilah and Brin were sleeping, so I took her for a walk."

Lady ran up to us. Kissed and wagged her tail more than ever. I stood up to allow Dan a moment with his baby girl.

"I'll make lunch," I said to Jesse. "Have a seat." I mouthed the words thank you to him and went into the kitchen to heat up last night's leftover chicken soup. I made three peanut butter and jelly sandwiches, poured the milk, and called them to the table. I set a smaller bowl on the floor for Lady. Of course, she ate the chicken first. "Eat your vegetables," I told her.

Jesse put a spoonful of soup in his mouth, swallowed, and told me, "You still make the best chicken soup in the world."

I laughed. "You're just hungry. How's the new cottage coming along?"

He pulled the sandwich back out of his mouth. "Frank's crew is insane. Right, Lady?"

Lady raised her eyebrows.

"I want to go and see it," I said. "Come on, after lunch." I eyeballed Dan. "We'll both go." My cell phone rang. "It's Kevin. Hello." He asked me if Dan and I had a minute.

Twenty minutes later, Kevin and Kourtnee came inside. Kourtnee had a basket filled with red and green apples. "I wanted your opinion on baking apples," she said as she set the basket down on the counter. "Hey little girl, no daycare today?"

Jesse laughed. "She got kicked out of school. No, she's hanging out with me today. Right Lady?"

Dan watched as Lady and Jesse left the kitchen. I offered Kevin and Kourtnee a drink.

"Water is fine," Kevin said as he sat down next to Dan at the table. Then he set the roll of plans on top of a notepad. "We spoke to Gina Marie, and she thinks it's a good idea to go over everything with the two of you before we start tilling up the soil or building the farm stand."

Dan looked at me. "You closed on the property, correct?"

"Yes," I replied. "I'm leasing the property to them for the first five years."

"Then you don't need our permission or opinion," he told Kevin.

Kourtnee sat down on the other side of Dan. "We

would like your advice on a few matters, and we need to ask a favor."

Kevin unrolled the plot layout. "I was thinking we could ask a local farmer to till our land this fall, and in lieu of paying him every year, we would offer him your hundred acres for his crops."

Dan glanced over at me, then back at Kevin. "Smart thinking. I'm sure a lot of farmers would be willing to barter with you," he told him. "Make sure you get it in writing… and see to it that whoever it is also rotates the crops."

Kevin took a deep breath. "Thank you. Wow, thanks."

Kourtnee opened the notepad. "We don't want them to do anything except till the soil every year. We want to work the ground ourselves." She turned the pages one by one showing us her designs. From tomato vines to berries to fruit trees. "The first four years, we're going to concentrate on growing. Hopefully, if my plan goes right, we will be able to sell our own fruits and vegetables by the fifth year. We'll offer homemade items such as preserves, salsas, pies, and fresh-cut flowers."

"Kourtnee's done a lot of research on the market. She's even created our own labels," Kevin added.

"I'm hoping to build community awareness by offering face-to-face interactions through direct marketing." She tossed her hand in the air. "Okay, the first year, I plan on giving away a lot of free samples." She smiled. "Christine said she would love to help me. We plan on offering products made from the garden.

Like samples of zucchini bread—oh, and Christine gave me a catalog that sells certified food bags and boxes."

"I love the idea that everyone is on board," I said. "Kevin, you can use the hundred acres any way you need to. Be sure to call the conservancy first."

Kourtnee turned to a page and read from the list of approvals. "We already contacted them. They said you will actually get a bigger tax deduction for using the land as farmland."

"That's right," Kevin said and then added, "We spoke to a local farmer who loved the idea. He actually grows corn for his cows who produce milk for Cabot Cheese." He looked at Dan. "He also said he will be rotating his crop every two to three years. And he'll plant rye in the fall."

Dan gave Kevin a big thumbs up.

Kourtnee hugged him. "I love you. We love you." Her cheeks turned red. "I'm sorry, Kevin is B negative and I'm B positive." She looked at me. "We went to our doctor the minute you told us Dan had liver disease."

# Chapter 36

THURSDAY MORNING, THE SUN was beaming in through the kitchen window. I had planned to stay close to home so I would not miss this week's Zoom class. Earlier in the week, I had read the schedule and thought every class appeared important enough to attend. This week, the subject matter was on liver champions.

Dan came into the kitchen and asked if I wanted to go to the beach and wait for him while he went to his appointment. "I have a ten o'clock session with Dr. Eastwood. It will only be for an hour, and then we can take a stroll down the beach and grab lunch at the Coast Guard House. What do you say?" He reached for the pot of coffee. "Refill?"

I held my empty cup up. "Please. Okay, sounds good—as long as I'm back by three. I need to attend today's class."

"Class?" he said as he poured my coffee. "Oh, yeah. Me, too."

We sat at the counter together. "Dan, I was thinking. Let's have an open house party. We'll invite Barbara and her sister. Rose can bring the children—"

He placed his hand on top of mine. "I don't think that's such a great idea. How about we host Thanksgiving dinner for our friends?"

"You're right. I like that idea, I'll get ahold of everyone and see what they think."

"Hey, did I tell you what I'm doing this Saturday?" He chuckled, got up, and grabbed the milk, cereal, and a bowl for himself.

"Do tell," I said and rinsed my cup out.

"I'm taking one of Gina Marie's painting classes." He raised his eyebrows. "We're painting landscapes."

"Seriously?" I set my yogurt down on the counter and pulled the lid off, added salad toppers from Lilly's Family Foods before sticking my spoon in for a bite. "Where?"

"Down at the pond. Kevin and Robert tied my old canoe off in it." He ate his cereal while I enjoyed my coconut Chobani.

When he was finished, he said, "I'm going to jump in the shower and get ready for my appointment."

"Dan, you haven't said much about your therapist lately. How's everything going?"

"Good," he said as he set his bowl in the dishwasher. "I trust him. He's non-judgmental, respectful, and observant. His advice is new every week. He listens to me before he explains why I'm feeling the way I do." Dan turned to face me. "You're breathing into your hand again."

I moved my hand away. "I'm happy for you. And just so you know, I was thinking about you and your therapist getting along. That's all."

Dan went into the bathroom while I rinsed out the coffee pot. My cell phone rang, and it brought an even bigger smile to my face. I plopped down on the sofa and answered it. "Hello, Frank."

I put my feet up on the coffee table, listening to him tell me about his double dinner date. "I need a secretary. I made the mistake of saying yes to two ladies at the same time."

"From your book club?" I asked, trying not to laugh.

"Yes, we read *Room* by Emma Donoghue. The ladies were crying, and I somehow said yes to both of them for the same day. And was at one house eating dessert when my cell phone rang from the other one."

"What did you do?" I asked while moving the stack of magazines with my foot.

"What any gentleman would do. I went to dinner. This book club thing is going to make me fat."

"I'm so happy for you. I'm glad you have a group of ladies to cook for you. What book are you reading next?"

"We've decided to read only self-published authors for a while. We're starting with a book based on a true love story. I suggested the author after I read a few reviews. You would love the cover. It has a yellow rose on it. *Still Crazy* by—"

"Yes, I read that. You're going to love the ending."

"Okay, sunshine, you have a nice day. Give Dan my best, and I'll call you when I'm ready for you to see the new bridal suite."

"Oh, wait," I said. "Frank, will you join us for

Thanksgiving dinner? Dan and I would like to host it at our house this year."

"I wouldn't miss it," he said, and the call ended.

Dan came out of the bedroom and asked who I was talking to. "Was that Gina Marie?"

"No, Frank. He's coming to Thanksgiving dinner."

"Great," he said and sat down to put his new camouflage Crocs on.

I laughed. "You know you're the only person who wears them that way." I flashed mine at him. "Everyone else puts the flap up."

He stood up and shook his head. "Not me."

"Let's go," I replied and headed out the front door. "I wonder if Lady misses us?"

Dan got in the truck before answering me. "Jesse said she sleeps next to the puppy every night." He pulled out onto the main road and told me about his upcoming meeting with the farmer. "Kevin wants me to meet him and the two young fellas he hired."

I was glad Kevin included Dan in on his new project. "When is your meeting?" I asked, wondering if it was during one of our online classes.

"Tomorrow morning," he replied and parked the truck in Dr. Eastwood's driveway. "I'll meet you back here in one hour," he said as he started to walk away, but then turned around. "Hey, wait. Why don't you come in and meet him?"

"Not this time," I replied and headed for the coffee shop. After I got my iced coffee, I took a stroll down the beach. "What the hell?" My Croc came off and almost floated away on me. I laughed aloud, glad Dan wasn't there to see it.

When Dan came outside, I was sitting in the truck with my feet up on the dashboard. I opened my eyes when he got in. "How was your appointment?"

"It was good," he said as he backed out of the driveway covered in clamshells. "I told him about my cirrhosis. He said to be careful until I receive my liver transplant. He asked me if I drank alcohol. I told him a cold beer on occasion, and maybe a rum and Coke with dinner when we dine out."

"I think as soon as everyone hears the word cirrhosis, they naturally assume you drank. Someone needs to educate people about how you can get the disease."

Five minutes later, Dan pulled the truck into the parking spot, turned the engine off, and added, "Dr. Eastwood said he didn't think I was the type to have a drinking problem. I told him I contracted it from a patient while I worked at the hospital."

When he got out of the truck, so did I. I thought about my poor husband having this disease eating away at his liver all this time. I wish I knew about it sooner and how to take care of him better. *Why didn't our primary physician call us when they started testing for it back in 1991?*

We strolled hand in hand down the beach until we reached the restaurant. It wasn't a bright sunny day as much as it was cloudy and overcast. Still, we saw numerous surfers, umbrellas, and people relaxing on beach chairs. I was close enough to the water to feel the mist on my face. "The beach is good for our souls." I kissed Dan's hand. "This was a great idea."

"I'm excited to try a new restaurant," he replied and opened the door for me.

# Chapter 37

DAN PUT HIS NAPKIN on the table. "I told Dr. Eastwood, I hope my donor is someone I don't know, and I would prefer if it was during the summer months so I would have time to heal before hunting season."

I wasn't sure my heart could wait until next summer. I wanted him to be saved as soon as the good Lord saw to it. "Dan, can I ask why you're hoping your donor is someone you don't know?"

"I don't want anyone to put their life in danger for me."

I was so busy wrapped up in being his caregiver that it never dawned on me until now.

As soon as we got back to the house, Dan said he wanted to talk to Jesse. I told him I had a few things to do before our Zoom class, and he promised me he would be back on time.

Dan walked in just in time for the Zoom class. About twelve people were in attendance. Dan and I were like sponges. I took notes the entire time. We listened as one of the women told everyone about her experience. She said, "Don't make the mistake of bringing anything with you when you come to the hospital." She laughed, telling us that she brought her laptop, makeup, jewelry, and money. "Trust me, just show up."

Someone else asked about the length of the surgery, and how long it took to get back up on her feet. The woman explained that her son-in-law was her donor. She told us about her recovery being smooth, however, he got a hernia and had to go back into the hospital. "When they say take it easy for the first three months, they mean it."

Another man said he was glad he attended the Zoom classes prior to his surgery. "I learned the universal signal for I'm ready to have this tube taken out." He motioned with his hand as if he were pulling the intubation tube out. "As soon as you're able to breathe on your own, you should let them know. I was so happy when they removed mine." He sat back in his chair, but then quickly leaned in closer to his computer. "Oh, one more thing. I highly suggest you take as many classes as you can. You'll learn something new every week, and make sure you have someone advocating for you."

The class ended about an hour later. Dan was glad he attended. "Not at all what I expected," he said and got up. "I thought a doctor was going to talk about the surgery."

I closed the laptop. "I read the schedule, they do have a few doctors, nurses, anesthesiologists, and I believe a few surgeons. These classes are important. Every Thursday at four," I said. "Let's start dinner. I'm dying to eat my leftovers from the restaurant."

We took our plates outside and sat on the back porch.

"I'm so glad we built a wrap-around." I glanced over at the grill and thought the inn's outdoor kitchen was more elaborate than my own. "Tomorrow night, let's cook on the grill."

He gave me a simpering look and replied, "You read my mind. I just picked up a few nice steaks from Tase-Rite Company the other day."

"When were you in Wakefield?" I asked.

He laughed aloud. "I took a ride with Jesse."

"Tomorrow morning, I have to run to CVS to pick up your prescription, so I'll grab a few lobster tails from Narragansett Bay Lobsters."

"Sounds good," he replied and sat back in his chair. "Maybe a nice salad to go with it."

"I'll pick the cucumbers and tomatoes when I go to the herb garden tomorrow morning. Anything else?"

He bit his bottom lip and gave me his seductive smile.

I slapped his leg and told him, "Later. Right now, I need to do some research."

Dan rested his chin on the back of his hand. "You go. I'm going to sit here and then go in and watch some TV."

We brought our dishes inside, set them in the dishwasher, and took out two slices of carrot cake to eat later. "I'm going to finish watching *Sherlock Holmes.*"

The next day, I went into town, picked up Dan's medicine, the lobster tails, and I bumped into Rose coming out of Champlin's Seafood. "Hi."

"Hey, Julie," she said and added, "How are you? How's Dan?"

"He's good, thanks." I reached out with my right arm to give her a hug. She embraced me with both arms. "I'm so sorry," I whispered to her.

She leaned back, put both hands on my arms, and said, "Thank you. I'll never understand his intentions. All I can do is thank God my children didn't see it."

I looked at her for a minute. She was going to be okay. I too was thankful for her children. I knew they would get her through the ordeal. "Would you like to grab a cup of tea?" I have no idea why I said that. Thinking I could console her or something.

"No, thank you," she replied.

"Rose," someone shouted, and we turned around to see a man approaching us.

I wanted to tell her how blessed and fortunate I felt when Dan told me he wasn't comfortable seeing another woman for even an hour, regardless of her profession. Instead, I simply said, "I'll let you go."

When I got home, Dan was waiting for me on a new porch swing. I sat down and told him that I loved the blue cushions. Then I noticed the vintage crock adorned with our house number.

"Frank just left. He said to tell you not to forget to name the roads and number all the houses."

I dangled my feet and rested my head, allowing myself to take it all in before telling him, "Stay here, I have to put the lobster in the fridge and put your medicine away."

I went back outside, holding two glasses of iced tea.

Dan took his, and I explained my chance encounter with Rose. "I saw Rose in town. Dan, did you explain to her why you changed therapists?"

Dan set his glass down on the side table. "I did," he replied. Turned to face me and added, "I told her that I would never allow another woman to come between us. I explained to her how sorry I was about her husband, but I was not about to get caught seeing a single woman, therapy or not. I was very clear with my decision to move on to a male therapist." He picked up his glass, took a sip, and said, "Besides, I like doc. He's funny. We have a good time. He's not as stiff as the women. His quality of candor is a refreshing change of pace."

"I'm happy you like him." I went to take a sip but instead said, "It means everything to me that you care about my feelings."

"I told you no more nightmares, and I meant it."

# Chapter 38

AFTER DINNER, DAN AND I decided it was a perfect evening to sit back and watch a movie. We settled into the family room, on the new reclining loveseat, with a bowl of popcorn smothered in parmesan, garlic, and black pepper. We chose *Transformers The Last Knight* starring Shia LaBeouf and Megan Fox. "She would make a great Wonder Woman," I said before asking if he wanted another glass of soda.

"No, I'm good, thanks. Hey, I met with Kevin's helpers. They stopped by when I was talking to the farmer. Jesse was telling Kevin about his truck not starting, and one of the boys was like, 'Hey, try checking the cables. Sometimes the connections get corroded.' Sure enough, he was correct."

"How old are the boys?"

"I'm not sure, but if I had to guess, fifteen." Dan fell asleep before the movie ended. I turned the TV off and started to cover him with a blanket, but he woke up. "I missed the ending," he said and yawned.

"Yep." I folded the blanket back up and set it on the back of his recliner. "Let's go to bed, sleepyhead."

I folded the bedspread down to the bottom of the bed, climbed in, and told Dan that I wanted to attend the author event we were hosting up at the inn on Sunday. "Tina's such a delight. She came here last year for some alone time so she could write her first novel. Now she's on book number three in the series."

"I'll be fine," he replied and rolled over onto his side. When I heard him snoring, I opened my book and read a few chapters before turning out the light.

The next morning, we went up to the inn together. I needed to get my list of herbs, and Dan wanted to talk to Kevin about building a dock for the kayaks and canoes down at the pond.

"Well, good morning, little one," Dan said to Brin. She was wearing her unicorn dress from her party.

"She will not wear anything else," Christine told us. "I'll be right back. I'm taking her to daycare, and then I have to bake for this weekend's book signing."

I blew them kisses as they left the foyer, told Dan about the shortbread cookies Christine was baking and putting the cover of the book on each one. "Sherry has a machine that prints edible paper. I saw a sample Sherry created for Christine, and it was an identical replica of the novel."

"Oh, hey," Teresa said to us as she came in from the kitchen holding a cup of tea in one hand and a glazed donut in the other. "Michael bought these fresh this morning," she said and took a bite.

"That looks good," Dan told her.

"What day is Tina checking in?" I asked as I turned one of the table lamps on.

"She'll be here Saturday. She wants to set everything up in the library and out on the back terrace. That's where she's planning on doing her reading and tea party as long as the rain holds off." Teresa took a sip of her tea. "We need rain, but why does it have to come when we have an outdoor event?"

I shrugged. "She can move everything indoors if she has to. I'm excited to see her."

Teresa sat down behind the desk. "Me, too. I've read both of her books, and I pre-ordered the third one."

"So did I. Let me check on the food for her party and see if we can do anything else for her."

I waited in the kitchen for Christine to come back from daycare. For some reason, she entered from the side door. "How are the plans for this weekend's book signing coming along?"

"Good, Tina is such a joy to bake for. I'm making petit fours, little tarts, cake pops, macaroons, and mini baklava." She went over to the corkboard, took down Michael's food list, and handed it to me.

I was pleased to see he had a variety of elegant choices. "It all looks wonderful. Thanks." I pinned it back up and let her get back to her baking.

Saturday night, Jesse, Sherry, Gina Marie, and Michelle all stopped by to challenge Dan and me to a game of pool. "I don't know too many people who have a pool table in their house," Sherry said after taking her shot.

"They've always had one," Jesse replied before taking his.

"Dan," Gina Marie said to him. "Hey, it's your turn."

Dan missed the cue ball entirely. He stood there frozen. Staring at the balls. I heard Gina Marie whisper, "You have high balls."

Dan's stick fell to the floor. Gina Marie grabbed hold of him from behind as he began to topple. Jesse moved in to stop him from falling over. Gina Marie took one look at Dan and shouted, "Call 911!"

I dialed the number, ran outside, and read the coordinates for the house to the dispatcher. I wasn't about to make the same mistake as I made when the cottage burned down. On the new crock, Frank had our house's latitude and longitude written in the center of the anchor.

I went back inside. Dan was pale, shaking, in and out of consciousness. When he told Jesse he had to go to the bathroom, Gina Marie, Jesse, and I moved him to the guest bathroom. Before we could get his belt unbuckled, he had soiled himself. When Dan started to vomit, Gina Marie handed him the wicker wastebasket. A few minutes later, an EMT arrived and took Dan's vitals.

I went into the bedroom, grabbed a pair of underwear and sweatpants. By the time I got back to the bathroom, Jesse had Dan totally undressed. Gina Marie was holding him up, singing in his ear. I grabbed a warm washcloth and cleaned him as best I could. Together, we dressed him. Sherry had wheeled the office chair to the foyer. Dan refused to sit down. He told the paramedics he could walk to the ambulance. Once they got him inside, Jesse,

Sherry, Gina Marie, Michelle, and I got in my Explorer. We followed them to the emergency room. Four hours later, Dr. Cummings asked Dan what brought him to the hospital. She explained to us that his blood work hadn't changed much from when he was last seen in September.

Dan tried to explain to her. "Earlier in the day, I couldn't use my cell phone. I tried calling Julie, but I couldn't. I don't feel right."

I explained what had happened at the house, and she said, "I'll be right back. Dan, I need to run one more test." Dr. Cummings went back to the nurse's station. I saw her snap her fingers, point to one person, and grab a clipboard from another.

A minute later, a nurse came over and took one more sample of blood from Dan. I'm not sure how much time had passed, but Dr. Cummings came back with a nurse and a small cup of medicine. "Dan, your ammonium levels are high. I need you to drink this." She took the cup from the nurse and handed it to Dan. After he drank it, the nurse filled it up halfway and handed it back to Dan. "Your liver isn't functioning properly, and therefore your ammonium levels are rising. We need to bring them back down."

"How do we do that?" I asked.

Dr. Cummings explained, "With medicine. The only way to bring your ammonium levels down is via your poop. I want you to drink thirty milliliters of Lactulose four times a day." She handed me a prescription and told me to pick it up on my way home. "In the meantime, I'm going to give you a few samples for tonight."

A male nurse came over to us, handed us Dan's discharge papers, and explained how important it was to stay close to a bathroom. "Lactulose works fast. You'll want to be near a bathroom at all times because you never know."

"How quickly?" Dan asked, and I thought, *We have a twenty-minute drive home.*

"For some people, within minutes of taking the medicine," the nurse replied, and Dan got up.

Dr. Cummings handed Dan a small bottle of Lactulose. "I'll send the report to Dr. Dove."

We both thanked her for testing further and not giving up on Dan. Before we got back into the SUV, both Jesse and Gina Marie hugged Dan.

# Chapter 39

SUNDAY MORNING, JESSE AND Sherry showed up with a basket of fresh eggs, homemade bran muffins, and a bag of prunes. "I got your back, old man. You eat these, you'll never have to worry about shitting again."

Sherry slapped Jesse on his backside. "Don't say that to him." Sherry handed Dan a muffin, "I added flax seeds and chia. It will help you to move your bowels."

Dan thanked her and asked if anyone wanted a cup of coffee. Before we reached the kitchen, Gina Marie knocked on the front door, hollered, "Good morning," and came inside holding a basket of almonds, walnuts, pumpkin seeds, sunflower seeds, more flax seeds, and Medjool dates from Lilly's Family Foods.

Dan stopped to give her a hug. "Thank you for everything. Would you like a cup of coffee?"

"Sure," she replied and gave me a wink. "Teresa said she had to see you about something. After we drink our coffee, I'm taking my fishing buddy down to the pond."

I mouthed, "Thank you," to her. "Dan, I'm going to run up to the inn and say hi to the writer real quick, and I'll meet you and Gina Marie down at the pond."

Dan gave me a kiss and told me not to worry about him.

That was hard, seeing him crumble. Instead of taking the path up to the inn, I walked past the old cottage, and my heart stopped beating. The ground was black. I sat down and cried. I'm not sure how long I sat there, but when I reached the inn, Tina was standing outside on the front porch. As I got closer to her, I could hear her talking on her cell phone. I took a deep breath and smiled up at her.

Tina's eyes opened wide, and she started jumping up and down. I heard her say thank you several times. When she closed her phone, she waved to me. "Oh, my goodness! That was Amanda Toney from Stage 32. They're turning my series into a movie." She hugged me and once again started jumping up and down.

"Congratulations!" I told her. "You must be ecstatic. I'm so happy for you."

"Thank you, I can't believe it. Stage 32 signed a deal with Netflix for the movie adaptation of my series."

Everyone within a mile could hear the excitement in her voice.

Teresa came running outside. "What's going on?"

Two seconds later, Kourtnee, Christine, and Tina's daughter Molly came outside. Cathy and Deborah ran over to the inn followed by Amanda, Jessica, and the babies.

I looked at Tina and told her to tell them the good news.

Tina started to cry happy tears as she gave them the news of her book deal. We all went inside for her to share the news with her editor, literary agent, book club members, and guests. Tina approached her editor and said, "Our story is about to become a movie."

Everyone jumped to their feet and hugged her. Christine opened six bottles of champagne. Kourtnee and Teresa filled the glasses while Deborah and Amanda handed each guest a glass. Cathy said, "Toast."

Molly held her glass up and toasted to her mom.

I slipped out and went down to the pond to see Dan and Gina Marie. When I arrived, they were sitting in Dan's flat-bottomed boat. Gina Marie hollered over to me. "I'm putting my paddle boat in here. You'll love it. It has a roof."

Dan gave me a look. "She doesn't like using the oars."

Gina Marie held her fishing pole up. "I need my hands for fishing, not rowing."

They appeared to be having a good time. I watched as Dan snagged a trout. A minute later, I pressed my index finger to my lips and with my other hand motioned to the south. A beautiful buck was making his way to my hydrangeas. Dan gave me a thumbs-up. I pointed toward the farmhouse and waved goodbye. They both tossed their hands my way.

When I reached the house, Dr. Dove's report was in my inbox. My heart sank, my eyes began to fill with tears. "What am I going to do? Oh, Lord." I Googled stage-four liver disease. Liver failure. When your liver can no longer function or heal itself. Why do I have to be a diabetic? I refused to tell Dan. Selfish? Maybe. I didn't care. His job from now on was to get better. Mine was to worry about the details.

Two weeks before Thanksgiving, Dan and I went to New York-Presbyterian Hospital for more testing. His first appointment was at eight o'clock for an echocardiogram, followed by an ultrasound of his carotid artery. Dan ended his day with a stress test. He was so hungry, we ate in the hospital cafeteria. "It's not Broadway Pizza," he said.

I told Dan not to worry about finding a donor. "I won't stop until I find someone."

I was surprised by his answer. "I don't want to see anyone go through surgery on my behalf. I don't want to put anyone else's life in danger. "

We walked outside, handed our ticket to the valet, and waited. I drove onto the highway as Dan looked out the window. We needed hope. "I posted on my Facebook page and wrote about you needing a living donor on my blog. Seven women volunteered to be tested. I heard back from two of them. One has a blood disorder, and the other woman was told she couldn't do it because she has lupus."

Dan reached for my hand. "Gina Marie called New York-Presbyterian too."

I stopped for the red light. Glanced over at him. "Seriously?"

"She said they advised her not to say anything to me until they knew if she was a match. She wasn't approved. I think it's going to be hard to find a good match."

After he said that, he closed his eyes. I don't think he

was sleeping as much as he didn't want to talk anymore. I pulled up to the house and told him we were home. I was surprised to see Lady come running from the backyard. Then I saw Jesse and Lucky.

Jesse opened my door. "How was your drive?"

"It was good. I'm getting better at finding my way home. What's going on with you?"

"I think someone is ready to come home," he said and waved to Dan.

Dan was petting Lady, telling her how much he missed her. "I'm glad you're ready to come home. Lucky can take care of herself from now on."

Jesse put his arm around my shoulder. "Sherry wants to bring the turkey on Thanksgiving. I told her I would check with you first."

"That's a great idea," I replied. "I'll let Michael and everyone else know right now." I stepped up onto the porch and sat on the swing. Dan and Jesse went to the other end of the porch and sat down on their own swing. I looked over at the six rockers next to me and thought, *I don't have cooties.* I sent a group text letting everyone know Jesse and Sherry wanted to bring the turkey, Dan was making dinner rolls, and I would be making my homemade cranberry relish along with mashed potatoes. Christine was the first to reply, "I'll bake all the desserts."

"A vegetable dish," Kourtnee wrote. We hadn't heard from Teresa or anyone else by the time I got up to go inside.

A moment later, Dan and Lady came inside. "I'm glad

Cathy, Amanda, and Deborah are joining us this year," I said to him.

"I'm grateful for all of them," he said as he filled Lady's bowl.

# Chapter 40

IT WAS SIXTY-TWO DEGREES outside. Who would have thought it would be so nice on Thanksgiving day? Dan and I set a few tables up on the side and back porches with a variety of drinks, appetizers to snack on, along with my new flameless candles, and we turned the stereo on, playing soft country. I was excited for Cathy, Amanda, and Deborah to see the place for the first time. Both Dan and I were eager to meet Deborah's new husband. While Dan relaxed in the family room, I set the table. I used a sage-colored tablecloth with matching napkins, our Portmeirion botanical plates, white-, green-, and peach-colored mini-pumpkins, and for the floral arrangement, I used white hydrangeas from my new flower bed along with some seeded eucalyptus Michael had ordered for me from Pleasantries Flower Shop on Main Street.

I glanced over at Dan. Lady was sound asleep. "Hey, what are you thinking about?"

He pursed his lips. "Just enjoying the view. If you need me to do anything, let me know."

I waved my hand at him. "I'm good. Relax. We have an hour before everyone gets here." I smiled when Dan started singing "Only the Lonely."

I went into the kitchen to check on the cheeseballs Dan and I had prepared earlier. Dan had shaped cream cheese into a ball, drew lines giving the appearance of mini pumpkins, rolled them in bagel seasoning, and put a stem on the top. For the place cards, I took a picture of the Ford and wrote: Welcome Y'all! on the top and their names on the driver's door. Of course, that damn song was still stuck in my head. "Know this feeling ain't right," I sang aloud and laughed. I looked at the clock and decided to put the charcuterie board outside. When the farmer had told us our corn would feed his cows and the milk was for Cabot Cheese, I'd decided to use all of their products this time. As I was cutting up the cheese, I had to stop myself from eating all the habanero and pepper jack.

I was on the side porch when two vehicles pulled up to the house. I hollered in the family room window for Dan to come outside. In the back of Jesse's truck sitting on bales of hay were Michael, Christine with Brin on her lap, Kevin, Kourtnee, and Delilah, along with Robert and Kate. Behind his truck were Sal and Teresa. Jesse turned the truck off, Sherry got out holding Lucky, and Lady ran right to her. I waved to Teresa as she handed a huge platter and a bag to Sal.

"Hey, she changed her dress," Dan said to Michael as he reached up to take Brin from him.

Michael laughed. "The laundry fairy has it. Thank God."

I kissed everyone hello and waved to Cathy's husband

Steve as he parked his Mercedes. Amanda came out of the backseat, smiling. She introduced Dan and me to her fiancé. "Gabriel, this is Julie and Dan."

He shook our hands and said, "You can call me Gabe. It's nice to meet the two of you."

It was sad to say, but the first thing I thought to ask him was his blood type. He was perfect. Same height as Dan, athletic build and Amanda said he was an extremely healthy eater, but I told him, "Welcome."

Dan hugged Amanda before saying, "Everyone help yourself to something to eat and drink."

Cathy followed Sherry and Teresa up onto the porch to put their dishes inside. "My green bean casserole needs to be warmed up," Teresa said.

Before I could turn around, I saw a 1971 Cuda convertible parked right in front of me. Under a brimmed hat, Deborah flashed me a smile. Her husband got out, opened the door for her, and introduced himself to me. Deborah stood behind him smiling. "Zachary's so full of light and love."

I was still listening to Deborah telling me about their honeymoon and her new house when Gina Marie, Michelle, and Frank pulled up in a Ford Model T with the top down. "Wow!" Zachary said.

Gina Marie and Frank got out. Michelle climbed out of the backseat, pointing toward Frank. "He had to buy it," she said.

"I love it." I gave them each a hug and introduced them to Zachary.

Frank smiled at him and pointed to the Cuda. "Yours?"

"It was my father's. Yes, she belongs to me now." Zachary handed the keys to Frank. "You're welcome to take her for a drive."

Frank rubbed his chin. "I'm honored. Next time."

"Whoa!" I heard someone say and turned around to see Kevin, Michael, Jesse, and Dan standing on the front porch. "I thought I heard a Hemi," Jesse said.

Dan and Jesse went directly over to the car. I introduced Kevin and Michael to Zachary. "Dan, Jesse, this is Deborah's husband Zachary." They both shook his hand and told him how much they liked his car.

"Umm, did anyone notice Frank's new ride?" Gina Marie said laughingly.

"Ha ha," Jesse told her.

"I took him to pick it up last week."

Dan shook Frank's hand. "She's a beauty. How does it ride?"

"Like a cloud," Frank told him.

I looped my arm through Frank's. "I made you your favorite corn pudding and sweet potato pie."

"Hey, *we* made the corn pudding," Dan shouted.

Jesse put his hands on Dan's shoulders. "He still loves her more," and Frank laughed.

Someone had changed the radio station. "Rockstar" by Nickelback was playing, and Deborah, Amanda, Kate, and Sherry were dancing. They each had a glass of wine in their hands.

About twenty minutes later, I took everyone on a tour of the house.

We entered from the kitchen door and made our way to the family room. "We spend most of our time in here," I said, and then went to the formal living room, dining room, Dan's office, and my study. "Down the hall are four bedrooms and bathrooms for guests. We're still waiting for the furniture for those rooms." I showed them our master bedroom and bath.

Cathy immediately opened the shower door. "Geez, how many showerheads do you have?"

Kate asked, "Is that really a Barracuda in the driveway?"

Gina Marie almost bumped into me to turn and answer her. "No. The 71 Cuda is a classic of its own. Just because it's a Plymouth doesn't make it a Barracuda."

"What's the difference?" Kate asked.

I smiled at Gina Marie and caught her rolling her eyes. "The Cuda has a Hemi." She glared at Kate. "A Hemi is a big block engine. Huge difference."

"Gotcha," Kate said and moved ahead of the line to go out onto the porch.

When we got back outside, Roy Orbison was singing, "Pretty Woman." Dan held his hand out to me. We danced for a few minutes before everyone else joined in. I kissed him and thanked him for the dance. "I want to check on dinner." I took a deep breath. "Save the next dance for me. I'll be right back."

I went into the kitchen, and out of the corner of my

eye, I saw Michael, Kevin, Steve, and Gabe playing a game of pool in the family room. Robert was sitting in the recliner reading *The Appeal*, a book I had picked up for Dan. He looked up at me and asked if I needed help with anything.

"No. Umm, actually, Robert, can I see you for a minute?" I pointed to the front porch. He followed me outside. "I was thinking about the cottage, and it's a shame to leave the space empty. It's such a peaceful site." I studied him for a minute. He appeared happy. I was glad he was a part of our family. "I'd like to rebuild the cottage for you and Kate."

Robert smiled. "Thank you, but that won't be necessary. Kate and I just bought a small ranch over in South Kingston. We got it for two hundred and fifteen thousand." He looked past me. Took a deep breath and said, "I'm not supposed to tell anyone, but Michael and Christine gave us the money to buy the house."

I heard laughter coming from the side porch. Kevin declared victory on the pool table, and my heart turned a page. I hugged Robert and told him I was delighted for him.

We went back inside when I heard Dan thanking everyone for coming. "You made my day," he said.

# Chapter 41

WE PUT ALL the food on the counters in the kitchen. Hot dishes on one side and cold food on another. Over in the corner, I set the floral arrangement and everyone's desserts on the round table. Everyone filled their plates. Delilah and Brin were both sitting in their high chairs feasting on turkey, mashed potatoes, and corn. We held hands, and I said grace. "Dear Lord, we thank you for this food, and for blessing us with the bond of friendship. Amen." I kept my eyes closed for a second to ask God to send Dan a donor.

"Who made the roasted vegetables?" Michael asked.

Kourtnee raised her hand. "Mmm, me. Sorry, I had a mouthful."

"The eggplant tastes wonderful," Michael added.

"Why are you not eating?" Dan asked me.

"I was just thinking how blessed we are to have all of them." I took a bite of my turkey and caught Robert smiling at Michael as he told everyone how the laundry fairy came in the middle of the night to wash Delilah's party dress, and I thought about his generosity.

Frank nudged me in my side. "Did you eat too many appetizers?"

I laughed. "No, I was just thinking how wonderful it

is to have all of you here with us."

"Julie, Christine, and I were wondering about Christmas," Kourtnee said. "We were wondering if everyone could sleep at the inn."

"On Christmas Eve," Christine added. "So we can wake up and open our presents together. Like a family."

I held back my tears. "I would love that," I said.

After we ate, we all gathered in the family room for a game of pool and dancing. At first, it was the women against the men. Of course, we won. Gina Marie and I were pretty good at shooting pool. I laughed so hard watching Kevin and Kourtnee dance to the Zac Brown Band's "Chicken Fried." Actually, they were very good dancers. "Who is ready for a cup of tea and a piece of pie?" I asked, and everyone stopped what they were doing.

A moment later, Gina Marie told us a joke she'd heard. "Two guys go into a bar. The shorter guy will not stop talking. He's annoying and whining about everything. The taller guy says, I bet you one hundred dollars I can drink this beer faster than you. The shorter guy tries and fails. When he continued talking up a storm, the taller guy says, I'll bet you two hundred dollars I can jump off the roof and land right back here on this stool. The shorter guy is mad he lost his money, takes the bet, and says, double or nothing I can too. The taller guy jumps off the roof and lands back on his stool. The shorter guy lands flat on his face outside. The bartender says to the taller guy, 'Superman, sometimes you can be a real asshole.'"

Everyone laughed at Gina Marie's funny story.

Some of us took our dishes and teacups out onto the front porch. I couldn't take my eyes off the Cuda, it was a beautiful car. We laughed at kicking the men's asses on the pool table. "I think they're in there practicing right now," Gina Marie said. "So, Deborah, how's life treating you these days?"

She took a sip of her tea and replied, "Wonderful, Zachary is a dream come true. He's pleasing on the eye, and he loves me. His mother told me he never talked about anyone the way he talks about me."

I held my cup up. "To finding love and knowing when you found the right one."

"To love," everyone said.

Kourtnee stretched her arms out. "Okay, bath time for a certain little girl who has pumpkin pie stuck in her hair." She got up and gave me a kiss on the cheek. "Later, Boss Lady. See you all tomorrow."

"For leftovers, right?" Gina Marie said, and I echoed her sentiments.

Michael was standing in the doorway. "We still have a few more turkeys. I could deep fry them up at the pool."

"But the pool is closed," Kate said.

"It sounds like a great idea," I replied. "Dan and I will bring all the side dishes up in the UTV. We'll meet at noon."

"I'll tell the men right now," Deborah said and went inside.

After everyone left, Dan and I took the dishes out of the dishwasher and put them away. "I'm going to check my email," I said to him. "I sent Carmie, Erin, and Lynnae each a happy Thanksgiving message this morning, and I want to see if anyone replied and hear about their day."

"Okay, I'm going to watch a movie in the family room."

I hung the dishtowel up and told him I would meet him in there in two seconds. I grabbed my laptop, sat down next to him, and read aloud, "We completed harvesting the olives today. Francesco said it was the best crop to date. I'm so excited. Good news, I have seven women who want to stay for the entire year to complete their manuscripts, and we have one male writer staying too."

Dan looked up at me. "I thought it was a women's writing retreat?"

I raised my shoulders and read, "He was a guest speaker. An editor from Penguin Random House. They were more than happy to have him stay. He's writing his memoirs. Francesco adores him. He speaks fluent Italian. I miss you and Dan very much. Give my love to Dan and tell him I am praying for him."

"Huh," Dan said and turned the volume up on the TV. "Did I tell you she told Gina Marie that she canceled her new dishwasher and used that money to send her daughter to the city?"

I wanted to cry. Before I could say what was on my mind, Dan said, "Order her a dishwasher, and tell her merry Christmas."

I kissed his cheek. "Sounds good. I'll have it shipped immediately."

I read Erin's email and shared her wishes for a lovely Thanksgiving with Dan. Nothing from Lynnae yet. Dan was still awake. I thought about telling him about the women who tried to become donors, but I thought otherwise. I did tell him about Michael and Christine's generosity. "I offered to build Robert and Kate a home where the cottage was, but Michael and Christine already gave them the money to buy a little house in South Kingstown."

He turned to face me. "Seriously?"

I nodded.

"That's great," he said and turned his attention back to the TV, but then added, "I'll bet it was more her idea than his." Then he closed his eyes.

I picked up my book and read the last nine chapters before I too fell asleep. "Hey, let's go to bed," I said nudging Dan on his arm. I shut the TV off and moved the blanket to the back of the sofa.

Dan got up, stretched his arms, and asked how long he had been asleep.

"Umm, you missed the entire second half. No, I'm not telling you how it ended."

I fell asleep in Dan's arms. When I awoke, he was

already in the kitchen preparing breakfast. "Good morning, my love," I said as I took hold of my coffee cup. When Dan didn't say anything, I asked him if he was okay.

I took his vitals and called Dr. Dove's office. "I left a message for her to call me," I told him. "I don't want you doing anything today."

# Chapter 42

AFTER BREAKFAST, WE SAT out on the front porch. The sun appeared in shades of golden tones, giving off a warm glow. "I'll be right back," I said to Dan. I went back outside and handed him a piece of apple pie. He smiled at me.

"I guess I forgot to serve it." I smiled back at him. "I made it just for you."

Dan set his plate down on the table and quickly got up. "I have to go to the bathroom," he said, and we both laughed.

I waited for him to return before eating my slice. Dan came back with two cups of tea, and I thought, *It's the little things in life.* I took the cup and thanked him. "Feel better?"

He sat down and took a bite of his pie before saying, "Now I do."

I looked up at the sky and said, "Before we know it, Christmas will be here. Any ideas on what you'd like?"

Dan laughed. "A new liver."

"Me, too," I echoed his sentiments. "I prayed for you. I asked God to send you a new liver that would be a perfect match."

I thought Dan had tears in his eyes. He closed them

and nodded. "I know I'm in your prayers," he said and opened his eyes. "I don't want you worrying about me. If that tick didn't bite me and make me so sick, I never would have known anything was wrong with my liver." He looked at me. "I'm not in pain."

I got up and hugged him. "I love you so much."

He squeezed me so tight before saying, "I love you more," and I quickly turned around when I heard a car pulling up to the house. It was Frank. We both waved to him.

"He can have a piece of my pie," Dan said jokingly.

Frank stepped up onto the porch and handed Dan a few cookbooks. "I just met with Gina Marie, she asked me to give these to you."

"Thank you," Dan said to him and handed the stack to me. "Would you like a piece of apple pie?"

Frank sat down. "If Julie made it, I would."

I read the book on the top. *The Liver Rescue Cookbook.* "I'll be right back. Would you care for a cup of tea or coffee?"

Frank glanced over at Dan's cup and replied, "Tea, please."

I cut a slice and had just put the pie back in the refrigerator when my cell phone rang. "Hello."

"Julie, it's Lauren from Dr. Dove's office. I received your message. How's Dan?"

I explained his episode to her, and she told me to make sure he took his Lactulose four times a day. "He needs to go to the bathroom three to four times a day in order to remove the ammonia." She reminded us of our upcoming appointment with Dr. Kato. "Be sure to tell Dr. Kato everything when you see him."

"Okay, we will, and thank you for calling me back. I feel better," I told her. In reality, I was scared to death. My insides were trembling. My heart was ready to explode any day. I was afraid to let Dan out of my sight. I let go of the counter, took hold of Frank's plate, and went back outside.

I handed Frank his tea and pie and sat down in the rocker on the other side of Dan. I listened to the two of them talk about deer hunting, and I wanted to scream, no. But I knew Dan lived for the outdoors. More than swimming in a pool or taking a vacation, he loved sitting in the woods waiting for something to walk under his stand.

"Julie and I were hiking the other day, and we saw a nice buck."

"I hope you're careful climbing up into your tree stand," Frank said to him.

Dan waved his hand at him. "Don't worry about me. Jesse and Kevin built a solid set of stairs for me to go up."

I leaned forward and told Frank how long Dan had been hunting.

"She goes with me during turkey season," Dan told him, and I thought, *Maybe I should start going for deer season, too.*

"Well, I was thinking. For Christmas this year, why

don't we all swap names?" Frank raised his chin at me. "What do you think?"

"I love the idea. Let me talk to everyone and get back to you."

Frank sat back and started rocking. "I already spoke to them. They love the idea. In fact, we're all planning on meeting here next Sunday to draw names."

I laughed out loud. "You're too funny."

Frank pointed his finger at me. "You're not to cook or think about doing one thing. We'll bring lunch and desserts. Kourtnee already made the list and cut out the names for everyone to draw." He winked at me. "The only name not going in the bowl is yours."

"What? How come? Why don't I get a gift?" I asked. Truly wondering why I needed to be excluded.

"Because I'm not good at buying baby clothes or kitchen gadgets for your chef," Frank said and stood up. "I'll see you next week." He shook Dan's hand and blew me a kiss.

Monday morning, Dan and I drove to New York-Presbyterian Hospital to see Dr. Kato. I wasn't going to say anything to him about the commercial we saw on television because I was sure he had heard it a thousand times before, but the first thing Dan said to him was, "I couldn't believe it when Julie told me I was coming to see you. I remember the little girl talking about you on TV."

Dr. Kato smiled at him. "Yes, she's all grown up now and attending college." Dr. Kato looked at his computer screen before adding, "She wants to be a doctor."

"I saw you ran the New York City Marathon recently," I said.

"Yes, I run every year," he replied. "Dan, I see you had complications with encephalopathy. How do you feel now?"

"Better," Dan replied. "I don't like the taste of Lactulose, but I drink it."

"You won't have to take it after you receive a new liver. Let me examine you." Dr. Kato had Dan sit on the examination table while he listened to his lungs, heart, and felt his abdomen. "You're in good shape, we're going to make you even better." Dr. Kato glanced over at me and back at Dan. "I'm going to give you something that will help keep your ammonia levels down." He smiled at Dan. "It's a pill." He handed his business card to both of us. "If you have any questions or concerns you call me, day or night."

We both stood up and thanked him. Meeting Dr. Kato was like seeing a rock star.

On the drive back to the house, I asked Dan if he felt better meeting the surgeon. "Dr. Kato is known all over the world. He's a great surgeon. The director of adult and pediatric liver and intestinal transplantation," I said.

"Did you look up his success rate?" he asked.

"Yes. And he has a one-hundred percent success rate. I trust Dr. Kato. In fact, I love everyone on your team."

"When do we meet with Dr. Dove again?" he asked, and I knew he respected her opinion the most.

"January," I told him. "I believe on the second." I saw Dan had closed his eyes. I thought about him being diagnosed back in September and wondered how much longer before he received a match. I was going to turn the radio on, but I reconsidered when I heard Dan snoring.

# Chapter 43

Sunday morning, Dan and I went for a stroll in the backyard. When we saw a buck drinking from the pond, I knew what Dan was going to say. "I should have put a tree stand up behind the house."

Poor Dan had been going out in the mornings from four a.m. to nine and seeing nothing. "Wait until the apple trees start flowering, you'll see deer then," I told him. "Come on, let's set the table before everyone gets to the house."

Dan opened the back door for me. "Don't worry, I named him Big Boy." I smiled, knowing Dan never shoots deer after he names them. He tugged on my hand. "Frank said you're not supposed to do anything."

A minute later, Gina Marie and Michelle were there with Kevin, Kourtnee, and Delilah. I held my hands out to her and she came running to me. "Ooh, you smell like lavender," I told her as I kissed her cheek.

"Yep," Kourtnee said. "I put it in her bath water at night. It helps to calm her down before bed. I order it from Pumpkin Blossom Farm in New Hampshire."

"Did you eat without me?" Jesse yelled.

Sherry slapped him on his chest. "Don't listen to him. Hey, I set the bowl with everyone's names in the family room." She looked at me. "I just noticed the house is the same shape as the inn."

I put my arm around her. "I wanted our guests to have their own private quarters."

"Oh, hey," Kourtnee said. "That gives me an idea. We could use your four bedrooms if we ever need—"

"No," Dan shouted. "Absolutely not. Don't even think about it."

"Geez, don't get your shorts all twisted up." Kourtnee looked at me and winked.

I ignored her, knowing how much Dan and I were both enjoying our privacy. Dan was correct. Our home was our space.

Fifteen minutes later, we were all gathered in the family room. We decided to let the men draw first. I was happy to see that Cathy and Steve wanted to be included even though they would be in Oregon for the holiday visiting his family.

After everyone drew a name, we had lunch. Frank had pizza delivered from Benny's Clam Shack on Sand Hill Cove. Ten pizzas in total. Two of each: veggie, BBQ, the Brooklyn, cheese, and pepperoni. Cathy and Sherry brought the drinks. Kourtnee had made a huge antipasto, and Christine had baked homemade cream puffs. She banged her hip into mine. "Don't tell anyone, but they're sugar-free, and I used dark chocolate instead of sweet."

I took a bite. "So good."

Teresa turned the music up a little and we all sang, "Santa Bring My Baby Back to Me." Sherry was holding

Delilah's hands, and Jesse danced with Brin in his arms. She smiled when he dipped her, and we all laughed.

After everyone left, Dan and I watched a movie on Netflix. When he fell asleep, I ordered my gifts for him and Christine. I liked the idea of no one knowing who drew their name, well except for me. I logged onto YouTube and watched a video about liver donors. I cried like a baby. A man had received a liver, and a year later, the donor's family wanted to meet him. The recipient refused by saying it would be too hard for him. I could imagine that would be the hard part—knowing someone else had died so you could live.

I closed my laptop and continued watching the show. About two minutes later, Dan woke up. "Are you okay?" he asked and tossed the blanket to his right.

"I'm fine," I replied as he got up to leave.

"I heard you crying, I have to go to the bathroom. I'll be right back."

When he returned, I told him I was watching sad videos on YouTube. "It was nothing you'd be interested in," I said and asked if he was thirsty.

"Sure, a glass of water," he replied and offered to get us each a glass. When he came back, I asked him how many times he had a bowel movement.

Dan shook his head. "Welcome to the senior citizen's center. Three, so far."

"Okay, because I was thinking you ate two slices of pizza, and nothing is more constipating than bread."

"Okay, doc. I'll eat an apple later." He sat down and

tossed the blanket over his legs.

I made a mental note to pick my battles with Dan. He'd always been a hard-working man. Had a mind of his own, and he knows what he wants. I knew better than to try and keep him down. At ten o'clock we went to bed. "Good night, my love."

"Night," Dan replied.

The next morning, I was sitting on the back porch drinking my coffee when six bucks entered from the side yard. I knew they were eating the last of my hydrangeas over at the pond. I heard Dan in the kitchen and whispered, "Shush."

He came outside, sat down next to me, and sipped his coffee quietly. No one had to speak. We just watched. After they left, Dan said, "A six, two eights, two tens, and a twelve pointer. Tomorrow morning, I'm sitting right here."

"Oh, no you're not." I got up and stretched my arms out. "I'm taking my shower." I turned back around. "You can join me if you'd like."

When Dan came into the kitchen, I was wearing only my panties. He took one look at me and grinned. I slowly took them off, dropped them on the floor, ran to the bathroom, turned all the sprayers on, jumped out, and hid in the linen closet. From behind the louvers, I watched him look for me in our bedroom, his closet, mine, and in the soaking tub. When he headed down the hall, I entered the shower stall, and he must have heard the door close because he quickly turned around and came in. "You're lucky I didn't find you," he said.

I was the first to step out and dry off. Romance is important as it should be in a marriage. Being playful—priceless.

# Chapter 44

CHRISTMAS EVE WAS UPON us, and yet my heart was full of aches and woes. It hadn't snowed yet, and that was only a part of it. "How can we celebrate Christmas if we don't have any snow?" I asked. "Hello, are you listening to me? Did you even hear a word I said?"

Dan got up and held his hand out to me. "Come with me."

I followed him down the hall to the guest rooms. He stopped outside the first room on the right. "Close your eyes." That room had all my furniture from the cottage. I just couldn't see anyone sleeping on my bed, our bed. It was also where Dan had put the little chair from the antique shop. He moved me in a few steps. "Open your eyes."

He'd hung the picture with our favorite quote over the bed. "It's not Hayden Lambson, but—"

"It's perfect," I said. "I love it there."

He read the quote aloud, "'To forgive is the highest, most beautiful form of love. In return, you will receive untold peace and happiness.' I wanted it there so everyone who walks by will see it. All I ever wanted was to make you happy."

I leaned back and rested my head on his chest. Looked

up and waited for him to kiss me, but instead he ran to our bathroom, and I laughed. "I'll just wait right here." The decor in our home was much like the house in New York, country with a flair for the outdoors. Except for the guest quarters; in those rooms, we stayed true to our Rhode Island lifestyle—nautical all the way. I read the quote one more time before going out to the family room.

I sat down in the corner chair. It was hard for me not to buy a token of my appreciation for each and every person at the inn. But giving them their bonuses made up for it. This year, we were giving them their biggest one to date. Kourtnee had enough in reserves, and she had an emergency fund. The inn was booked solid for the next two years, we had a wedding scheduled every weekend, twenty-six of them had over three hundred guests, and that meant we were financially secure.

Friday morning, Dan and I carried our gifts up to the third floor, and we noticed our staff had already set up the Christmas tree in the conference room. "I need to see Kourtnee for a second," I told him.

"Okay, I'll meet you in the kitchen," he replied before asking me if I wanted a cup of tea.

I shook my head and went into the office, but no one was there. I noticed Sherry had a photo of Jesse on her desk along with a piece of mistletoe tied with a red ribbon taped to the top. Considering we had guests staying with us, it was very quiet. Usually the inn buzzed with excitement before a wedding or big holiday such as

Christmas. I heard voices coming from the kitchen. Michael had his own staff coming in for the wedding and another big event, but they wouldn't be here until Saturday. Sunday's wedding was taking place in the library followed by dinner in the large dining room. I went into the kitchen, and Dan was talking to a couple I had never met before. "There she is," Dan said and motioned for me to come closer. "Julie, this is Emily and Corey. They're getting married here on Sunday."

I held my hand out to them. "Congratulations."

"We were just telling your husband about our dilemma. Apparently, our guest list is more than we anticipated. By any chance, do you happen to have five more rooms?" she said.

I thought for a moment. "Of course we do. Follow me." I saw Dan look at me. Knowing every room was occupied by guests and our staff. I already knew the groom was paying for every room, so it was easy. I didn't need to ask for anyone else's credit card. They followed me out to the lobby, and I pointed to the staircase. "All of the rooms are on the third floor."

The bride hugged me. "Thank you so much."

"I'll let our chef know you have a few more guests attending the ceremony and dinner."

They went up to their room, and I went back to the kitchen to explain to Dan. "We need to move our gifts back down to the farmhouse." After that, I sent a group text letting everyone know I was calling a meeting in one hour in the kitchen at the farmhouse. "Dan, we need to call Cardi's and put a rush on those beds. Next, we need to go shopping for a Christmas tree."

Dan's eyes lit up. "I'm on it. Jesse and I will get the tree, you call the furniture store."

We drove the Polaris back to the house, Dan got in his truck and drove as far as Jesse's. I went inside and called Cardi's Furniture Store. "Hi, this is Julie Holliday at The Inn in Rhode Island, by any chance can you send over the beds we ordered, we don't need the rest of the bedroom furniture right now, we just need the beds."

"Julie, hang on one second." She put me on hold. I looked around; with everything going on with Dan, I didn't decorate one thing in the house. Two seconds later, she said, "The truck is on its way. Is there anything else we can do for you?'"

"Seriously? Oh, my. That's wonderful." I thought for a second. "Can you also send over two cribs and a twin bed?"

"No problem." The call ended.

I went down the hall. "I'll put Michelle and Gina Marie in the first room, and across the hall will be Teresa and Sal. At the end of the hall, I'll put the cribs for the babies and their parents. Deborah and Zachary can have our room. Dan and I will sleep in his office on the pullout, and Frank can sleep in my study." I said to myself. "Perfect." I went out to the garage, opened the bins labeled Christmas decorations, and set them in the living room. I ran to the kitchen and pulled down my china, linens, and candlesticks before setting them back and grabbing my flameless.

One by one, they all came inside.

"I love it," Gina Marie said, and everyone echoed her sentiments.

"Are you sure?" I said and then told them how excited Dan was.

"Oh, my, where is he?" Teresa asked, looking around.

"He went with Jesse to get a tree." Sherry held her hand up. "Jesse will take care of him."

Michelle clapped her hands together. "We'll help you decorate."

Delilah started clapping. When Brin decided to join in, she slapped her father in the face. Everyone laughed.

Gina Marie turned the Christmas music up, and everyone went to work.

By the time Dan and Jesse arrived with the Christmas tree, the entire front porch, door, and home was decorated.

# Chapter 45

On Christmas Eve, the inn overflowed with joy. The guests were meandering around as if they owned the inn. They were celebrating in every room. Beautiful Christmas carols streamed from overhead speakers. I glanced into the large dining room and had to catch my breath. Behind the bride and groom's table were strings of white: stars, shiny Christmas balls in different sizes, and wedding bells. Every table was adorned with all-white flowers. The table linens— white. The only other color in the room was the deep burgundy napkins wrapped in sterling silver napkin rings with the word "Shipmates" etched on each. I loved every aspect of it.

I went into the kitchen, handed out the bonus checks to Michael's staff, and thanked them for always coming to our rescue.

"It's our pleasure," a woman said to me wearing a chef's coat that read: "Culinary Institute of America" under a gold flame. I recognized her from previous weddings. She was diligent, much like Michael.

I held my hand out to her. "I'm very grateful."

She beamed as she held up a tray of smoked sausage and brie topped with a dollop of warm cranberry. She picked one up by its toothpick and asked me if I'd like to try a sample.

"How can I refuse?" I said. "They look delicious." After I took the first bite, I wanted to take the tray back to the farmhouse with me.

She looked at me and smiled. "I'm glad you like it. We're sending down a sampling of everything we're making for this weekend's wedding to your house. The groom insisted."

"Wow, that's very kind of him."

I left feeling good about giving up the entire house to such a beautiful couple. "Generous couple."

"Did you say something?" Kourtnee asked.

I stopped and looked in her office. "What are you doing here? Why aren't you home?"

She tilted her head as usual at me and held up a stack of envelopes. "Bonus checks."

I clapped my hands. "I'm glad you're on the ball."

She shut off her light and followed me. "Is it ever going to snow?" I asked.

"They're getting a blizzard out west. Maybe, we'll get the tail end of it."

"By tomorrow, I hope," I replied and asked her if she was truly excited about spending Christmas Eve at the farmhouse.

"Kevin and I both feel like this is our home." She put her arm around me. "I'll always be here for you. I pray every night for you and for God to send Dan a new liver." She banged her head against mine. "Delilah asks God to send Poppa Dan a new wiver, instead of liver."

I laughed out loud. "I love that she calls him Poppa Dan."

"Hey, that's what she started calling him. Every morning, when she's eating her cereal, she says, 'I see Poppa today?'"

"As long as she doesn't call me Boss Lady, I'm good." We were on the path to Kourtnee and Kevin's house when I saw a snowflake. I pointed up to the sky. "Is that?"

"Oh, yeah," Kourtnee said and started running. "I'll see you in a little while, Boss Lady. I have something very special to do."

Before I could reach my front porch, I heard laughter, music, and I saw two people dancing in the family room. I opened the door and saw Steve swirl Cathy around. She waved her hand to me and said, "We got turned around."

Steve added, "Our flight was canceled."

I looked at Dan, he was grinning from ear to ear. When he waved his finger at me, I went over and stood next to him. Then I saw Amanda and Gabe in the kitchen, they were making cookies alongside Jessica, Gina Marie, and Michelle. Jesse and Sherry came in holding a stack of pillows, blankets, and several air mattresses. Before Dan and I could go over to help them, Deborah and Zachary came in. We put our hands out just as Teresa and Sal walked in carrying similar items. Teresa looked around and started singing. Then we heard the babies, and we knew Kevin, Kourtnee, Michael, and

Christine had arrived too. When Dan kissed me on my forehead, I started to cry. I was overwhelmed by all the love.

Teresa gave me a kiss and told me, "Cathy and Steve are going to stay in our room."

Kourtnee turned around and said, "Christine, Michael, and Brin are staying with us at the end of the hall. Jesse and Sherry can have our room."

I looked around and saw Jessica waving her hand. "I'm staying in the family room with Amanda and Gabe."

I wiped my eyes and said, "Well, Merry Christmas, everyone."

We heard a knock on the door. Jesse opened it and took several boxes from one of the sous-chefs. She nodded at him and said, "Merry Christmas, these are from Mr. Corbett."

"Merry Christmas," Jesse told her, as did the rest of us.

Dan took a few boxes and so did Michael. "Try the pockets, they're stuffed with crab and lobster," Michael told him.

In the kitchen, you could smell cookies baking, and you could hear laughter. I smiled when Gabe told Amanda they should get married at the inn.

"Oh, we're having our reception here," she told him. "But I have to get married in a church, or my mother won't be happy."

I glanced over at Kourtnee, and she held up two

fingers. I wasn't sure if she was telling me in two years or giving me the peace sign.

Dan, Jesse, Michael, and Kevin were playing pool when it dawned on me. Someone was missing. I picked up my cell phone and dialed his number. "Hello," he said, standing behind me, next to Robert and Kate. "I picked these two up on my way. Figured you had plenty of room." Frank put his cell phone back in his pocket.

I hugged them and told them, "Welcome."

Robert handed me a small box and told me to open it. I cried just looking at it. It was a set of coasters. With an anchor and the words: "Storms Don't Scare Me. They Teach Me How to Sail My Ship." I hugged him and Kate before thanking him.

She pointed her finger at Robert and said, "He picked you, and he was so happy he did."

I saw Frank wink at me. "Come inside. Let me take your coats." I hung everyone's coats up in the hall closet. For some reason, they all forgot how and where to put their coats.

I whispered in Dan's ear, "We need to set up a few more tables in the dining room."

He gave me his famous smile. Kissed my temple and whispered back, "Teresa and Cathy took care of it." Then he grinned. "Gina Marie told them where to find everything."

"Okay, who is hungry?" Michael shouted. "Dan, why don't you go first, and we'll all follow you around the kitchen table."

Dan picked up his plate, and of course, he started with the steamed clams. The zuppa de peche was in small crocks and easy for everyone to grab. I saw Dan smile when he took hold of two slices of garlic bread. "This calamari looks divine," he said.

"There are fried oysters too," Michael said. "Save room on your plate for the flaming-hot garlic wings, they're my favorite."

I helped myself to the lobster bisque and made myself a fish taco for starters. I laughed when I saw Kevin's plate overflowing with focaccia bread. Once everyone had filled their plate, we all went into the dining room to eat. I noticed someone had placed a few candles in the window, and I immediately thought about Erin and Kyle. I included them in my prayers along with Carmie, her family, Francesco, Nico, and Aria. "Let's eat," I said.

The food was delicious. I was glad Michael was at the table and not up at the inn. I felt Dan's hand on my own. "I'll be right back," he whispered in my ear, and I thought he was going to the bathroom, but he came right back, sat down, and read a Christmas message. "There's more, much more to Christmas than candlelight and cheer; it's the spirit of sweet friendship that brightens all year." He folded it and handed it to me. Dan held his glass of water up. "To the friends who will always be here for Julie. God bless you all."

# Chapter 46

CHRISTMAS MORNING, OUTSIDE MY window was a blanket of white. "A dusting, but I'll take it." I ran through the house and turned on all the candles, lit the tree, and made coffee. Dan and Jesse, in true tradition, were up before anyone else, even me. I found them out on the back porch, coats, scarves, gloves, and talking about me. "Promise me you'll stay in Rhode Island and watch over her."

I stepped outside wearing only my pajamas and robe. I gave each of them a kiss and said, "Merry Christmas." Then I told Dan he wasn't going anywhere. "I have faith in God. I trust Dr. Dove and Dr. Kato. We're going to find you a liver. Do you hear me?"

Jesse got up. "Yeah, that's right." When he went inside, I sat down next to Dan.

"I won't lose you. I can't. God brought us together for a reason. Look at me."

He did. "I'm a realist, Julie. Only twenty percent of my liver is good. How long—"

I stopped him. "I believe in miracles." I stood up. "And so should you."

Frank came outside and put his hand out to me. "Go inside."

I closed the door behind me. Looked out the window at my husband and my secret keeper and prayed for God's healing hands to be upon my husband. I felt Jesse's hands on my shoulders. He didn't say anything, he just stood there for a moment before going back to his room. In the family room, I heard Amanda tell everyone she smelled coffee. I turned the cold water on, splashed my face, blew my nose, and wiped my eyes. "Good morning," I whispered, but everyone just waved me off.

"I need coffee," Gina Marie said.

Lady brushed up against my leg. I bent down and patted her on the head. "Where did you sleep last night?"

"In our room with the puppy," Sherry said and added, "Merry Christmas, everyone."

I laughed when Gina Marie and Amanda held their cups up.

A half-hour later, everyone was up, drinking coffee, tea, juice, and cold-brewed coffee. I put Brin and Delilah in their high chairs and gave them each a serving of scrambled eggs. After breakfast, we went for a walk down to the pond so Santa could get ready. "Oh, no," I said. "This way, Delilah. We have to go in the front door." I rang the doorbell. Knocked on the door and opened it.

Brin saw him first. Santa was sitting in the wingback chair with a stack of presents all around him. Lucky knocked over one of the dollhouses. Under the tree sat two balance tricycles, each with its own basket on the handlebars and helmet on the floor. Christine bent down to put Brin on hers and looked up. "Thank you, Dan."

"I couldn't buy just one," he replied.

We let the girls open their toys before we exchanged our gifts to each other. I watched Dan smile every time someone opened their gift, and I wondered what he was thinking. I didn't want him to worry, or to think about the what-ifs. I picked up my cell phone and glanced at the calendar. We had an appointment with Dr. Dove the first week in January. Maybe she could give me some advice on how to lift Dan's spirits.

Jesse stood up and announced he was hungry, and everyone laughed. Gina Marie said, "Again? You just ate."

He went into the kitchen, and Dan, Frank, Michael, Kevin, Steve, Robert, and Sal followed him. The women stared at Gabe and Zachary, waiting for them to get up, but they didn't move. "And that is why you are both in great shape," Sherry said as she gathered all the wrapping paper.

"Where are you going?" Cathy asked Teresa.

"To see what they're cooking up."

"Me, too," Amanda said as she followed her to the kitchen.

"I'm tired. I need a nap," Gina Marie said and stretched her legs out.

Michelle tossed a blanket on her before sitting in the chair next to her. "When in Rome."

I noticed Kate rubbing her belly. "Are you full?" I asked.

"Five months pregnant," she replied.

Christine sat down next to her. "We're throwing you a baby shower."

Everyone congratulated her. Then she stood up and said, "Actually, that bacon smells really good."

We all went into the kitchen, and the guys were making turkey BLTs with the leftover turkey from the night before.

After lunch, everyone said they were going home to take a nap. I was sad but also delighted to be alone with Dan. We sat on the loveseat holding hands, watching a movie. I'm not sure where my mind was, but it certainly was not on the characters in front of me. I closed my eyes for a second and asked God to please send him a liver.

The following week, we went to see Dr. Dove. I didn't have a chance to ask her about how to keep Dan's spirits up. She was more concerned about Dan accepting a liver if given the opportunity. "If you get a call, I want you to take it."

"Do you think I'll hear from someone soon?" Dan asked.

"We never know when the right match becomes available." She looked down. "It's based on everyone's MELD score."

Dan's was only at twelve, and I knew that put him near the bottom of the list. "Thank you, Dr. Dove." I turned toward Dan. "Ready?"

"Let's grab a slice of pizza," I said, hoping to turn his frown into a smile.

"I'm not hungry. You get one if you want. I'll wait in the car."

"We'll eat when we get home." I handed my ticket to the valet and took my keys from him. I drove straight home. Dan only said a few words the entire way. I tried to think of things to say, but all I could do was wonder, where do we go from here? What was I supposed to do? Was there something I should be doing? Could be doing for him?

When we got to the farmhouse, I told Dan I was starving. I wasn't. I just wanted to see what he would say.

'I'll make you a steak sandwich," he said, knowing they were my favorite. "Let me call Jesse and see if he wants one." Dan got out of the Explorer adding, "I promised him I would tell him what Dr. Dove had to say."

"Okay, I'll get everything out and ready for you."

When I opened the door, Lady was inside waiting for us. Dan hugged her. A moment later, Jesse walked in. "How the hell did she get down here? I left her in the daycare."

Lady wagged her tail at Jesse.

Amanda hollered in through the kitchen door. "Lady, let's go, baby." She looked in. "Hey, I was taking the girls for a walk, and Lady saw a rabbit and a bunch of deer in your backyard. I didn't want her to chase them, so I put her inside."

Amanda was the absolute best. Not only did she take good care of the babies, she wanted to watch the dogs too. She claimed they kept her company when the babies were taking their naps. Both Delilah and Brin held their hands up for Dan and Jesse to get them. "I'm making steak sandwiches for lunch," he said to Amanda, and she closed the door behind her.

"Yum."

Jesse took Delilah out of the stroller first, then Brin. When they both hugged Dan's legs, I thought, *Children know the exact moment when you need to feel loved.* Once more, my heart was sad for never having children of my own.

# Chapter 47

January rushed out as winter rolled in. Unlike our December bride, January's was the total opposite. The entire inn was covered in red velvet. Teresa stopped me at the front desk. "Look at this," she said, holding up a pair of red velvet high-heels. "Come here." I followed her to the library and saw ten red velvet men's suit jackets hanging on the bookshelves. "Even the table runners are red velvet. She'll be the only person in white."

I smirked at her. "Until the wicked one shows up wearing white, ivory, or cream on purpose." We both laughed and ran out to the front room as we saw a red velvet antique sofa go by the doorway.

"Hi," Teresa said to the men. "Can I help you with that?"

"Over here," a very staunch woman said to the men. "Follow me."

Teresa and I just looked at one another.

"Oh, that must be the wedding coordinator," Teresa said and we both made a scary face.

"I'm leaving before I get into trouble," I said.

"Hey, wait," Christine said to me before I reached the front door. "Kourtnee and I were wondering if you would like to go to a yoga class with us next week.

We're dropping the girls off at Tumbling Tots for a half-hour and—"

"Aw, how cute," I said. "I'd rather stay and watch the girls."

Christine shrugged. "You can do that too."

I made a mental note to see if Jesse could stay with Dan while I went with Kourtnee and Christine. Lord knows I could use a girl's day away right about now. I went down to the farmhouse, opened the door, and heard Dan on his cell phone. "Great. Yes, thank you. I'll let Julie know as soon as she gets home."

I closed the door. "Know what?" I asked.

Dan hugged me. "I'm on the transplant waiting list."

I tried not to show my emotions. I knew from taking the classes that in order to be on the list your liver had to be bad. They factor in everything. Still, it didn't mean he would get a liver right away. "That's good news," I said and hung my coat up.

"I knew the news would make you happy. "

"It's what I've been praying for. Hey, next week, I'm going into town for an hour with Christine and Kourtnee to watch the girls tumble. I'll ask—"

"I'll be fine. Kevin and Robert want to go over to the new farm. I'll have them stop by then."

He was starting to read my mind, and that scared me.

Tuesday morning, I sat in the backseat with the girls listening to Kourtnee and Christine talk about trying not to pass gas during yoga class. I smiled at Delilah and

Brin. "Mommies are being silly. I'm so excited to see you tumble." They clapped their hands. "I see someone found her dress."

Christine turned around to face me. "It was either that or Daddy buy a dozen more."

Kourtnee and Christine dropped the girls off at the door. I wasn't allowed inside until they got the girls settled in. I stood behind the glass. Read the sign: "No waving to the children. No cameras and no flashing lights." Okay, don't distract the kids. I watched as five females moved the girls on the mat like they were ragdolls. I loved how protective Delilah was over Brin. I didn't mean to laugh when she pulled Brin away from the instructor and almost hit her. When they were done, Kourtnee and Christine found me in the parents' waiting room.

"How'd they do?" asked Kourtnee.

"Great," I replied.

"Okay, we have to wait here until they take the girls outside."

Kourtnee looked at me. "You never can be too cautious."

When the dance room was empty, we headed down the hall to leave. As soon as we opened the door, Christine bolted. "STOP!" she screamed as loud as she could. Both Kourtnee and I ran after her. A woman was putting Brin in the backseat of her car. Christine grabbed the woman by her hair and threw her to the ground. She picked up Brin and hugged her. I held my hand out to the woman to help her up.

She pushed my hand away and jumped to her feet. "Give me my daughter."

Kourtnee took hold of her. Telling her, "That's not your daughter. The baby's name is Brin. Now stop."

The woman scanned us with her eyes, reached out, and attempted to take hold of Brin one more time. Several women approached us.

Christine took one look at the woman and said, "Are you crazy?"

When Christine started to walk away, I looked into the girl's eyes. "Wait," I shouted. From behind she was Brin's identical. I held my hands out to the little girl. When she smiled at me, I knew. "Christine, put her down. That's not Brin."

Christine looked at the baby's face, her hair was exactly how Christine had done Brin's that morning and she was wearing a rainbow party dress. The only thing missing was the unicorn headband. "Who?" Christine said to her, and the little girl started to cry.

We saw a security guard, the dance instructors, and Delilah holding Brin's hand.

Christine dropped to her knees. I stood over her. Kourtnee gathered the girls, and the woman picked up her daughter.

"What the hell?" Christine said to the woman. She began to cry before saying, "I'm sorry. Oh, my God, I'm so sorry." She stood up. Looked at the little girl and said, "Honey, I didn't mean to scare you like that. I'm sorry, pumpkin."

The woman was staring at Christine with a desire to kill her. "They do look alike," she said.

Christine met her eyes. "Who's her father?"

"You know as well as I do," she replied, and I thought, *Oh, no.*

Christine clocked her. The woman did a complete circle before falling to the ground.

I told Kourtnee to take the girls to the car. "Now," I said as I grabbed ahold of Christine. "Look at me. Take a deep breath." Before I could take hold of her, she collapsed in my arms.

# Chapter 48

THE RIDE HOME WAS anything but sunny. Christine cried the entire way. I had Kourtnee take Brin home with her, and I got out of the car at Christine's. I was hoping Michael was up at the inn, but he was inside on his cell phone talking to the other woman. Christine turned to face me. "I've got this. You have enough on your plate. Go home and take care of your husband. I'll deal with Michael." She gave me a hug and said, "Go home, Julie."

Michael and Christine's home was less than a ten-minute walk from the farmhouse. I didn't go inside, I sat on the front porch. I knew how she felt. Terrible. I couldn't do anything for her but be there. A moment later, Kevin dropped Dan off. I waved to him and Robert. Dan sat down next to me. "Are you okay?" I shook my head.

"What's the matter?" he asked as he leaned in closer.

I explained everything to him, and he agreed with me. We don't get to take sides. Still, I wanted to slap Michael upside his head. I was disappointed in him. "How? Why?" I asked. "He loves her so much. Why would he do that to her?"

"To them," Dan replied.

He was correct. What Michael did affected not only

himself, but Christine and Brin, too. "They could be twins." I thought for a second. "She dressed her daughter in the same unicorn dress. Was that a coincidence or done on purpose? And her hair, wrapped up in a tight bun." I thought I heard a loud noise in the distance. "Did you hear that?"

Dan stood up and listened. "They'll work it out, but just in case things get out of control, let me call Jesse." He took out his cell phone. "Hey, Michael and Christine are fighting over something. Can you come down here?" Dan closed his phone. "He's on his way."

"I need a glass of water," I said and went inside. I poured two glasses and called Kourtnee to see if she needed help with the girls, but she told me Christine had picked Brin up two minutes ago.

"She left him, Julie. She's not coming back."

I went outside and told Dan. A moment later, Jesse pulled his truck up to the house. Dan and Jesse went to see Michael. I wanted to go, but I thought maybe it would be best for Dan to talk to him. I tried to call Christine, but she wouldn't pick up. I left her a voicemail. "I love you. I'm here for you. Please let me know if you're okay. Christine, I'm sorry this happened to you."

A week went by, and no one heard a word from Christine. Michael was a hot mess. I asked him several times to please call the woman from the culinary, but he refused. "Michael, she was great during the holidays. She's been here enough to know what we expect. Call her so I don't have to worry about you. You need a good sous-chef."

I was sitting in the library remembering all the times Christine told me he was in town, and I had to wonder if he truly did love her the way he said. So many times, I thought he was buying fish, when really he was seeing that woman. I was sick to my stomach. My cell phone rang. It was Christine. "Hi, honey."

"Hey, I'm down at the pond—"

"I'm on my way," I said and ran out the door.

Brin was sitting in one of the Adirondack chairs. I could barely see her. Only her feet were hanging off. As soon as she saw me, she climbed down and gave me a hug. I picked her up and held her as if she were mine. "Are you being a good girl for your mother?"

She kissed my lips.

"She loves kisses," Christine said as she sat down.

I sat down in the other chair with Brin on my lap. "Are you okay?"

"I can't stay with Michael. Every time I look at him, I'll see his baby-momma, his—" she caught herself, "child. I'm only here now because of you. I wanted to tell you myself. I can't work with him. I won't be in the same room as him, let alone a kitchen."

"I understand."

"Do you? Because, I'm far from—"

"Christine, no one more than me knows what you're going through right now. I know exactly how you feel. I respect your decision. I will support you in any way I can. Do you want to know about Michael?"

"No," she said a little louder than she needed to.

"It's okay. Mommy is yelling at the ducks. See the ducks?" I pointed toward the pond. "Do you need money? Where are you staying?" I looked at her. "I would never betray your trust."

"I know you won't," she said and added, "Mary is letting me stay with her for the time being. She's good with the baby, and she makes me rainbow Italian cookies."

"Let's take a walk," I said and stood up. I took hold of Brin's hand and headed toward the old cottage grounds.

"Julie, thank you for everything, for putting up with me during my postpartum depression, and for all my bonuses. Because of you, I'm financially set. I'm not desperate to take the first offer that comes my way."

"You'll let me know where and when you get settled in, right?"

"I will. As soon as I figure it out," she said and flashed me a smile.

"I heard what you did for Robert and Kate."

"That was the last thing we did together. It warms my heart knowing they will have a safe place to live. Michael and I made sure it was a house they could afford. The taxes are low, and—it is affordable."

"Robert will always have a job here at the inn."

She thanked me. "Let me know if anyone has a baby shower for them. I'll send a gift." She kicked the dirt. "This is a shame. I always loved your cottage."

"I did too. Promise me you'll keep me posted and let

me know where you are." I reached out and touched her arm. "We're family, Christine. I love you with all my heart."

"We love you, too. Right, Brin?"

I sat with Brin watching her play with her toy. Knowing Christine and Brin would not be living at the inn any longer brought tears to my eyes. As much as I tried not to get too close to the children, I knew my heart would miss Brin. I received a text from Dan telling me he would be there to pick me up in five minutes. I said goodbye to Christine and Brin. Sat in the backseat and cried.

# Chapter 49

VALENTINE'S DAY WAS IN three days. The entire inn overflowed with sweet messages. Someone had bowls filled with heart candies declaring love, happiness, and other cute sentiments. On the lobby table sat small bottles of champagne in ice buckets for the taking, and flowers were in every room. This year's theme—red, pink, and ivory. I went into the library and laughed. On a tray sat square dishes filled with chocolates wrapped in red and silver foil, hard candies, and confections in every variety.

I went back out to the reception area and asked Teresa, "Who has the sweet tooth?"

She rolled her eyes. When she started to bite the inside of her mouth, I knew she wasn't pleased. "Michael hired a new sous-chef. She has heart-shaped red-and-white ramekins and for dessert, she's making one item. Mixed berry mini pies with vanilla-bean ice cream." She shook her head. "From the store."

"She's not making the ice cream from scratch?"

"No." Teresa sat behind the desk. "I give up."

"I'll be right back," I said and headed for the kitchen. On the counter sat sixteen desserts that looked delicious. Her crust was light and flaky, sprinkled with coarse sugar. She had blueberries, raspberries, and

a blackberry on top, with vanilla ice cream slowly melting. They looked good to me. But Teresa was correct. If they wanted store-bought ice cream, they would have stayed home.

She scared the hell out of me when she stood up. "Oh, hey. You must be Julie. Michael has told me so much about you. I'm sorry about Dan—"

"Julie," Michael said as he entered the kitchen carrying a crate of lobsters.

I glanced over at the menu board. "Can I have a moment with the two of you, please?"

Michael set the crate in the walk-in cooler. Sat down at the counter. "Everything okay?"

"I'd like to go over the menu for this weekend." I looked at her. She was still standing over by the oven. "I'm sorry, I didn't catch your name."

"Heather."

"Heather, please take a seat." When she sat down, I couldn't help but notice her crystal blue eyes.

After she sat down across from Michael, I asked them, "What are we serving this weekend?"

Michael said, "Duchess potatoes, chicken with spinach in creamy parmesan, red wine short-ribs surrounded by mashed potatoes and brown gravy, lobsters in herbed butter, and risotto. House salad and balsamic mozzarella with beets and crumbled blue cheese on a lettuce wedge. Oh, and lobster rolls for lunch."

"Sounds delicious. And what are we serving for dessert?" I asked.

Michael looked at Heather and back at me. "Julie, I'm trying. What do you want from me?"

My heart sank. I tapped his hand. I looked at her. "Heather, the pies look wonderful, but the ice cream is unacceptable."

"Michael told me you would be upset. We ordered the heavy cream, if it's not here by this afternoon, I'll go into town and buy it myself," she said sounding upset.

"Julie, I called Munroe Dairy. They'll have it on today's truck. I promise."

"Julie, wait," Heather said as I went to leave. "I promise you, I'll make everything from scratch, even if I have to change the menu."

"Thank you."

I stood in the hallway. He looked terrible. Dan told me Michael was devastated by what he had done, not only to his own family, but to the other woman as well. I didn't know the whole story and honestly, I didn't have the time or desire to know. I just wanted to make sure my guests were taken care of in the manner they expected. I went by Kourtnee's office and overheard her and Sherry talking about giving Kate and Robert a Jack and Jill baby shower, and I thought it sounded like a great idea. "We'll talk to Julie first, but March works for the inn. We can have it on a Sunday afternoon after the wedding guests have all gone for the day," Kourtnee said.

I didn't go inside or say anything. I was too upset. When I approached the lobby, I heard Dan and Jesse asking Teresa where I was.

"She's in the kitchen with Michael," Teresa told them.

"Jesse, get out of that candy dish," I said to him.

"I made reservations for us at Spain of Narragansett for tonight," Dan said, and I saw Teresa's head pop up.

"Tonight?" I asked.

"Yeah, it won't be too crowded," Dan said. "Jesse and Sherry are coming."

I am not sure what Frank said to Dan that day out on the back porch, but he seemed much happier this past month. In the past, it had always been Dan and me on Valentine's Day. I turned to Teresa. "Would you and Sal like to join us?"

"No, thanks, we were there last night. The food is so good. You're going to love it. Gosh, do all men think alike?" She laughed. "Sal said we were going early to beat the crowd too."

"Okay, I wonder if anyone else wants to go," I said. "Let me check with the others, I wouldn't want to leave anyone out."

Teresa waved at me. "Kevin's taking Kourtnee to 1230 Ocean Bistro tonight." She shrugged. "I made the reservations for him. They're going with Cathy and Steve. They asked us, but we already celebrated."

Jesse tugged at my elbow. "Umm, I wanted it to be just the four of us."

I looked up at him. "So, no Gina Marie and

Michelle?"

"No," he replied.

Teresa smiled. "Umm, they have plans too. Michelle is taking Gina Marie to New York to see *A Streetcar Named Desire*." She cocked her head adding, "They're going for three days. Oh, and Frank is having dinner every night this week with a different woman."

"Now, that I knew." I looked at Jesse and Dan. "Okay, I guess it's just the four of us. Wait—"

"No," they both shouted.

We stepped outside and heard a tractor running. "The farmer is tilling the soil for this year's crops," Dan said. "He'll do it again in the spring right before he plants the corn."

"Why does he do it twice?" I asked as we stepped outside.

"He's putting down lime to kill any weeds," Dan replied.

Dan and I went down to the farmhouse. "You didn't even notice," he said to me.

I stopped walking. "What? Oh, my. I love it." Someone had put road signs in the ground at the beginning of every road. Ours said Holliday Lane with an anchor. Underneath were the words Private Road. "I want to see all of them," I said.

"Come on, I knew you would." We got in the Polaris and drove down every road. The corner sign leading to Kevin, Kourtnee, Michael, and Christine's was Rhody Road also displaying an anchor and the words Private

Road. That sign reminded me of the magazine. Then Dan showed me a new road leading to Gina Marie's house.

"Canvas Drive," I said.

"We had to get them approved by the town. I had one put down at the cottage too, just in case you ever decide to build again. That one says Cottage Circle, because it's a circular driveway. Christine named her road," he said and looked at me before adding, "She said they were all Rhody's now, including Michael."

"They're perfect, I replied.

# Chapter 50

"ARE YOU READY?" DAN asked, standing next to the entryway. "Wow, you look gorgeous." He held the door open for me. We drove my Explorer and picked Jesse and Sherry up at their house. She looked beautiful. Her hair was curled, and she had lipstick on. Jesse was as dapper as usual.

"I'm excited about this restaurant," I said. "I've never been there before."

The restaurant was spectacular. Elegant with a rustic feel. We sat in the corner near a window. "I like the way they wrapped the beam with white lights," Sherry said, and I agreed.

"They give the room a soft touch." Sherry picked up her glass of water, and I noticed she had nail polish on. "Wow, you painted your nails."

"Teresa took me to the salon, and Cathy did them for me." She moved a curl to the front and added, "She did my hair too. Teresa said it was a fancy restaurant."

The server came to the table, handed us each a menu, lit the glass oil burner, and asked if anyone would like a cocktail. Jesse ordered a bottle of wine. "Blumond Blue Bubbly."

"Nice choice," the server said. "It has a sweet,

refreshing, light flavor. I'll be right back."

Dan opened his menu and said, "Look at the Paella Marinara. Anyone else want to share the calamari?"

"I don't know yet. Let me read the menu first," I said. "Oh, wait. They have rack of lamb." As soon as I told Dan about the lamb, I knew he would ask me to get the paella.

"How about," he paused. "You want the salmon, huh?"

"Yep." I closed my menu. "But I'll order the calamari for everyone to share."

Sherry asked Jesse what he was having. "I'm getting the baked stuffed lobster," she told him.

Jesse nodded. "Mmm, I guess I'll have the New York sirloin." He picked the menu back up. "Let's get the clams in the garlic sauce too."

Everyone agreed. I read the menu and didn't find Jesse's wine on the list anywhere.

The server brought the bottle and poured each of us a sampling. Dan put his hand out for the man to stop pouring after the first splash. He held his hand over his heart. "Bad for my ticker."

"Sorry," the gentleman said and set the bottle down in the ice bucket.

Jesse picked his glass up and toasted to friendship. We banged glasses. "Here's to you, and you." He leaned over and kissed Sherry on the lips. "And here's to you."

She blushed. "This is my favorite wine." She looked at Dan. "You don't have to drink it, it's okay." She went to take a sip but stopped.

I looked at her. We all did. She started to cry. Jesse got down on one knee and said, "Sherry, will you spend the rest of your life with me?"

First, I looked at Dan. When she set her glass down, I saw it. Sparkling white-gold band and what looked like a two-carat Tiffany-setting ring. I started to cry.

Sherry leaned forward and hugged Jesse before looking him in the eyes and saying, "Yes."

Dan had tears in his eyes. I kissed his cheek. Our server came back to the table, and Jesse gave him a high-five. "Good work, I can't thank you enough."

Apparently, he was in on the whole episode. "Did you know anything about this?" I asked Dan.

Dan rested his chin on his hand. "Maybe."

Jesse sat back down as the server poured Sherry's wine into an empty glass. He wiped the ring dry and handed it to Jesse. Jesse slipped it on her finger, and her eyes filled up again.

Laughingly, she cried, "I love you so much. I promise to always be here for you."

He kissed her and told her he would take care of her and give her whatever she wanted. He waggled his eyebrows at her, and she blushed again.

"Okay, is everyone ready to order?"

"Sure," Jesse said. "Dan, why don't you start?"

We placed our orders, and the server told us he would be right back with the appetizers. I held my hand out to Sherry. "Let me see. I'm so happy for you."

She put her hand in mine, and my heart turned a page. "Oh, Jesse."

"Don't start crying," he said, adding, "We've had enough of that tonight." Then he pointed at Dan. "Will you be my best man?"

Dan couldn't speak. Tears were running down his face. He nodded. Sherry and I were fine until Jesse got up and hugged him.

"I have to use the ladies' room." Sherry and I both got up. We looked back and saw the men still holding each other. "They've always been close," I told her.

We returned to the table just in time, our food was waiting for us. Dan and Jesse had a sampling on their plates. I held the calamari up for Sherry to take what she wanted.

Jesse took a bite, swallowed, and said, "Remind me to thank Teresa. She was the mastermind behind the whole thing."

"What do you mean?" Sherry said and then asked, "Did she really come here last night?"

Jesse laughed out loud. "Yeah, and I paid for it." He winked at Sherry. "She brought the ring and the wine in for me and gave it to Trevor." Jesse pointed toward our server. "It was Teresa's idea for you to get your nails done. She said, 'every woman will wish she had her nails polished.' Yes, your hair looks good too."

Sherry kissed him. "You make me so happy." She leaned back. "Wow, the garlic is strong."

"Good. Sleep at the inn," he teased. "Nah, you can go

in your craft room."

"Like hell I will," she said teasingly.

Dan shook his head. "They sound like a married couple."

I glanced over at Dan. He had something to look forward to. I hoped Jesse would get married at the inn, but wherever they chose would be fine too. "Any ideas as to where and when?"

Sherry smiled. "We want to get married on the beach and have our reception at the inn. If that's okay with you?"

"Hey, I was kidding when I said that." He rubbed her back. "I'm joking. Whatever you want."

Dan tapped my hand. "He's going to make a great husband."

I nodded, looked over at Jesse. "Whatever makes the two of you happy." *The playboy found someone he loved more than any other person in the world.* Jesse is getting married. Our food had arrived, and everything was amazing.

"This tastes like heaven," Dan said.

"Not yet, old man." And we all laughed.

# Chapter 51

I DROVE HOME FROM the restaurant listening to Jesse and Sherry talk about their intimate wedding on the beach and how they wanted it to be romantic. "We want to surround ourselves with everyone we love, so they can share the best day of—"

"Your life," Jesse said to her.

I heard her slap him. "And yours."

Dan looked back. "That would be the day he saw you in the window at Deborah's shop."

I pulled into their driveway, stopped the vehicle, and told them congratulations. "We love you both so much."

"Yes," Dan echoed my sentiments. "Hey, don't forget we're going to see Frank tomorrow morning for coffee."

"I'll pick you up right after I drop her off for work," Jesse replied.

After they got out, I asked Dan, "Why wasn't I invited for coffee?"

"He invited me and Jesse. Ask him. Let's go. I have to use the bathroom."

I drove as quickly as I could to the farmhouse, parked in the garage, and told Dan he had to take his medicine too. "Monday, we have to start your weekly blood work at Quest Labs."

"Yeah, I'm not looking forward to that," he said and went inside.

I sat in the family room and read a text message that I had gotten earlier from Christine. When Dan came out and sat down next to me, I asked him, "When you go see Frank tomorrow, can you drop me off at Mary's Bakery and pick me up afterward?"

"Sure, are you thinking about buying your desserts from her?"

"No, I'm meeting Christine there. She needs to talk to me about something. What time so I can let her know?"

"Eight," Dan replied, and I texted her back.

We watched a movie for about twenty minutes before we both started to fall asleep.

Dan was in the bedroom taking his lounge pants off when I asked him, "How do you feel?" I tossed the throw pillows onto the chair next to the window and turned back around, waiting for him to answer me.

"Except for feeling bored, I would never have known anything was wrong with my liver."

Dan is exactly like me. He has to have something to do. In New York, if he wasn't working, he was hunting, riding in his car, or on his motorcycle. "Let's get the Cobra back on the road," I said.

He climbed into bed, covered himself, and shrugged. "Not now," he said, and I thought, *Don't talk to me now or don't put the car on the road now?*

He kissed me good night. "I don't want to drive the car. What if I have an attack? Let's stick to walking on the beach."

He was right. I felt bad for suggesting it.

"I drive as far as Jesse's, and that's it. I only drove to the restaurant because you and Jesse were in the car with me."

"I'm sorry. That was very insensitive of me." I said my prayer aloud, "Dear Heavenly Father, I ask you Lord to please bless Dan with a new liver. Watch over him, place your healing hands upon him. Thank you. Amen."

Dan reached for my hand and squeezed it.

The next morning, we walked up to the inn and had coffee with Teresa, Gina Marie, and Kourtnee. When Sherry came inside, Dan and I left. I didn't tell anyone where I was going, I just said I would see them in a little while.

Jesse dropped me off at the bakery, and I was happy to see Brin was there too. "Where's Mary?" I asked as I kissed Brin on the top of her head. She was sitting in a high chair eating apple slices.

"She went to the wholesaler. She'll be back later. Coffee?"

"Please," I replied and sat down next to Brin.

Christine came over and handed me my cup. "I've decided to stay in Point Judith. This is my home. I was born and raised here. Why should I go?"

"You shouldn't," I said and sipped my coffee.

She flashed me her big smile. No red lipstick, but still.

"I bought the bakery from Mary. She said she's ready to retire."

I got up and hugged her.

"I'm going to be open from eight a.m. to three p.m. only, so I can close and prepare my soups and muffins."

I looked at her waiting, knowing there was more.

"From four to seven every evening, Brin and I are going to open our back door and feed the homeless." She raised her eyebrows. "I'm not opening until eight so I can make your desserts for the inn every morning." She pointed her finger at me. "He's not to call me or pick up. In fact, my driver will deliver to your inn."

"Sounds good. Thank you."

"Yeah, well. It will keep me busy, and my mind off him. I filed for divorce. So if you hear slamming and banging in your kitchen, it's my fault. He can have shared custody of Brin. Julie, I just can't be near him."

I reached over and put her hand in my own.

She shook her head. "Michael was my world. When he walked in here and ate every damn one of my samples, I couldn't take my eyes off him. I knew that day I would marry him. When he sent you in here to offer me a job, from that moment on, I couldn't imagine my life with anyone else." She made a fist. "When I was sick, he told me he would give me my space. He said, 'I'll come back to you when you're better.'"

She drank her coffee, and we both knew what Michael was telling her that day. "Can you imagine? The nerve of him. While I was battling depression, he was getting a piece of ass."

I shook my head.

She handed me a piece of paper. "Every week, I'll

have a list of items for you to choose from."

I looked at her list. "You send me whatever you want. By now, you know what I'm looking for. As long as my guests are happy, I'm good. I'm glad you're staying in Point Judith."

"Oh, Julie. I'm so sorry." She got up, took several pastries out of the showcase, and set them down on our table. "How's Dan?"

"He's anxious to get a new liver. It's not easy watching him."

"I know how much you love him. We all do. I pray for him every night," she said. "I'm sorry that I'm not his blood type."

# Chapter 52

March rolled in, bringing us warmer weather and Dan a new attitude. It seemed like everything bothered him. I had never seen him that way before. Yelling at me, biting my head off. "I can do it myself." or "Just let me do it." No matter how I tried to help him, he refused, telling me he could do it by himself. I knew it wasn't him. He was scared, but so was I. If I asked him how he was feeling, he would snap and tell me, "I'm fine." In reality, we both knew the silent killer—cirrhosis of the liver—was a ticking bomb, and it was inside his body. Not mine. I attended every class the hospital offered, made notes, blogged about it, wrote a letter to AARP magazine, and posted on my Facebook page. The only place I didn't talk about it was at work, until now.

I went up to the inn to go over the spring calendar with my staff. I decided to only meet with those on payroll. No need for Jesse or Dan to attend. On my way up, I stopped along the driveway to take a look at the orchard. The star magnolias were in bloom, shades of white, pink, and fuchsia. My favorite will always be the cherry trees with their delicate blossoms. I still prefer the buds over the flower.

"Hey," Gina Marie said as I stepped up onto the front

porch. "Good morning."

"Good morning, how are you this morning?"

She got up and followed me inside. "I'm good. I met Michelle's sons last week."

"Michelle has children?"

"Yes, and she has two granddaughters. Oh, my goodness, they are so cute. They live in New York. Her other son lives in South Carolina. He flew all the way up just to meet me."

"Getting serious," I said and asked Teresa if everyone was in the kitchen yet.

"We just have to knock on Kourtnee's door and get her and Sherry," she replied.

Teresa told Kourtnee that I was ready to get started. When Gina Marie and I entered the kitchen, Michael was holding his head in his hands, leaning on the counter. Kevin was rubbing his back and trying to console him. I cleared my throat. They both looked up at me and saw everyone coming into the room. Kevin opened the side door and let Robert, Amanda, and Cathy in. A moment later, Teresa entered, followed by Sherry and Kourtnee.

"It's so nice outside," Cathy said.

On the counter sat a tray of fresh-baked muffins, pastries, croissants, and strawberry cream cheese, and I knew Christine had sent it in early for the meeting.

Amanda put her hands on my shoulders. "Good morning, I told Jessica I would fill her in after the meeting. She's watching the babies and the doggies." She winked at me. "Brin is in the daycare if you want to stop by and see her."

Kevin came over and told me Michael saw Christine drop Brin off, and he fell apart. "Maybe you should let him take the day off or something."

I went over to Michael and asked if he would like to go see his daughter. "Why don't you go and spend some time with her?"

"After the meeting," he replied to me and sat down. Gina Marie put her hands on his shoulders. "You okay, Bud?"

He patted her hand and groaned. "I miss my wife."

"Give her some time," Gina Marie told him.

"Good morning, everyone. Grab your coffee, tea, whatever, and let's get started." I took a cup of black coffee from Kourtnee and thanked her. I sat down next to Gina Marie and started the meeting. "First up, we have our annual garden tour this month. We also have a wedding down by the pond, and at the end of the month, we are booked solid with visitors for the annual food truck on the beach event. I have the menu for the season, but I don't have the flower list or the finances yet."

Sherry got up and ran to the office. When she came back, she said, "Sorry." And sat back down.

Kourtnee handed the folder to me and added, "I only have one proposal for this year. To buy more flameless candles for all of our events."

Michael shook his head. "I don't need anything. I'm all set."

Gina Marie asked him if the kitchen needed anything.

"How about kitchen supplies? This year's seafood budget? Did prices stay the same?"

He dropped his head. "I'll take a look and get back to you by this afternoon."

"Oh, Michael," Gina Marie said softly, and she told him she'd add five percent to his food budget just in case. "Don't worry about it. Hey, we're family. We understand. Breathe."

I looked around at everyone sitting at the table and thought, *Now.*

Teresa handed a piece of paper to Gina Marie. "Sherry and I were thinking about making our own signature line of cards. We could start with two hundred dollars and see how it goes."

"We can sell them to our guests," Sherry said, adding, "We want to make postcards, recipe cards, and note cards too."

"Mostly nautical and of our gardens," Teresa said as she bit the inside of her mouth.

I liked the idea. I looked at Gina Marie. "A thousand dollars is fine by me."

I saw Teresa and Sherry both smile.

"I'm sorry I'm late," Deborah said as she entered the kitchen. "I overslept. We were up all night picking out new furniture for the house."

Everyone laughed. Deborah was always late, and she was forever working on something new. "Grab some coffee," I told her.

I waited for Deborah to sit down. "I have tried

everything to find Dan a donor."

Michael shook his head.

"I have to ask. By any chance, are any of you A positive?"

"I'm O positive," Michael said. "But I can't donate because I have type 2 diabetes."

"I'm sorry. I should have known."

He gave me a wry grin.

Kevin said they went to the clinic and got tested last month, but neither one of them was compatible.

Sherry raised her hand. "Jesse and I both tried too."

"I swear you are the best of the best." I felt depleted. I could have cried. "Thank you for trying. It means everything to me."

After the meeting, Michael went over to the daycare to spend time with Brin. I started to go back to the farmhouse, but I instead went to the rose garden. I opened the gate and sat on the bench. I felt lost, like there was nothing I could do. I spent the rest of the week asking everyone I bumped into if they were type A.

My UPS driver pulled up to the farmhouse, knocked on the door, and before he could set my package down, I opened the door and asked him if he was type A. "By any chance, is your blood type A positive?"

"I don't know what my blood type is, to be honest with you."

I picked the box up, went inside, sat down, and cried.

# Chapter 53

EASTER SUNDAY, WE HELD an egg hunt on the front lawn for all the children. The bride had three boys, and the groom had two daughters. Christine's desserts arrived on time every day, and the more decadent they were the more in demand they became. The chocolate bunnies filled with raspberry cream were everyone's favorite. I loved the Italian Easter pie the best. Sherry and Teresa spent their evenings in Sherry's craft room creating the most beautiful stationery. Kevin and Kourtnee were busy with the new farm stand. Robert and Kate were happy to be in their new home, and in less than a week, Kate would be giving birth to their first child. A boy. Gina Marie kept her promise. She'd been spending most of her afternoons with Dan. From fishing, to flying his drone, to playing video games on Oculus, to getting ready for turkey hunting. I was so grateful for her. Dan always seemed to be a little calmer after visiting with Gina Marie. I laughed when Jesse yelled at her: "Get your own friend. He's mine!"

Gina Marie told him he could tag along, but sitting in a boat and waiting for a fish to jump wasn't how Jesse wanted to spend his afternoons.

I was in the living room dusting when I heard Gina

Marie tell Jesse, "Please stop asking Dan to go riding.

He's not comfortable going down the road on his motorcycle yet."

"I forgot about that. How's he doing?" Jesse asked, and I heard her whisper.

"Shh. I'll talk to you later."

"Jesse, what's up? Does anyone want something to drink?" Dan asked as he opened the screen door.

Gina Marie and Jesse came inside, and I stopped cleaning. "Hi, everyone. What does everyone want to drink?"

"Got any beer?" Jesse asked, and Dan stood up to get him one.

I saw Gina Marie shoot him a look.

"I'll take a soda or whatever you have," Jesse yelled to Dan.

Dan came back and handed him a Corona with a slice of dill pickle in it. "Just because I can't drink, doesn't mean you can't enjoy one."

"That's right," Jesse said and held his bottle up. "Dan, what are you doing on July sixth?"

"Whatever you want," Dan replied.

"Good, because that's the day she wants to get married."

"On a Wednesday?" I asked and set a tray of cheese and crackers down on the coffee table.

"It's the only day in July that Michael had available," he said and grabbed a piece of pepperoni before adding, "We're getting married on the beach and having a barbeque at the pool."

I hugged him. "I'm so happy for you."

Dan shook his hand. "I'll be there. I promise you."

Jesse drank his entire beer. "I know you'll be there." He pointed to Gina Marie and me. "You, too."

"I wouldn't miss it for the world," Gina Marie told him and went into the kitchen.

I followed her and asked, "How was Dan today?"

She sat down at the counter. "You can tell it bothers him, but he's getting better. Any news on the donors?"

I shook my head. "Seven woman stepped up, but none of them was a match."

"No men?" she asked.

"I thought that was odd too, but women are the ones who know what it feels like to give life to another person."

"Where would the world be without strong women?"

I opened my laptop and logged onto Facebook. "I have a message from a Malichi McGhee." I looked at her. "He said he saw my post and wanted to help." My eyes started to fill up. "He's O positive, and that makes him a universal donor."

Gina Marie got up and stood over me. "Oh, my God, he already called the hospital and went for blood work." Gina Marie read aloud: "Mrs. Holliday, I'm trying. I'll keep you posted and let you know as soon as I hear back from my team."

I grabbed my heart. "They assign teams. Dan has one, and the donor always has their own. Oh, Gina Marie. He could be the one." We both started to cry. I wiped my eyes and closed the laptop. "Should we tell him?"

"I don't know. Maybe we shouldn't get his hopes up," she said, and I agreed.

"Yeah, he has Jesse's wedding to keep his mind busy." I sat down, as did Gina Marie. "When Malichi's blood work gets approved, then we'll tell Dan."

"And Jesse," she said. "He's a bigger pain in the ass than Dan. How long have they been friends?"

"More like brothers. At least thirty years. Jesse's known Dan longer than me."

"You talking about me again?"

We turned around and saw Dan and Jesse standing in the doorway. Dan winked at me. "Would you like to take a stroll down the beach?"

Gina Marie stood up and said, "I'll catch you later. I have a friend request to send out."

"See you tomorrow morning," Dan told her.

"Dan's therapist said we could say our vows in front of his place," Jesse said to me. "I want to take Sherry there so she can get an idea of how she wants to set everything up, and I thought you might like to tag along."

"I would love to," I said and stood up.

Because Jesse had had a beer and only a few crackers, I drove my Explorer to pick Sherry up at the inn. "I'll run in and get her, I want to say hi to Teresa and see how things are going," I said and got out. I felt guilty for not giving all my attention to my guests. When I stepped inside, Teresa and Sherry were setting up a small table in the lobby.

Teresa turned around. "Look what we created," she said, beaming with pride.

I picked up a box set of note cards and envelopes. "Ten dollars for ten. That's inexpensive."

"Too cheap?" Teresa asked.

"Not at all. I want to buy this one." I held the box to my chest. Aww, you put a blue anchor on the card."

"Oh, but—" Sherry started to say something, but Teresa stopped her.

"We'll put it on your account," Teresa said to me.

"Thank you," I replied and told Sherry the men were out in the car waiting to take her to the beach.

Sherry got in the backseat with Jesse and told me, "Only two cards have anchors, the others are different. They're in pairs of two: anchor, sailboat, whale, lighthouse, and a ship's wheel. If you want, we can make you a set of just anchors."

I stopped at the end of the driveway, turned around, and asked her, "Am I your first customer?"

"Yes."

"No givebacks." I pulled out onto the main road and headed for the parking lot near Dan's therapist.

We arrived, and Sherry stood there in awe. I looked back and saw Dr. Eastwood reading on his back deck. When he looked up, I waved to him. He put his book down and came over to us. Dan shook his hand and introduced us to him.

"It's my pleasure," he told Jesse and Sherry. "I'm sorry

my home isn't big enough to throw a party in."

"This is great," Sherry told him.

"Thanks again," Jesse said and shook his hand one more time.

Dr. Eastwood rubbed his chin, looked over his glasses, and told Dan, "She's everything you said."

Dan grinned. "Thank you. I'll see you next week."

Jesse picked Sherry up and swung her around in a full circle. She kissed him. "I love, love, love you."

# Chapter 54

THERE WERE OVER THREE HUNDRED people at Friday's wedding. On Saturday, the bride and groom asked if they could stay past eleven o'clock on Sunday to use the pool, but we had to say no considering it was Mother's Day and we were booked solid. Every table in the dining room, out on the terrace, and on the porches was reserved. Michael's crew worked flawlessly, and he seemed to be handling life a little better these days. He usually saw Brin Sunday afternoons till Tuesday evening; however, because of the holiday, they agreed Christine could keep her home until Monday evening. I had no idea Kourtnee was their liaison.

Outside, the sun was shining, the flowers were blooming, and my gardens were overflowing with new flowers that I had never seen before. I loved the way Kourtnee had tagged all the flower beds. I walked down the path past March, April, and May to discover June's ranunculus, dailies, coneflowers, and black-eyed Susan were way ahead of schedule. Even the alliums had begun to open earlier than usual.

I waved to Teresa as she spoke to a guest on the phone about a reservation for next summer. She flashed me a smile and gave me a thumbs up. Standing outside

Kourtnee and Sherry's office, I overheard Sherry ask Kourtnee, "How long do you think Dan can live with only twenty-five percent of his liver functioning?"

At first, I wasn't going to go in, but then I heard Kourtnee tell her, "I Googled it too. He'll be fine. Don't worry, your wedding gives him something to look forward to. Hopefully, he's thinking about the two of you and not how long he has to live." I heard a drawer close. "We have to stay positive for both of them."

"You're right, but I'm worried about Jesse. The other day, I asked him if he wanted to invite Julie and Dan over for dinner, and he said it's hard for him to see Dan sick."

I tapped on the door. Kourtnee's face was red. Sherry jumped to her feet. I sat down in the chair between their desks. "My husband will receive a new liver. He'll stand next to his best friend on July 6th, and, yes, staying positive is the only attitude acceptable around here." I patted the seat next to me for Sherry to sit down. "Dan and Jesse have been best friends for a long time. If Jesse's heart hurts knowing Dan needs a new liver, it's okay. He can feel sad." I laughed. "You know you're marrying a big old teddy bear, right?"

She nodded. "I'm sorry, I didn't mean to sound selfish. I'm worried like everyone else."

I thought about what she said and knew how hard it must've been for her to watch Jesse knowing there wasn't anything either one of them could do. "I want you to focus on your wedding, your guests, and your honeymoon."

She shook her head. "Jesse won't leave." She looked at me. "And neither will I. We'll take our honeymoon when Dan is better."

I looked over at Kourtnee, who had tears in her eyes. "Julie, we love Dan."

The door opened, and Dan entered holding a stack of mail, small packages, and a new box of flameless candles. All three of us stood up to help. "Thanks, Dan," Kourtnee said, taking the box from him. "You just made my day."

Sherry took the mail from him, and I grabbed the packages. "I'm hungry. Let's go to George's for lunch." I looked at him. "Please."

"Let's go." I followed him outside.

Once we were in the car, I asked him if he wanted to go to dinner up at the inn. "How do you feel about having dinner out on the terrace tonight?"

He laughed. "Is that all you have on your mind today, food?"

"Michael's serving rack of lamb."

"His lamb is the best I've ever eaten. Hell, yeah," Dan replied.

"Good, we'll just share a few appetizers for lunch and save our calories for dinner, because I'm dying to try his new lemon-roasted salmon with escarole." A few minutes later, I pulled up to George's and saw the parking lot was full. "Let's go to Aunt Carrie's and sit outside." Dan agreed, and I drove as slow as I could down Ocean Road. I wanted to be away from the house, inn, and everyone. I wanted Dan to breathe the fresh ocean air, smell the salt water, and get a taste of beautiful Rhode Island. I didn't want him overhearing anyone doubting his prognosis. Maybe, I took the drive for myself too. No, I was pretty sure I wanted to take Dan away, to make his day as bright as God's plan.

As soon as I pulled up to Aunt Carrie's Restaurant, I saw four empty Adirondack chairs down by the water. "I'll grab us a seat if you get lunch," I told him. "I'll eat whatever you want."

Dan went inside and came out holding a red tray with two baskets filled with coconut shrimp, fried clams, and an order of onion rings. I took a basket from him. "I thought we were eating light? Where are our drinks?"

Dan popped an onion ring in his mouth, pointed behind himself with his thumb, and a young man set our iced teas on the arm of my chair. "Thank you," I said as he walked away.

Dan sat down and said, "Living here is like being on vacation every day of your life."

I smiled warmly at him. "Thank you for saying that. You have no idea how much that means to me. I want every day of your life to matter, to feel special, and to be exactly what you hoped for."

He reached over, took my hand in his, kissed my palm, and said, "I hope to spend the rest of my life with you by my side, right here."

We ate our lunch, took a walk, and smelled the salt air among the fried food billowing from Aunt Carrie's rooftop. "Ahh," Dan said. "I'm full. Let's walk for a while longer."

Hand in hand, we walked down the shore. Laughing about Delilah calling him Poppa. Lady falling in love with Jesse's puppy, and about Jesse finding true love. "I wonder if they'll start a family right away," he asked. "I'm not sure how Sherry feels, but Jesse would have a baker's dozen if it were up to him. He's great with the girls."

"Yeah, and he was good with Kyle too," he said.

"I hear the wedding plans are coming along great. Everyone is staying at the inn Tuesday and Wednesday nights. Gina Marie told me she heard them arguing over a traditional wedding cake or large cupcakes."

"Let me guess who wanted the cake. Sherry?"

"Huh, no." I laughed. "Jesse. Sherry won. Christine's making vanilla cupcakes filled with chocolate custard and whipped cream frosting. By the way, we have to go shopping. We're supposed to wear ivory, white, and tan."

"Yeah, Jesse told me to wear khaki shorts and a white button-down shirt."

"What's he wearing?" I asked when I heard shorts. "He told me he's wearing the same."

"We'll go to Crosswynds Traders on Monday, I'm sure I can find something for both of us there."

As soon as we arrived home, Dan took a nap. I went into my study to see if I had any messages. Malichi had sent me an email. He went to New York City and met with his entire team. He had an MRI, a CAT scan, and a stress test performed. Everything was looking good, according to his team coordinator. I thanked God when I read, "I should know by next week if I'm approved. By the way, the psychiatrist was impressed by me."

# Chapter 55

MONDAY MORNING, I TOOK Dan shopping for a new pair of tan Dockers shorts and the perfect ivory cotton button-down. I chose a tan gauze dress with a hint of lace on the bodice and shoulders. "I need new shoes," I declared as Dan went to go out the door.

"Seriously?" he asked, and I followed him.

We walked about one hundred feet and found a little sidewalk sale going on. I picked up a pair of tan wedges with an ankle strap that matched my dress perfectly. I held them up. "Done."

"Good. Let's go home," he said.

I paid for my shoes and drove home. I wanted to tell Dan about the man from New York, but I thought otherwise. Until he asked me, "Were any of those women a match?"

I inhaled deeply before replying. "No, but a young man saw my plea on Facebook, and he—he's very close to becoming your donor."

"Really?" Dan said, sounding more excited than I had heard in a very long time.

"Yes, he's already had his blood drawn, he traveled all the way to the city for testing, and he's just waiting to hear back from his team. Dan, Malichi feels good about everything."

"Is he A positive?"

"He's O positive," I replied and pulled into our driveway.

"That means he can only give me a part of his liver."

"Yes, but as you know, it will grow to full size within twelve weeks. Dan, this is good news."

"We'll see," he said and got out of the car.

I refused to let his doubt stop me from believing in this donor.

Dan went into the family room and took a nap while I hung my dress up. A half-hour later, Jesse and Sherry stopped by. I was standing in the kitchen and saw Dan sit up quickly when he heard their voices. "Where the hell are you?" Jesse hollered.

Dan rubbed his face. "Right here."

Jesse sat down next to him. "Women stuff," he said and then asked Dan how he was feeling.

"Good, we just got back from buying our clothes for the wedding," Dan told him.

Sherry set her box on the counter and sat down. "Would you like something to drink?" I asked loudly enough for the men to hear me.

Dan and Jesse came into the kitchen. "Iced tea is fine," Sherry said, and they too agreed.

"We wanted to say thank you for letting everyone stay at the inn and for hosting the barbeque both nights." Sherry opened her box and showed us her guest list. "We want it to be as unceremonious as possible. In fact, I wrote casual attire, and bring your bathing suits on the invitations."

"Yeah, I want everyone to relax and have fun," Jesse said.

I set our drinks down and asked, "Is there anything we can do to help?"

"Nope, just be there and have a good time," she said.

"We'll be there," Dan replied, and Jesse drank from his glass, emptying it entirely.

"Bet your ass you will," Jesse said and then asked, "Where are the snacks? I'm hungry. What's for lunch?"

"Hang on," I said and started taking food out of the refrigerator. I created a charcuterie board for everyone to enjoy. After we ate, Dan challenged Jesse to a game of pool.

We were tippy-toeing around Dan, and he could feel it. Normally, Jesse would be busting his ass or teasing him about something. By now, we would have been riding our motorcycles. Dan took his shot and missed. No one said a word. Then I remembered he needed to take his medicine. I handed my stick to Sherry, went into the kitchen, came back, and told Dan to drink.

After Dan took his medicine, Jesse suggested we sit out on the back porch. Sherry made a pitcher of lemonade, and I put pistachio biscotti on a plate. Just as we both sat down next to the guys, we heard Gina Marie call out for Dan.

"I'm out here," he told her.

She had a glass of lemonade in her hand. Before sitting down, she took hold of a cookie. "Why is it every time I see you, there's food?" she said to Jesse. "Dan, we're still going tomorrow, right?"

"Yes, four o'clock," he replied.

Jesse snapped his neck to ask, "Where the hell are the two of you going? Oh, count me out."

Sherry looked over at me and pursed her lips. "Turkey hunting," I told her.

"Oh, Michelle wanted me to tell you thanks for the invitation to your wedding," Gina Marie said to her.

"We're both looking forward to it. We even have our outfits."

"Oh, let me show you what I'm wearing," I said and stood up.

Sherry, Gina Marie, and I went into my bedroom. They sat down in the two chairs, while I showed them my dress.

"I love it," Sherry said to me, and Gina Marie agreed. "Mine is layered with lace. It's short with a halter top."

"Sexy," I said and sat down on the edge of the bed.

Gina Marie gave me a look. I inhaled, got up, and shut the door. "I heard from Malichi. He's not a match. His liver isn't big enough. Everything else was frigging perfect."

Sherry gasped.

"It's okay," I said. Then I remembered. "I told Dan about Malichi." I started to cry, as did Gina Marie. "I wish I didn't give him that hope. What the hell am I going to do now?"

"We'll find someone," Gina Marie said, and Sherry agreed with her.

"Yes, we'll all ask our family members and friends to look into it," Sherry said as she reached for a tissue.

I have no idea why I started laughing and crying at the same time, but I did. "I asked the UPS driver if he was A positive. I even asked Delilah the other day."

"I honestly thought Malichi was going to be the person. He sounded so upbeat and positive when he told me about all the tests coming back. His MRI, CAT scan, everything came back great. Except for the size of his liver. Seventy-two and twenty-eight." Gina Marie was sobbing. "They won't do it."

"What does that mean?" Sherry asked. "I'm sorry, I don't understand."

I explained to her as best I could. "Our liver has two parts. Dan needs sixty percent of a living donor's liver. A liver can be sixty/forty, or seventy/thirty to be a good match. In order for you to give Dan what he needs, you must be left with at least forty percent. If they took sixty percent of Malichi's liver, he would be left with only twenty-eight percent on one of his lobes. Malichi's recovery would be too risky."

Gina Marie stood up, went into the bathroom, and came out crying even harder. "He told me he's ready to accept his fate. That he knows he's going to die from liver disease."

I stood up and hugged her. "He's going to be okay. I have faith."

She leaned back and told me about Michelle's granddaughter, Eva, searching online to see how old a person had to be in order to donate their liver to someone else.

We all needed a tissue.

# Chapter 56

THE FOLLOWING MORNING AT three-thirty sharp, Gina Marie came into the house dressed in full camouflage. "It's not my army gear, but it's close enough. Let's go, Dan."

I laughed. "Remember, no talking, cell phones, or coffee." Then I whispered in her ear, "Thank you so much."

Dan came out of the bathroom. "You made it." He picked up his gun, mask, and hat, kissed me goodbye, and followed Gina Marie out the front door and into the Polaris Ranger.

As soon as the sun came up, I went hiking. I passed Kevin and Kourtnee's place and turned around; I didn't want to go by Michael's and think about Christine not being there.

I was sad Teresa didn't live on the property. I could have used a cup of tea and a few of her hymns at that moment. I decided to run back to the farmhouse. Once inside, I dialed Frank's number. It was only seven o'clock, but I knew he would be up.

"Good morning, young lady," Frank said.

"Good morning. Are you busy right now?"

He laughed, and I knew whatever he *had* planned was

about to change. "I'll be there in twenty minutes." He hung up the phone before I could ask him to meet me at the old cottage site. I jumped in the shower and sat outside waiting for him. My idea was perfect.

Frank pulled up and waved. "Are we staying here or going for a drive?"

"We can sit out here if you'd like, or we can go inside, and I'll make you a cup of coffee."

Frank came up onto the porch and said, "Out here is fine. How is everyone?"

"The inn is busy, thank God. Michael and Christine seem to have things worked out for the time being. Kevin and Kourtnee are excited about their new venture."

"Yes, I was there the day they put up the farm stand and fencing. How's my songbird?"

"Teresa and Sherry have been spending a lot of time together creating their own line of cards. Robert and Kate had a baby boy. Kevin gave him six weeks off to stay home and help with the baby, and I was glad."

"You have the best staff I have ever seen. Almost as good as my own. I'd like to have Once Upon A Child send over another gift. What's the little fella's name?"

"Thomas," I replied.

"How's Dan holding up these days?" he asked.

"He's turkey hunting with Gina Marie, so right now, he's happy. We got word of another donor not being a good match. Frank, my heart is breaking. I can't lose him. We just found each other. Our lives are perfect. Dan is happy. He loves Rhode Island as much as I do."

"Well, let's do something. Can't we take an ad out in the paper, or—"

"I blogged about it, put it on my Facebook page, I've tried everything." I told Frank about Malichi and about Gina Marie's granddaughter. "I need to do something that will keep Dan's mind off his liver. I want to build a new pole barn for Dan to put all his equipment in, but I don't want to tell him."

"I can do that, but don't you think he'll want a say in the design?"

I smiled, got up, and went into my study. When I came back out, I handed Frank the plans for Dan's dream garage.

Frank unrolled it and said, "Where?"

"On the other side of Kevin and Kourtnee's farm stand. Then Kevin and Robert will have access to the equipment too."

"And Dan will think all the noise is coming from the farm."

"My goodness, how great minds think alike." I laughed. "Do you own a pair of khaki pants? We could go shopping if you'd like."

"Jan was very happy to take me shopping the other day."

"Why, Frank, I do believe you are blushing."

He shook his head. "You're the only person who can tell when a Black man is embarrassed. I have no secrets from you. I saw Cathy and Steve the other day down at the bookstore. He's a tall fella. They make a good couple.

She was telling me about Amanda's wedding plans."

"Weddings and babies. They can have it," I said laughingly. "Between the inn, garden tours, author events, and Dan, my hands are full."

"I have a thought I'd like to run by you."

"Yes," I replied and sat back in my chair.

"I played a round of golf with Judge Abrams the other day, and he asked me about you. Wanted to know if you would consider using your cottage as a safe house?"

I looked at him. "Absolutely," I said. Feeling privileged. "I'll pull the funds out of my personal savings. We don't have to worry Gina Marie with any of the details. Besides, she's worried sick about Dan."

Frank smiled warmly. "I'll call the barn-raising team and let them know my lady needs us… one more time."

"Frank, please tell Judge Abrams I'm honored he still thinks of me, and it will be my pleasure to help women, children, and their pets."

Frank stood up. "I'm off to the building department. I'll see you next week. If you hear any noise, stay away."

"Frank, we'll have to tell Kevin and Jesse so they can dig the foundation hole."

Frank shook his head. "According to these plans, Dan's putting it on a slab. A little grading, and that's it. I'll let Kevin in on the surprise. And I'll let Jesse know to keep Dan away."

I kissed his cheek. "What would I do without you?"

He laughed as he walked away.

Gina Marie and Dan went hunting three days in a row.

They only left for a few hours in the morning. Poor Dan had to wake up two hours before they would leave so he could take his Lactulose, which he hated the taste of. And if he didn't go to the bathroom before they left, Gina Marie said he would stop along the trail.

One afternoon, Dan, Gina Marie and I were up at the pool, Dan was in the water, and we were sitting in the chaise lounge chairs discussing their adventures.

"One time, I turned around just to see if he was okay, and I saw his poop go flying out of his butt."

I laughed harder than she did.

"He sprayed the poor tree behind him. I walked away and waited for him near the Polaris."

We both watched as Dan swam from one end of the pool to the other.

"Are you okay? I'm worried about you."

I gave her a wry grin. "I'm scared. I can't lie. That man is my every dream, desire, and prayer. Gina Marie, he's my life."

# Chapter 57

JUNE BRIDES ARE THE happiest in the world. This weekend's was no different. "I love her colors," I said to Dan. "Hey, did you hear me?"

"Yeah, something about colors," he replied.

I took one look at him. "How many times did you go to the bathroom yesterday?"

He held up two fingers.

"No more bread or bagels." I opened the refrigerator and took out eggs and bacon. "No toast either. You have to go to the bathroom at least three times a day, if not four."

"Tell me something I don't know," he said and grabbed the frying pan. "I'll make breakfast."

I put out a bowl of berries for him to snack on while he was making breakfast. I sat at the end of the counter and watched him. "I took another class this week. It was on medications. At first, you'll have a lot, but after a few months, it will taper down to just your antirejection medicine and a couple of vitamins."

Nothing. Silence.

"Dan, I have faith."

He handed me a plate.

We stayed in the entire day. Gina Marie stopped by

in the afternoon and tried to get Dan to take his drone outside, but he didn't feel like it. She asked him if he wanted to do something on Oculus or shoot a game of pool. When he said he wanted to watch a movie, she agreed to let him be. Nine o'clock, we went to bed. At ten-thirty that evening, the phone rang. I heard Dan say, "Hello, do you know what time it is?"

"Who is it?" I asked and sat up.

"Oh, yes. I'm sorry," Dan said. "Yes, of course. Can I put my wife on the phone, please?"

My heart sank. Something had happened. My first thought was Lynnae. "Hello."

"Mrs. Holliday, this is Dr. Kato. I have a liver for your husband, and I believe it is a perfect match."

I knew from taking the classes to ask, "Did you do any testing on it?"

"Yes," Dr. Kato said. "I can do further testing, but only if you are here at the hospital. How long before you can get here?"

"Three hours," I replied and added, "Dr. Kato, thank you."

When I hung the phone up, Dan was on his cell phone with Jesse. He told me to call Gina Marie. I called her, and she said she would be over in five minutes. "Don't leave without me," she said and hung up.

"Jesse's on his way," Dan told me and immediately jumped in the shower.

"Take your wedding band off," I told him. "You can't have anything on you." I took it from him adding, "I'll give it to you in the recovery room." I kissed him and told him I loved him. "We got this. Dan, it's happening." He closed his eyes, and so did I. *Thank you, Lord.*

I could have driven to New York-Presbyterian Hospital with my eyes closed at that point, but I was too nervous, so Jesse drove. Gina Marie sat in the front seat with her GPS on in case there were any traffic problems. Dan and I sat in the backseat. They were talking the entire way. I had no idea what they were saying. I was praying, thanking God, and hoping Dr. Kato was in possession of a clean and healthy liver.

"We're almost there," Gina Marie said, and I looked up and noticed we were on Riverside Drive.

Then she asked Dan, "Did the surgeon say anything about the donor?"

I glanced over at Dan.

He answered her. "Dr. Kato said it was from a forty-two-year-old male."

My cell phone rang. "Hello. Yes, we're close. Okay. Sounds good. Thank you. They said to drop Dan off at the front door, and for us to park the car and they will bring us to him."

After Jesse turned onto 168th Street, I told him to stop at the light and let us out, and to park in the parking garage on the right. I was so nervous, I almost blacked out, but instead, Dan and I got out of the car. I leaned in and told Gina Marie and Jesse the hospital is right there. They'll bring you upstairs."

"Go," Gina Marie said to us. "We'll find you."

We crossed the street and noticed Jesse was still in the same spot. Dan looked back. Jesse yelled over to us. "I love you guys."

Dan said, "Love you, too."

We entered the hospital, and within seconds they escorted us to the fourth floor. While Dan got undressed, I texted Gina Marie and told her where we were. Moments later, I saw her and Jesse sitting outside the room. The corridor was dark. I saw several people lying in beds. Nurses scurried around, and then Dr. Kato came in with Gina Marie and Jesse. "I've tested the liver. It looks great. I'm going to call the anesthesiologist in, and I'll start prepping you for surgery."

I knew based on the classes I had taken the tests they run prior to surgery, and I felt comfortable knowing Dr. Kato would be Dan's surgeon. "Thank you, Dr. Kato."

"Yes, thank you," Dan, Jesse, and Gina Marie said to him as he left the room.

A moment later, a nurse came in and said, "Your team is on their way in." She turned to us adding, "You can stay with him until they arrive." She touched Dan's shoulder. "You're in good hands. Dr. Kato is a great surgeon. He's performed more liver transplants than anyone else."

When I realized I was pacing the room, I sat down on the end of the bed. Jesse kept telling Dan, "You got this."

Gina Marie told him, "We'll take care of her. You need to stay positive."

"I feel good," Dan replied, and his anesthesiologist

came in and introduced herself.

She smiled at Dan and said, "You're my wake-up call. You're cute." We all laughed.

She sat down next to Dan on the side of the bed. "I'm going to take good care of you. I don't want you to worry about anything." She stood up and faced us. "You can walk with us to the entrance door. Dan, let's go."

He sat up. "I'm walking to surgery?"

"Yeah," she said and laughed. "Come on."

We followed him down the hall. First, Jesse hugged him, then Gina Marie, and then me. We watched him walk away laughing and talking as if he was going to a ball game.

"I didn't tell him I loved him," I said, and they just hung their heads.

We sat in the nurse's waiting room on the fourth floor. At two o'clock the next day, my friend, anesthesiologist Margaret Sagsveen, found us and said Dan was in the intensive care unit. She brought us upstairs and introduced us to Jay, Dan's pain management nurse.

Gina Marie held Dan's feet in her hands. Jesse collapsed in a chair. I took one look at his drip bottles and said, "I want him off the fentanyl. Immediately."

Jay looked at me and said, "It's used for pain."

I didn't care. I knew how highly addictive the drug was. "Give him something else. Anything," I said, and he left the room.

# Chapter 58

WE SAT WITH DAN for thirty minutes. Talking to him, rubbing his feet, hands, arms, and his forehead. I kept telling him to wake up. I told him, "I love you so much."

Jay came in and introduced me to one of Dan's doctors. "Mrs. Holliday, Jay is the best pain management nurse I know. He knows what he's doing. You need to trust him."

I held my hand out to him. "It's not a matter of trust," I said and pointed toward Dan. "I have been taking care of that man for thirty-six years. I'm not stopping now. I do not want him on fentanyl. Give him something less addictive. Please."

Twenty minutes later, Jay came back in and said, "I've started reducing the fentanyl."

"Thank you," Gina Marie said to him.

I thanked him too and asked, "When will he start to wake up?"

"He should be waking up soon," Jay replied and moved to the other side of the bed.

From taking their classes, I thought about people suffering from high ammonia levels having a harder time waking up from anesthesia. "What can we do to pull him out of his sleep-like state?"

Jay yelled, and I mean he screamed in Dan's ear, "DAN!"

Gina Marie jumped five feet in the air. Jesse jumped to his feet and said, "What the hell is wrong with you?"

Jay yelled three more times in Dan's ear. Finally, he opened his eyes. Jay turned to me and said, "You're up." He left the room, and we all started talking to Dan.

About an hour later, Dan was awake enough to tell us he wanted the endotracheal tube removed. The head nurse Stefanie came in with Jay and asked us to give her a minute. We stood out in the hall. When Jay told us we could go back inside, he also mentioned, "If he keeps pulling on his tube, I'm going to have to strap his hands down."

I looked at Stefanie and then Jay and told them, "He's not trying to pull it out. He's telling you he's strong enough to breathe on his own, and that he's ready for you to take it out."

She looked at me. "Seriously?"

"Yes, come here." We all went back in, and I asked Dan if he was ready to have the breathing tube taken out, and he motioned with his hand again. Never touching the line at all. "We took your classes, and that's the sign for I'm ready to have this removed."

Stefanie asked Dan if he could breathe on his own, and he nodded.

She told us they would be right back.

I was pleased to see Dan's fentanyl drip was empty. Every now and then, he would close his eyes for a minute, but every time I saw Stefanie go by his room, I told him to open his eyes. "She needs to know that you're awake and capable of breathing on your own."

Gina Marie stood near one foot, and Jesse stood next to the other. Each time someone walked by his room, they would tap his feet.

As soon as they removed the tube, he was ready to leave. "Easy Superman," Gina Marie teased him.

Jesse and Gina Marie told Dan one story after another. Finally, Dan was allowed to use oral swabs. While Gina Marie moistened his lips, I reserved a room for us at the closest hotel. That night, Jesse drove home, and we went to our hotel in New Jersey that offered shuttle service.

As soon as we got in the elevator, Gina Marie said, "You realize neither one of us has slept or had a bite to eat all day?"

"I'm too tired to think about anything except sleeping right now."

In our room, Gina Marie ordered from a local deli that delivered. "I have to eat something in order to take my medicine," she said. "And you need to eat so you don't fall down on me. I thought you were going to pass out on us when you got out of the car."

I made us each a cup of tea. "Thank you for coming with us."

"I promised Dan," she said. "Done, the sandwiches will be here in ten minutes."

Gina Marie texted Michelle, and I sent a group text to

my staff letting them know how wonderfully Dan was doing. After we ate, we both lay down on our beds. The TV was on, but we both just kept talking about Dan and what a miracle it was to see him. "I'm so grateful Dr. Kato was his surgeon. I prayed he would be the one to perform Dan's operation."

"I just told Michelle how proud of you I am. You did great today."

I looked over at her. "I'm so glad I took the classes the hospital offered. I wasn't about to stop standing up for Dan, not now."

"Every person needs to have a health advocate," she said, and I agreed.

"They're called liver champions."

I woke up at four o'clock, ready to see Dan. I quietly slipped into the bathroom, made myself a cup of tea, and sat in the chair next to the window thanking God. At five-thirty, Gina Marie woke up and asked me, "How long have you been up?"

I stretched my arms out and replied, "Only a short while. I'll make the coffee."

She went into the bathroom while I poured our coffee. "I told our driver to take us back at eight-thirty," I said and handed her a cup.

"Dan is so lucky to have you. You're calm when you need to be and strong when he's not."

I looked over at her. "Thank you. One day, I'll tell you our love story." I got up and said, "I'm going to take a shower and get ready."

"Okay, but they won't let us in until nine."

I stopped in the doorway, "I'll pace the halls."

She laughed. "I'm right behind you."

We arrived at the hospital in time to stand in a long line. At one point, an officer hollered out, "Please move forward in the line." And I thought, *Yes, I'd like to see my husband, thank you very much.*

"Are you excited to see him?" Gina Marie asked, and I took a deep breath before answering her.

"I can't believe we are standing here. It's over. He did it."

A few minutes later, we stood in front of the line. "Next."

As soon as we received our name tags, we were off and running. "Slow down, you'll get there," another officer said to us, and we both laughed.

We stood in the doorway, staring at him. He was sitting in a chair. Stefanie moved past us and said, "We've tagged him Super Dan. He's incredible. No pain medicine, ready to go home, and he walked already."

We both gave him a kiss. "I'm so proud of you," Gina Marie said to him and went to sit on his bed, but then jumped up.

"You can go to sleep for all we care. We like when family is in attendance." Stefanie winked at Dan. "Visitors are important, right?"

"I wouldn't be here if it wasn't for my wife," Dan told her. "I did this for her."

Stefanie smiled. "I love that."

# Chapter 59

A LITTLE WHILE LATER, Janine, Dan's nurse for the day, came in and said, "Hey, Super Dan, we're trying to get you out of the ICU, but there's no rooms available on the ninth floor. So you're stuck with us until a bed opens up."

Dan introduced Gina Marie and me to her. She smiled. "He's doing great. We've never seen a faster recovery or had a more pleasant patient. We're tempted to send him home." She tapped Dan on his foot. "Kidding." She checked his saline-solution bottle and added, "You can have liquids today."

A few minutes later, Dan's breakfast arrived. Pudding, Jell-O, tea, coffee, and juice. Dan offered his coffee to Gina Marie.

"You're the best," she told him and took the cup off his tray.

"Did you eat?" he asked me, and I told him Gina Marie ordered from the local deli for us. "We'll take turns today and get something from the cafeteria."

Dan stayed in his chair all day. Lunch and dinner were the same as breakfast. The next day, he was sent up to the ninth floor, where he had a view of the Hudson River. Stefanie came up to check on him. "We're kind of missing you downstairs. You're our new poster guy for liver transplants."

Dan held his hand out to her. "Thank you so much for everything."

She waved goodbye and told him to keep in contact. Dan invited her to stay at the inn. "Please let everyone know, you're all welcome to stay at The Inn in Rhode Island any time."

After she left, Dan started to cry. Gina Marie stood in the doorway. Sobbing. I hugged him and told him, he did it. "You are so blessed. I love you with all my heart."

Gina Marie came over and hugged him. I was in the bathroom getting a tissue when I heard him tell her, "I survived because of Julie. I did this for her. She asked me for thirty more years. I think I'll give her thirty-five."

I stood there looking at him. The love of my life. I was so proud of him. He fought the fight and beat the odds.

Gina Marie kissed his cheek. "Quick, Julie, tell him what else you want. He's feeling generous."

On the very last day, the pharmacist came into the room and had me set up Dan's medications for the week ahead. Bergen Pharmacy sent over all of his medications, pill boxes, you name it, it was in the duffle bag.

June twenty-third, Jesse came back to take us home. This time, I drove so he could sit in the back with his best friend. Oh, we heard a few nurse stories, but that was okay. Because they were the greatest of the great. "You should have told them you needed an in-home nurse," Jesse said, and Gina Marie yelled back at him.

"I'm joking," Jesse said. "He has the best nurse in the world taking care of him, and he knows it."

Gina Marie was steadily texting. I was certain she was letting everyone know about the past few days.

I glanced back, and Dan winked at me. Three hours later, I pulled up to the farmhouse, and everyone was on the front porch. There was a banner that read, *Welcome Home! We love you Dan!* But what brought me to tears was seeing Lady, Delilah, Brin, and Jesse's puppy holding signs of their own. As soon as Dan got out of the car, Delilah started jumping up and down calling out to her Poppa Dan.

Jesse had parked my Explorer as close to the house as possible, opened the door, and took hold of Lady. "No jumping, little girl."

Dan reached his hand out to pet her as she sat down by his legs. Everyone blew kisses as he stepped up onto the porch. Frank gave him two thumbs up, and when Teresa started singing "If I Can Dream," there wasn't a dry eye to be found. When she was finished, Dan walked up to her and hugged her.

Gina Marie put her hands on his shoulders. "Come on Super Dan, it's nap time."

I wiped my eyes and laughed knowing she was ready to finally close her eyes. I thanked her for everything and blew kisses to my staff. Inside was an array of fruit baskets, flowers, plants, and a stack of cards.

Jesse and Gina Marie walked with Dan to the

bedroom where he was happy to lie down. I set his medication up in a cabinet in the kitchen. He only needed to take it twice a day. At nine in the morning and at night. After Dan fell asleep, Gina Marie said she was going to see Michelle. Jesse said he was going up to the inn before going home. "If you need anything, call me," she said, and Jesse echoed her sentiments.

I looked back and replied, "I promise."

Dan and I stayed home, watching movies on Netflix. We both texted Gina Marie daily, letting her know his progress. Jesse stopped by every day to see if we needed anything. I told him he could come inside, but he insisted Gina Marie would kick his ass if he went near Dan the first week. "She's insane. She said I can only visit you if you come outside."

One time, Dan went to go outside, but Jesse told him not to. "Stay there and get rested up. You have to stay germ-free for a week. I'm just checking up on your old ass."

An hour later, we heard Michael on the front porch. I opened the door and saw a tray with two plates. "Michael, thank you," I shouted as he climbed into the new Kubota utility vehicle. I brought the tray inside and showed it to Dan.

"He's something else," Dan said and got up. "There's enough here for an army. Call Gina Marie. She loves lamb."

"She's with Michelle," I said, but I knew exactly where she really was.

Michael had sent down Dan's favorite lamb chops along with my herbed salmon.

The next day, Gina Marie and Frank stood on the front porch. "Dan," Frank hollered.

Gina Marie opened the door and told Dan to come outside. She grabbed one arm, and Frank took the other. Dan was doing well. He was in great shape and eager to get outside. It was perfect timing.

Gina Marie and I sat in the back. Frank drove the Polaris with Dan by his side. We drove down the road toward Kevin and Kourtnee's, and when Frank kept going, I heard Dan ask where we were going. "Is the farm stand open?" he asked.

Frank turned the corner, and there it was. Gina Marie whispered in my ear, "The building inspector said it was bigger than the firehouse."

We got out and stood near Dan. Frank walked over to him and put his hand out to him. "She's a beauty."

Dan held Frank's arm as he went inside his new garage. When he stood under the lift, he cried, "This is fantastic."

I hugged him. "Thank you for going through the surgery, for fighting, and for loving me."

When Dan went back outside, everyone put their masks on. "I told them no hugging." Gina Marie took hold of Dan's arm. "We can't take the chance of you getting an infection."

A few minutes later, everyone went home, Dan took a nap, and I wrote my letter to the donor family. My instructions were that it had to be handwritten, no personal information, just a simple thank you. I thanked them for the gift of life.

# Chapter 60

DAN WOKE UP FEELING wonderful. He made breakfast for Gina Marie, Michelle, and me. When he started singing, "Book of Love," Gina Marie and Michelle jumped off their stools and started dancing. As soon as breakfast was ready, we took our plates out to the back porch and sat down on my new patio furniture. I held my glass up and toasted to Dan. "Here's to the best husband in the world, to long walks, rainy days, and going back to Italy."

"Here, here," Gina Marie said tapping her orange juice to mine.

"To Julie, for putting up with me," Dan said.

Everyone laughed before eating their omelets. I looked over at Gina Marie and thought it was a perfect solution. "Gina Marie, how do you feel about becoming the inn's new innkeeper?"

She put her fork down. "What?"

"Think about it. Everyone comes to you for budget answers. Dan and I will be able to travel and not worry about the inn."

"I think it's a great idea," Michelle said and raised her eyebrows. "You live here, and it's all you talk about. Why not?"

"I agree," Dan said. "Come on, you love it here. Frank

said you couldn't wait to build next door. Julie's right, you're good with the employees, they all like you and feel comfortable coming to you for advice."

"Gina Marie, you have the best people working here. You don't have to do much," I said, hoping she'd say yes.

"I'm not digging in the dirt or planting one bulb," she said.

"Yay." I clapped my hands.

When I met with my staff to get their reactions, everyone agreed with me.

"Gina Marie runs the meetings better than you," Teresa said.

"Well, there you have it," I said and laughed. "I know she does. She's great with numbers, and she respects each and every one of you."

"I think it's a fantastic idea," Michael said. "I'd like to see you and Dan take more vacations. You both worked hard, and you've been through a lot."

"Thank you," I replied. "I'm hoping to take Dan to Alaska."

"Can he travel?" Kourtnee asked.

"We wouldn't go until next spring. I wouldn't want him to catch an infection. In fact, he can't even go in the swimming pool."

Kevin stood up and stretched. "I'll have Kourtnee's helper assist me in the gardens."

"Oh, she would love that," Kourtnee said.

Fourth of July, I was standing in the kitchen rinsing

our glasses when I saw Dan out in the backyard. He bent down and picked up one of the rocking chairs. I threw the towel on the floor and ran outside. "What the hell are you doing?"

When he turned to face me, I saw a huge wet spot at the end of his incision. His T-shirt was covered in wet blood. I could tell he was uncomfortable, his chest was rising and falling. "Dan," I yelled at him. "Are you trying to pull your stitches out?"

He touched his stomach, looked at his hand, and said, "I wanted to move the chair out of the sun."

I blew out a breath. "Come inside, I need to look at your sutures."

Dan followed me inside. "Sit down. I'm going to grab some gauze and a new drainage bag just in case." He sat down, and I went to our bathroom to grab my supplies. When I returned to the kitchen, he had taken his shirt off. The entire area was soaking wet. "You better hope you didn't just give yourself a damn hernia. Why would you pick up the heaviest item on the back porch?"

He didn't say anything. He didn't have to. We both knew he did something wrong. "I need to take this off," I said and removed everything before cleaning him up. I wiped the area as gently as I could with a saline solution. After cleaning the area with eight four-by-four gauze pads, I was finally able to stop the wound from discharging.

"It looks like bloody fluids," he said.

I wanted to slap him, but instead I told him, "It's your

body removing bodily fluids at the surgical line. It helps to speed up the healing process and decreases your chances of infection." Then I added, "I have to call Lauren and let her know."

"Why?"

"In case you gave yourself a hernia. Dan, you could have pulled a muscle. She needs to know."

He gave me a pointed look. "She'll think I'm ungrateful."

I rolled my eyes. "I'm sure you're not the first man or woman to do something stupid."

"Thanks," he replied and stood up.

I pointed my finger at him. "Don't even think about picking up anything else." Dan went to the family room, and I tossed all of the bloody gauze pads in the garbage before I called his nurse practitioner, Lauren.

July sixth, the temperature was perfect. The breeze felt inviting, and everyone looked great. Most of the women wore summer dresses. The men wore tan shorts or pants and white T-shirts. The archway was made of birch branches, and it was covered with ivory tulle. The aisle was created using silver-dollar eucalyptus and flameless candles in various heights. Up at the altar was a row of four chairs on each side, followed by five, six, and in the back, there were seven on each side. The forty-four gold Chiavari chairs with ivory cushions had tulle tied to the back, along with Sherry's favorite bouquet of white daisies.

I read the sign stuck in the sand. "Shoes Optional for

Sherry and Jesse's Wedding." On a table lined with silver ice buckets sat coconuts and straws for everyone to stay hydrated. On another table, shot glasses with lime wedges. I read the sign, "Cheers to the Bride and Groom."

My staff occupied the two back rows. I sat down next to Gina Marie, Michelle, Frank, Teresa, and Sal. When Christine sat next to Michael in the row across from us, Gina Marie tapped me on my leg, and I thought, *Let there be peace among us.* Up front, sitting in the first row on the left, sat Sherry's mother. Across the way, I saw Jesse's mother crying. I walked up to her and handed her a tissue. She whispered in my ear, "Thank you for watching out for Jesse all these years." She kissed my cheek and added, "I'm so proud of you."

I waved to the rest of his family. When I heard, "One Love" playing in the background, I took my seat.

First, Jesse, Dan, and Craig walked past us and stood up front. I cried when Jesse's father stood up and hugged Dan before Jesse. We laughed when he stopped, turned around, and shook Craig's hand. Sherry's sisters came down the aisle. When they turned to face us, Sherry and her father walked toward Jesse. Her dress was a gorgeous short, sexy, sequin-halter with matching flat sandals. Jesse took her hand in his, then extended his other hand to her father.

During the golden hour, Jesse and Sherry said their vows. Everyone stood as "Kiss The Girl" played. We all cheered, and Jesse dipped her low, kissed her as she kicked her leg out towards the ocean.

Right there, a page fluttered in my life book.

# Chapter 61

Dᴀɴ ꜱᴛᴏᴏᴅ ᴜᴘ ᴀɴᴅ tapped his knife to his glass. Everyone held up their glasses. "To Jesse and Sherry, may God bless you with many years of happiness and a house full of children."

"Cheers," we all shouted.

Dr. Eastwood came outside holding a big, flat, white package adorned with a big white-and-silver bow. When he handed it to Jesse and Sherry, she cried, hugged him, and thanked him for allowing them to get married at his home.

"I made a small token for the two of you to remember this day by."

Jesse reached out and shook his hand. Sherry asked if she should open it. And when he nodded, she tore the paper off of it. Tears ran down her face. I looked over Dan's shoulder and saw that Dr. Eastwood had taken a photo of the two of them the first day he'd met them. Jesse picked Sherry up and swung her around. The sun was glowing like a big yellow burst perfectly behind them.

Sherry kissed Dr. Eastwood's cheek, and Jesse teased him by saying, "You have a new admirer."

Michael's crew was standing by to load the chairs,

archway, and cocktail tables back to the inn. One by one, we all said our goodbyes to Dr. Eastwood and went back to the pool for an evening of celebration.

I sat next to Dan. "Can you believe it? Jesse is married. What is the world coming to?"

"I never thought he'd find someone," Dan said. "I always thought he'd be a single man, but look at him."

Jesse was standing behind Sherry, arms wrapped around her chest, kissing her face, listening to the music. As they stood there watching their family and friends dance to "Celebration," he never looked happier.

"What do you say we head on over to the house and take a little nap before the barbeque?"

I looked at him. "Sounds good to me. They'll be dancing and drinking for another hour before dinner."

The pool was a short walk from our house. We entered through the back door. Dan stopped in the kitchen and grabbed himself a glass of water. I saw a stack of mail on the counter.

"I'm going to rest in the family room," he said.

"Okay, I'm going to make myself a cup of tea, and I'll join you."

I took my cup of lemon tea, the mail, and went in and sat next to Dan. When I saw a letter from New York-Presbyterian Hospital, I opened it. It was a reply letter from the donor family. I held it up and told Dan who it was from. Then I read it aloud, "Dear Dan and Julie, I received your letter. I was surprised by how quickly it came. I am so glad the surgery went well. My husband was on his way home from work when a drunk driver hit his car head-on. They said the woman was driving fast and lost control of her vehicle. The impact was so hard, no one survived. Even in his death, he did so much for others. He can rest easy knowing he was your donor. Our children had to grow up fast. Only ten and twelve, they are fascinated by the fact that their father was able to save another's life." I glanced over at Dan, we both had tears in our eyes. I looked past the first page. There were several other pieces of paper attached. *Documents*, I thought. I continued reading her message. "I have enclosed a copy of the letter Daniel's mother wrote to him before she passed away a year ago, along with a few other reports."

"His name was Daniel?" Dan said.

I looked at him and continued reading. "I want you to know, Daniel drove to New York to see you, he wanted to tell you in person, however, you had moved to Rhode Island. When he went to see you there, he was told you were on vacation in Italy."

Dan touched my leg. "What's going on?"

I grabbed a tissue for both of us. "Wait," I said and remembered. "Robert saw a man parked at the end of the driveway. I just assumed it was Chad looking to see if you and I were still together. He told me the man asked about you. Dan?" I too was unsure as to what was happening.

Dan reached for the letter. I started reading the other documents. "This is a copy of Daniel's birth certificate.

It says father unknown." I glanced at the letter his mother wrote to him. "Daniel, I'm sorry I kept your father from you all these years. He was much younger than I was. Only seventeen when you were born."

Dan set the letter on the coffee table. "I was sixteen when she broke up with me. She started dating this guy she was seeing at her job." Tears appeared once more. I think we were both in shock. "There was no way I thought that baby was mine." He cried, "I'm such a fool."

"I'm so sorry. Dan, you have a son?" I swallowed the lump in my throat, feeling bad for him. Then I read the Ancestry report. "Father. Son." I showed the paper to Dan. "When was the last time you looked at Ancestry?"

He shook his head. Ran his hands through his hair.

I grabbed the tablet, logged on, and saw the green leaf blinking. I tapped on it and read, "DNA Match. Close Family. Son." I set the tablet down and hugged Dan. Then I searched the letter for a return address, phone number, and saw a small envelope. I handed it to Dan, but he handed it back to me.

"It's addressed to both of us, you open it," he said.

Inside was a lovely family photo. With tears in my eyes, I cried, "We have a daughter-in-law and two beautiful grandchildren."

# Acknowledgements

FIRST AND FOREMOST, I must thank God for His healing hands. To the staff, nurses and doctors at New York-Presbyterian Hospital, my heartfelt thanks. To every donor and especially to their families, you are my heroes.

Black Hawk Literary Agency, Jan Kardys and Barbara Ellis – the best in the business. Thank you for standing by me.

Hopeful cheers to success as we break from the world of book publishing to movie adaptation. Thank you, RB Binotto and Amanda Toney for welcoming me into your world at Stage32.

To my team, I could not have done the Be Strong Enough Series without all of you. Thank you, Susan McGurl, Natasja Hellenthal, Donna McFarland, Karen Sheff, Claudia Armann, and to my new brilliant editor, Erika DeSimone, you are the lyrics in my song!

To my dear family, followers, fans, and book friends, thank you from the bottom of my heart for your support, reading time, reviews and for sharing my stories with your book-loving friends.

To learn more about me and my books, please visit my website and sign up for my monthly newsletter, where you can also join my book club and street team.

Blessings,
Judy.

judyprescottmarshall.com